THE INSPECTOR

THE
INSPECTOR

JAN DE HARTOG

NEW YORK

ATHENEUM
PUBLISHERS

1960

THE INSPECTOR

One evening in the early spring of nineteen forty-six, a train sped through the flat Dutch landscape toward the sunset. As it approached a level crossing it whistled, a long wailing sound that trailed mournfully through the dusk, and a middle-aged man in a dimly lit compartment remembered the night of his wedding day, twenty-five years before. For a short, nostalgic moment an image came back to him, faded and quaint, like a photograph in a dead relative's album: Susie, dressed in cornflower blue, with a white cloche hat, reaching up to lift her vanity case from the luggage rack. He saw her sturdy legs under her short skirt, the white fireman's helmet of her hat; as she lifted her arms, a few scraps of confetti fell out of the cuffs of her coat.

Then he saw the conductor approach in the dark corridor, checking tickets, glanced at the couple sitting by the window, got up and went out. The conductor was about to enter the next compartment when the man accosted him.

"Inspector Jongman, Criminal Investigation," he said, showing the conductor a card. "I have no ticket, but I don't want the two people in my compartment to know that. Could you write one out now, and punch it when you come in?"

"Certainly, Inspector," the conductor said eagerly, taking out his ticket book. "Where are you going?"

"Make it the Hook."

"Are you expecting trouble? If so, just call me. I was with the Parachutes."

The inspector smiled. "No, thank you," he said. "I think I can handle this. Thanks all the same." He took his ticket, paid for it and went back to his compartment. When the conductor came in, after a martial rap on the glass with his punch, he looked a little sheepish as he saw that the only other occupants of the compartment were a young couple. The man looked elegant and slight, and the girl was a little wisp of a thing with big dark eyes and a beret on short black hair, certainly no quarry for the fat copper clumsily dozing in the opposite corner.

The train sped along through the night, stopping only at The Hague and Rotterdam on its way to the coast. In Hook of Holland everybody got out and trooped toward the customs building. Behind the crippled façade of the bombed-out station loomed the silhouettes of the ferryboat and the military transport steamer. The platform was crowded with soldiers in battle dress and full pack, British troops on their way to Germany for occupation duty. The inspector was unobserved as he left the crowd and, after watching the couple go inside, entered a side door of the customs building. In the office, a sergeant of the military police sat yawning behind a newspaper while a bulky private, booted and spurred and slung with guns, sat typing a form with two fingers. The sergeant looked over the edge of *The News* and said, "Hullo, Inspector, long time no see. What are you hunting this time?"

The inspector gave him a quick half-smile. "I'm on an emergency case," he said. "I haven't been able to notify my wife, and I should also like to tell my British opposite number what's coming up; will you send a couple of telegrams for me?"

"Any time, Inspector, any time," the sergeant said, taking his feet off the edge of the desk, and folding his newspaper with military precision. "What's up? Dope smugglers again?"

"Of a sort," the inspector said. "Look, there is the couple I am after." He pointed them out among the crowd, through the small glass pane in the office door.

"I would like you to have a look yourself and see if, by any chance, you can get a London address out of the man's passport."

"There won't be any," the sergeant said. "All it will say is 'London,' if he's a resident. Is he a Dutchman?"

"No. I don't quite know what he is. My guess is he'll be a Panamanian this time. Do aliens have to fill out embarkation cards at this end?" He answered his own question. "No, of course not. Well, all right, that will have to wait till we get to the other side. Just take a look at those passports, will you?"

"I can bring them in here, if you like," the sergeant suggested.

"No, thank you," the inspector said. "I don't want them to suspect anything. I don't think they know that they have been spotted."

"Any way you want it," the sergeant said. "You're the boss."

The private in the corner growled, glared at his typewriter and started hammering out a line he had typed with the sound of a small steam hammer.

"Be careful," the inspector said as the sergeant got up and put on his gun belt. "The man is a wily customer. He might get away from me on the other side if he knew I was there."

"Don't worry, Inspector," the sergeant said. "I blend into the background." He put on a peaked cap that made him seem enormous and entered the inspection hall, creaking with leather.

SORRY NOT HOME FOR SEVERAL DAYS, one telegram read, OFF ON UNEXPECTED ENGLISH JOB WRITING LOVE PETER. The other: WILL CONTACT YOU SOONEST AFTER ARRIVAL TOMORROW SIX A.M. PLEASE CLEAR ME WITH HARWICH JONGMAN

5

"Do I give these things to you?" he asked the private in the corner.

The private frowned. "What are they?"

"Just telegrams."

The private read them, his lips moving, then he sighed, shook his head and said, "All right."

Through the glass pane in the door the inspector watched the sergeant take up position majestically behind one of his subordinates at the inspection desk. He blended into the background like a statue in the desert, but he checked all passports, which was something, at least. The line of subdued human cattle moved slowly past the desk, and after terrifying some old ladies by frowning at their passports and giving a clergyman of the Church of England an undressing look, the sergeant, with Passion Play histrionics, merely glanced at the passports of the couple and dropped them as if they were of no interest. He then fastened his feline stare on the collar button of a nervous passenger behind them, and the inspector sighed. It was well-intentioned but it must have been obvious to the elegant traveler; the sergeant had shown him the negative of his suspicion instead of its print. He came back eventually with the information that their passports were in order. That of the man was Swiss, and his name was Thorens, the girl was Dutch, name Held, Anna, age twenty-one.

The ferryboat lay in the night, ablaze with lights. The passengers, carrying their own luggage, staggered across the windy expanse of crane rails and cobbles between the customs building and the gangway, where a self-conscious old sailor with a beribboned cap bearing the company's name apologetically checked their tickets. The inspector watched the couple go up the gangway, then went toward the front of the ship where, in the darkness, was another gangway, unguarded, which led to the crew's quarters. He climbed aboard with the assurance of familiarity, and watched the ship leave.

When the outer buoy had slipped by, he went to find the captain in his quarters. The rooms looked like the bridal suite of a provincial hotel in the 'twenties. There were mirrors everywhere, and the doors of the wardrobes were inlaid with wooden roses. The ceiling light was cubistically modern with stained-glass facets; in the corner was a marble statue, surreptitiously riveted to the wall, of a Grecian goddess pulling on an invisible stocking; the head of the goddess was temporarily hidden by the captain's cap.

On a low table, in front of a sofa flanked by two club chairs, stood a tray with two glasses, bottles of geneva, whisky and sherry, and small dishes of peanuts, sausages, cheese cubes and gherkins. The two glasses would soon be three.

"Captain?" the inspector called.

"Who is it?" an angry voice growled from the shower.

"It's Peter Jongman."

"Inspector!" the voice cheered. A hairy old man came out of the shower, a towel around his loins, vigorously drying his ears. "What brings you here?"

"Go and dress first," the inspector said.

The hairy old man said, "Won't be long. Make yourself at home," and hurried back into his sleeping quarters. The inspector took off his coat, dropped it on a chair, picked up a cheese cube and looked, munching, at a framed photograph on the wall, of the captain and his wife smiling nervously at the camera, surrounded by potted palms. Then he heard a sneeze in the corridor and in came a rotund, genial man in resplendent uniform, wiping his neck with a handkerchief.

"Hullo, Chief," the inspector said.

The chief engineer was also pleasantly surprised. He beamed as he cried, "Well, if it isn't our favorite bloodhound! What are you tracing this time?"

"A wily fox," the inspector said; then the captain came out of his sleeping quarters in a bathrobe, sat down on the sofa and whistled. In his bedroom sounded a double thump and in waddled a reluctant dachshund, graying around the muzzle. "Watch this," the captain said. "Just name a number below ten. Any number. Go ahead."

The inspector, who knew the routine, frowned in thought while the dachshund, resigned, hoisted himself on to his haunches. "Eight."

"Okay," the captain said, "now watch this."

He put a cheese cube on the dachshund's muzzle, lifted an admonishing finger and counted sternly to eight. Then his finger came down and the dachshund, quick as lightning, snatched the cheese cube from the air.

"Perfect!" the inspector said. "What about the Hitler-Churchill gag? Does he still know that?"

"He?" the captain asked. "He never forgets a trick. But that's out of date now. You can't go on hating a dead man. What will it be? Geneva? Sherry? Whisky?"

"Hold it a moment," the inspector said, "let me tell you what's up first. I had to leave in a hurry because I didn't know this case was coming up, so I haven't got anything with me; pajamas, toothbrush, that kind of thing. Could you people help me out?"

"Sure," the captain said, filling his glass with geneva; the dachshund followed the proceedings with a sidelong glance and rose once more at the captain's knee. The captain, with a conspiratorial wink, put a gherkin on the dog's nose, brought the glass to his lips but, to the dog's dismay, he did not drink. "Wait a minute!" he said. "Does that mean that you have come without your gun?"

"Of course," the inspector said. "I never carry one."

"I'll get you mine," the captain said, rising; the dog, seeing him go, considered the signal given, snatched and spat simultaneously, after which he disappeared under the sofa, leaving his tail sticking out. The chief nudged the inspector and whispered, "Cheers."

"Here!" the captain said, coming out of the bedroom, and he held up an old Detective Special. "It may not look like much, but it will be the fastest gun you've ever handled." He put the gun into a pocket of the inspector's overcoat. "Now I've done my share," he said. "You give him your pajamas. Anything else you want?"

"Listen, I really don't need the gun," the inspector protested, rising to take it out.

The captain said with authority, "You leave that gun where it is, and tell your story. But let's first. . . ." And there came the geneva again.

The inspector looked at them with a mixture of envy and irritation. The irritation was with himself, for unlike them he did not hold his liquor very well. He had only had one glass and already he felt with pleasure and alarm the first smoky spirals of tipsiness envelop him. He must not, tonight of all nights he must not. On the other hand, there he was, safely imprisoned on this island of steel lumbering through the night, and so was his quarry.

"What about that story of yours?" the captain asked.

"It's a sordid story," he replied, "one of those things that make a man of our age wonder what the hell has happened to the world," and he proceeded to tell them about the Canadian soldiers of the Army of Liberation who had promised their Dutch girl friends that they would send for them as soon as the war was over. Only a fraction of them had done so, so there were a lot of girls in Holland now who were waiting to go to Canada

9

and would go on waiting. A particularly obnoxious type of crook had taken advantage of this situation by picking out the ones that had no relatives and no steady jobs, and promising them a visa for Canada at very low cost. The only thing the girls had to do was to follow their guide to London from where the transatlantic liner would leave, bound for Canada. Only it did not go to Canada, it went to South America.

"I see," the captain said. "White-slave trade, huh?"

"Does this mean that we have one of those girls on board right now?" the chief asked.

"Yes, with one of the kingpins of the ring."

"What are you going to do? You won't let him ship her, will you?"

"Not if I can help it," he said. "I'm going to find out where the man lives, in London or elsewhere, and then my friend Scott and I will close in on him."

"Who's that?" the captain asked.

"A commander at Scotland Yard," he replied. "We've known one another for twenty-five years now. Work together like this." He raised two crossed fingers and frowned at this sign of drunkenness. He should not get garrulous now. It was none of their business how he felt about Jim Scott's being a commander now. Jim was very decent about it but he could not be expected to change the mechanics of their service. Inspectors dealt with inspectors, that was all there was to it. But this time he would go over the head of Burke or Bruce or whatever the youngster's name was. This was a case that needed special handling and only Jim had the power and the independence to act.

"No wonder you're on this case yourself," the chief said. "How did you cotton on to it?"

"Oh, I was just doing a routine check-up," he answered

casually, "when I happened to spot him on his way with another victim. So, here I am." Should he tell them that seeing the girl had made up his mind for him? No, it was none of their business.

"What kind of girls are they?" the captain asked, filling the glasses once more. "Tarts?"

"Now what has he been explaining to you all along?" the chief asked. "If they were tarts, he wouldn't be here. It would be a business transaction between two independent parties. They are jilted fiancées of . . ."

"Yes," the inspector said recklessly. "She just broke my bloody heart, standing there in the hall of the station, with that little beret and those big dark eyes. All she could be was twenty, twenty-one at the most, and there was this suave swine dealing in innocence and despair and loneliness. I just decided that this was my turn."

"Your turn to what?" the chief asked, frowning.

But the inspector didn't hear him. He looked tipsily at the wall, seeing the hall of the station, the trim little figure under the clock, hearing the gruff whisper of Detective-Sergeant Wolters, "There's the next one. Jewish girl. No parents. Out of a camp. A natural." And then he saw her smile of recognition, the debonair stranger who put his arm around her shoulders and joined the queue in front of the ticket window. "I'd better get a ticket myself," Wolters had sighed, "unless you want me to leave it here. There isn't much else we can do, is there, apart from reporting to the British?" He had hesitated, and then said, "All right, Wolters, you go home. I'll take over from here." The tough old detective had looked up, amazed; the captain and the chief understood at once. It was not necessary to tell them that this had been the flash point of all the resentment and guilt and powerless indignation pent up inside him ever since the war started. That girl with her little beret underneath the clock in the hall of the station had been his call to action.

He thought of all the calls he had let go unheeded during the war; the cranes sabotaged on the waterfront, by others; the German freighters blown up, by others; the launches of drunken soldiers tricked into collision, by others; all he had done was to turn his back and let the saboteurs escape. Now he was going to do something himself. He picked up his glass and lifted it at the wall. "Here goes," he said grimly. "If it takes all I've got: this one they shall not have."

"Attaboy," the captain said, and poured out another round.

When the inspector finally came out into the cold night air, dragging his overcoat behind him, he was quite drunk, and knew it, and enjoyed it in a sloppy way. He nearly tripped as he crossed the high threshold of the captain's cabin, and he found it a huge joke. He hit the glass wall of the promenade deck, hopping on one leg to keep himself from falling, and knocked his hat over his eyebrows. He laughed so much that he had to take out his handkerchief and wipe his eyes, and screamed like a woman when he felt something dead and cold in his pocket, a finger. He yanked the handkerchief out, and the finger fell on the floor. It was a gherkin. Relief and the memory of the dachshund spitting out the gherkin made him burst out laughing once more. At the same time he began to sober up deep down inside, for the thought floated to the surface that he was lucky the ship would take another five hours before it got to Harwich. It was a pity that he had let himself be tricked again into one of those drinking bouts that seemed to be inevitable whenever he crossed the North Sea on this ferry. But if he went about it in the right way, there would be no harm done. Steady now, Peter. Go to your cabin, boy, lie down and. . . .

As he turned the corner, he heard somebody coughing in the distance, and he saw her. She stood at the far end of the empty promenade deck, looking out at the dark sea, her forehead resting against the glass. The sight of her did not sober him, it just made him realize that he must turn around; she should not see him. If only he had not drunk so much he would have been able to stroll casually past her and lean on the rail a few windows further down and start a conversation. Now, he had to turn around and slouch to his cabin in the other direction.

He could not forget the way she stood there, all alone, her forehead against the glass, facing the darkness of the future. What guiding star did she think she saw? What hope? What illusion drew this pathetic little moth to perdition with its eerie light? He leaned on the rail himself on the other side of the ship and rested his forehead against the glass and stared out. All he saw, in the pale reflected light of the electric bulbs sparsely strung along the ceiling, was the face of a middle-aged drunk with a hat crushed out of shape, bags under his eyes and the jowl of virility run to seed. He forgot about her and thought about himself. He certainly had not made a success out of life. Part of him again voiced his resentment that Jim should be a commander of Scotland Yard whereas, this much was certain, he himself would remain a nondescript footslogger for the rest of his natural life. But the other part hurried to his aid with the old excuses at once. One could not compare Scotland Yard, with its thousands of staff, to the Amsterdam Police Criminal Investigation Department. There must be a score of superintendents with Scotland Yard, the Amsterdam Police C.I.D. had only one. But this time he refused the salve that had so often soothed the smarting of his ego. He stared at the man mirrored by the night with bitter objectivity: a failure, a cowardly, henpecked failure. Ah, for the days. . . .

He could not remember any particular days; what surged within him at this wave of nostalgia was a tumble of images. A row of girls' heads, peering down from the sun deck of an East Indies liner; seagulls wheeling in the sky; a cheeky little tugboat spanking across the harbor; a buoy with a flashing green light, a patrolboat of the Harbor Police tied up to it, an old helmsman yawning in the foc'sle while he, as a young subinspector, stood gazing up at the stars. Twenty-five years had gone by with nothing about them bright enough to dim the sunlit joy of his one season as a subinspector with the Harbor Police. Perhaps he was getting old, old people started to remember their youth, so they said. But what about the captain, or the chief engineer? They seemed happy enough, and were certainly not haunted by nostalgic visions of their youth. He sniggered again as he remembered the captain putting the gherkin on the dachshund's nose; then he heard a door squeak in the echoing vault of the promenade deck and saw Thorens look up and down the empty corridor. With a sudden stiffening of his muscles, his body tautened in pugnacious determination. Whatever the cost, this one they would not have!

But even as he thought these pompous words, he realized that all this was an empty show of hollow aggressiveness. In Harwich he would start shadowing the two to London, find out where they went, then he would phone Jim, who would have Thorens arrested on a trumped-up charge. That was all there was to it, and the only way in which he himself could possibly influence this inevitable course of events was by not losing sight of them between Liverpool Street Station and wherever Thorens might take her. He sighed and found his cabin, fed up with himself.

But he could not forget Thorens, and as he stood

brushing his teeth in front of the washstand mirror, he looked at himself again. Seen in normal light, he was not so bad. True, he should have watched his weight a little and perhaps used a hair tonic, but his eyes were still young and he still had all his teeth, and if he were to dress as nattily as Thorens he would be a fine figure of a man, despite his fifty-three years. It was Susie's idea that he should dress the way he did, or perhaps not Susie's alone. It was the idea of the crowd he lived in, a crowd of graying people in a gray world of office hours, midmorning breaks, pension schemes and fruitless marital discussions about asking for a raise. That world had survived the war unscathed; empires might crumble, millions of innocents might be tortured and gassed, their very town might be blown sky-high outside the planked-up windows of their offices, they had still filled out their forms in triplicate and taken their imitation coffee at the hour of eleven and put their jackets over the backs of their chairs after the first of June. During the war it had been a sort of haven, that office, after prowling through the jungle of the harbor with its gangs of saboteurs and its lurking bands of hunters in the shape of the German Naval Police, the Gestapo, the S. D. and whatever else they might call their organizations. Now the haven had turned into a prison. Now he occasionally caught himself thinking of the jungle with nostalgia. He shrugged his shoulders, finished brushing his teeth and went to bed.

After putting out the light he lay listening to the creaking of the walls, the soft clatter of the carafe over the washstand, the throbbing of the engine and the slow shuffle of his overcoat brushing the door with the swell, until he fell asleep.

He was awakened by a knocking on his door and called, "Come in" before he knew where he was. In came a smiling English constable, and he realized this was Harwich.

2

"Hello, Inspector," the constable said. "How are you today?"

"Fine, just fine," he answered, but as he sat up his head felt as if there were something loose inside.

"I saw your name on the list," the constable said. "I thought I'd come up to see if you needed anything."

"Are the passengers through customs yet?"

"They're just about starting. Anybody in particular you want us to keep an eye on while you have your breakfast?"

"I'll have breakfast on the train," he said, swinging his legs out of bed and feeling a wave of dizziness as a result. "Thanks all the same."

"Want me to notify London? Need a car at Liverpool Street?"

"I don't think so, thank you. My party is probably going to take a taxi and I think I prefer to trail them in a taxi myself."

"Just as you wish, sir. Been nice seeing you again. If you should think of something before the train leaves, I'll be at the door to the platform."

"Fine, thank you," he said. The constable had already opened the door when he called after him. "By the way! You say you found my name on the list?"

"That's right, sir."

"London did not tell you I was coming?"

"Not that I know of, sir. The message may have come in, though, since I left."

"Okay, thank you."

"That'll be all, sir?"

"That'll be all."

The constable left. Wonderful manners, these English. So Jim hadn't bothered to notify Harwich. He could consider it without qualms. In Jim's place, he would probably not have bothered either. Scotland Yard had other things to do than to notify its ports that an obscure Dutch inspector was appearing with a feeling of importance. Jim was probably thinking of him at this very moment, if he were up this early, wondering how to tell his boyhood friend not to go over the heads of his own rank on his visits to England. Jim took his job very seriously.

The steward brought the customary sweet cup of tea and asked whether he wanted his shoes polished, which was a rhetorical question. He asked the man to change ten guilders into English money and gave him the generous tip stewards seem to expect all over the world. He felt a little shaky and his mouth tasted of gherkins.

As he came out on deck, he found the morning was mild, so he put his coat over his arm. There was still a long queue at the aliens' side of the customs at Immigration, and he went through the British side with an adolescent feeling of superiority. The constable at the entrance knew him and greeted him with that unique mixture of courtesy and superciliousness that no other nation could imitate. The immigration officer shook him by the hand, which signified that, despite his acceptance, he was still rated as a foreigner.

"I'm following a man that travels under the name of Thorens on a Swiss passport in the company of a girl called Anna Held, Dutch passport."

"Anna Held?" the Englishman asked. "Haven't I heard that name before somewhere? Isn't she a singer of some sort? Opera? Something to do with a nightingale? Swedish nightingale, or was it Hungarian?"

"Whatever it was, I wouldn't rack my memory for it," he answered with a smile. "The child is twenty-one years old. The name Thorens, however, is probably an alias: whoever thought it up probably looked at his watch."

"Pardon?"

"It sounds like a Swiss make of watches."

The Englishman gave him a pained little smile, the joke had not been very good. Come to think of it, it hadn't been a joke at all. God, he felt faint. Better go on board that train and get some breakfast, quickly.

"Anything else we can do for you, Inspector? I needn't remind you that we would like to be notified the moment you hand these people over to the Yard."

"Of course," he said, going toward the door to the platform. "If you could slip me a note with the man's address on it before the train leaves, I would appreciate it. I mean the address he writes out himself on his disembarkation card."

"Certainly, with pleasure."

"Do you think you could see your way to giving it to me personally? I'll be in the dining car, and I prefer not to be seen with policemen in uniform just now."

"Will do."

"Thank you."

The fresh air on the platform felt soothing to his burning eyes and he took a few deep breaths of the salty, foggy sea air before hoisting himself into the stench of humid plush, stale cigar smoke and frying kippers. An attendant like an undertaker asked him whether he had a reservation, in a muted tone as if he inquired whether he were a relative of the deceased, then directed him to a corner. The compartment quickly filled with breathless

Germans heaving bulging suitcases into the luggage nets, only to be ordered to take them down again by the attendant. An old lady, holding her ticket firmly in a gloved hand, asked him if this train went to London. A leathery Englishman in bowler hat, striped trousers and with a rolled-up umbrella trod past him like a stork and came back again a minute later with a newspaper, behind which he vanished on the opposite seat. Thorens and the girl came out of Immigration and he saw them look up and down the platform. The constable who had woken him up guided them to the dining car, which was kind but unfortunate. They came in, were given a table and when Thorens' eyes met his, he knew he was recognized, not as a policeman perhaps, but as somebody he had seen before. Then the immigration officer from the British section came in, said, in a ringing voice, "Ah, there you are. Well, here's the information you wanted. I hope our friend does not shake you," and at the look of dismay on his face, he added apologetically, but still with the volume of the barracks, "Oh, I'm sorry. Well, cheerio, and happy hunting."

He closed his eyes wearily, thinking that this just could not be true. The man must bear him a personal grudge. But no. This all came somewhere, somehow, under the heading of the secret that won the war. The undertaker's assistant appeared at his table and looked down on him as if he were lying in a coffin. "Breakfast, sir?"

"Yes, please."

"Orange juice, sir?"

"No, thank you. Is there a menu?"

"It will be either bacon or kippers, sir. That is to say, if you want breakfast. There is continental breakfast, of course."

"I'll have kippers, and coffee."

"Very good, sir."

He saw that Thorens was given the same treatment. It was an unexpected tie between them that created a feeling almost of companionship. He no longer felt any personal antagonism, nor did he think again of this being his great moment of decision or whatever it was he had felt when he was getting tipsy in the captain's cabin last night. He just felt tired and neutral and hungry. A whistle throbbed on the platform, some people came running and the train left. It would not stop before Liverpool Street Station, so he could have his breakfast in peace.

The kippers came and went, the Englishman opposite read his paper, folding it smaller and smaller as he became conscious of his fellow traveler reading the back, which also had to do with the great secret. Thorens had finished his breakfast too and leaned back in his seat, his eyes closed, tweed cap on the bridge of his nose, but his sleep looked as convincing as that of a crocodile. The girl sat looking out of the window at England's green and pleasant land. The morning fog had lifted, smoke rose from the chimneys of red brick houses and of distant farms in the fields.

The ticket collector came and was less easy to handle than his Dutch opposite number. He cursed himself for not having foreseen this. The man brought out a writing pad on a steel base, a book of fares, a spectacle case from which he produced a pair of steel-rimmed glasses, and a pencil with eraser that came from his cap. He wrote out, in triplicate, as if for the entertainment of the bored travelers in the dining car, that the undersigned, Jongman, Peter, had taken a seat in a second-class compartment of the London North Eastern Railway without a valid ticket, and without notifying the conductor prior to the commencement of the journey. The undersigned admitted these facts and would be notified of court proceedings by the proper authorities in due course. For the time being, he paid his fare, for which he received a receipt. All this could probably have been fixed if he had shown the man his card, but he might as well have passed it among the audience. The look Thorens gave him after the show was over was one of sly amusement, contrasting with the cold stare he received from the gentleman opposite, whose paper now measured four inches square. With all this, time passed quickly and he found himself on the platform of Liverpool Street Station with no English money left worth speaking of. He stood a moment in doubt as to whether to let Thorens go and assume that he would indeed travel to the address he had given to Immigration, or boldly to board a taxi in pursuit and hope for the best.

He did the latter and it all worked so smoothly that it almost looked as if Thorens cooperated. They drove through the sad ruins of the City of London that seemed to invigorate the English, who strode briskly from the catacombs of the tube to the catacombs of their offices. The taxi driver gave a long monologue of jokes in cockney, with a stage accent and a strange rolling motion of his torso as if he were cycling. The traffic was slow, courteous and on the wrong side of the street; the taxi with the couple in it was not difficult to follow. As they turned into Sloane Street, after crossing Hyde Park and Knightsbridge, it became obvious that Thorens was indeed heading for the Chelsea address he had given to Immigration and the taxi meter mounted steadily. They ground their way down Kings Road, turned left at the far end and headed for the river. The taxi ahead of them stopped in front of a block of flats, one side of which was missing. He told his driver to pass and round the next corner. In passing, he checked the number and saw that this was the address on the card. He had better give Jim a call now.

He asked the taxi driver to stop at the nearest call box. It was on the Embankment. The river lay wide and glinting in the early light, the tide was high, muddy water swirled through the pilings of the police dock and between the barges restlessly chafing at their moorings against the quay. The Battersea Power Station, half finished, smeared the sky with a trail of smoke. The city seemed strangely unconscious of the river flowing through its heart, it seemed as if it had turned its back on it. He stood looking out of the grimy little windows of the call box, while the switchboard of Scotland Yard tried to locate Commander Scott for him. The sight of the river through those little windowpanes was melancholy and still wintry. No birds, no boats, just the cold, muddy, restless water, tumbling and swirling mindlessly to the sea. There was no launch at the police dock and not a man to be seen. If this were a village, he would have said that there was a fair somewhere or a parade, and that all the villagers had gone to join the fun, leaving him dismal and alone in his glass box, its windows slowly steaming over.

"Jim? This is Peter. Sorry to bother you this early, but did you get my cable?"

"Just found it this minute on my desk." The voice was precise and impersonal. It sounded far away, like the villagers. "What is it this time?"

He smiled sourly to himself. He probably would have put the same question in Jim's place. "I have just followed the leading suspect in the white-slave racket to his London address from the Hook. He has another victim with him. I think it's about time we moved in."

"You followed who?"

His smile clung on tenaciously. "An alien, from your point of view, who seems to be the kingpin of the white-slave ring that ships those girls to South America. Remember?"

"Of course, of course. I'm sorry, the line is bad. Where are you now?"

"In a public call box somewhere on the Embankment in West Chelsea. Right opposite the police dock as a matter of fact."

"And where's your man?"

"At his home address, according to his disembarkation card. A block of flats in Ashburnham Road, just around the corner."

"All right. Now, let me see. Perkins?"

"Pardon?"

"Sorry, I'm talking to the sergeant. What are my appointments this morning?" A man's voice mumbled in the background. "All right, give him a call and tell him that I'm out on a case that has matured unexpectedly." Mumble, mumble. "I should be back by then. Peter?"

"Yes."

"If you drive on along the Embankment about a quarter of a mile toward the city, you'll find behind a little parklike thing, a sort of lawn, a small restaurant called the Golden Pheasant. You can't miss it. It has a sign outside with a bird on it. Wait there, order a cup of coffee, I'll be with you in about twenty minutes."

"All right. Golden Pheasant. But, Jim, by the way . . ."

"Yes?"

"I have a taxi waiting that I took in Liverpool Street and I haven't any English money left. Sorry to bother you with this, but what do I do?"

"Oh, I see." The voice was bland, careful not to betray any irritation. "I don't quite know who is on duty this morning, but there are two waiters at the restaurant. One is called Albert and the other Oscar. Both of them, I am afraid, are Cypriots. Just tell them, either of them, that I would be obliged if he would pay the taxi for you and will be around presently."

"Okay, thank you very much."

"That's quite all right, old boy. I'll be there shortly."

"Thank you, Jim. I . . ." but Commander Scott had hung up.

"The Golden Pheasant," he said to the taxi driver. "It should be about half a mile down the road on the left-hand side."

"I know it," the taxi driver said. "Classy joint. Used to be a hangout for tugboat captains during the war. Now they've got candles."

The sign showed a bird painted by an amateur. The door was lemon yellow and in the window, half covered with net curtains, there was a little sign saying, *"Table d'hôte* from 6 to 8 P.M. for the discriminating."

One of the men who Jim had been afraid was a Cypriot stood staring swarthily over the net curtains as he got out of his taxi. There was a little doorbell, a smell of cold frying oil, and a shrill-voiced angry little dog answering the doorbell. A disembodied Levantine voice said, *"Couche,"* and half a Cypriot advanced from the shadows in a short white coat and black trousers.

"Good morning, sir."

"Good morning. Are you Albert or Oscar?"

"Oscar, sir."

The little dog's hysterical bark drew closer and the waiter growled, between his teeth, *"Couche,* Sally, or I . . ." and there followed a few words in what he supposed must be Greek that changed Sally's yapping into Cheyne-Stokes breathing.

"Commander Scott of Scotland Yard will be here in a quarter of an hour or so, and he told me to ask you to pay my taxi for me. I've just come from abroad and I don't have any English money. So if you'd be so kind. . . ."

The waiter looked at him from under lowered eyebrows. Even the dog had fallen silent as if amazed; it was still invisible but its presence hovered somewhere around the Cypriot's invisible ankles.

"I assure you that I am quite trustworthy," he said. "My name is Jongman. I am an inspector of the Amsterdam Police."

"Certainly," the Cypriot said. "How much is it?"

"I don't know. Perhaps you would ask him?"

The doorbell tinkled as the waiter went out, and Sally waddled into the light. She was a small fat pug with black and white markings, the kind of creature the French call, benevolently, *"chien de concierge,"* with one opaque milky eye and half-cocked ears that looked like a hat of the Gay 'Nineties. She started to growl at him and he said, "Shut up, Sally," in Dutch. The little dog fixed him with her milky eye and panted. The Cypriot came back and said, "It was eight and six, sir, including tip. Would you like something while you're waiting for the Commander?"

"A cup of coffee—and thank you very much for your trouble."

"It's a pleasure, sir. Come along, Sally," but the little dog, fascinated, went on staring at him, panting. The waiter brought him a cup of coffee that managed to look bad even before he tasted it, but there was a lump of sugar and Sally's panting accelerated. "All right, Sally," he said in Dutch, "Let's see if you can sit up and beg.

Come on." He held out the lump of sugar, tantalizing her, but Sally would not beg. Instead, she panted frantically and, when the lump was not forthcoming at once, she waddled while sitting down, as if stamping her feet, and gave an angry hoarse bark. "All right," he said, "here it is," and he threw the lump of sugar on the floor in front of her. She did not look at it. She did not even sniff. She just sat there panting, fixing him with her milky stare, waiting for something that existed only in her mind. He wondered what a dog's mind looked like, for want of any better thought; then a car stopped in front of the restaurant.

Like all things British, it was discreet. No one who did not belong would have recognized it as a police car. Out came a dapper man in a checked sports coat with leather patches on the elbows, and a soft hat. He had not changed much since the day he had come down the gangway in Amsterdam for the first time, only he had a mustache now as if to hide the deepening of the lines around his mouth. Commander James Scott, Scotland Yard, looked the very image of success, as he gave the driver an order and headed for the café, and Peter felt a sudden twinge of envy. It was the war that had done it; Jim had been able to go on building up his career during the hostilities, the bombings of London had improved his chances for promotion instead of retarding them, whereas he himself, caught in the rattrap of Occupied Holland, had seen his chances wane. He had had to let those saboteurs escape and close his eyes to scurrying food thieves during the great famine of the last winter of the Occupation. All those liberties he had taken with the law, those moments of voluntary blindness and ham-acted stupidity had been patriotic actions at the time, regarded by his desk-bound colleagues with envious respect. Now that the war was over, their respect had

turned into suspicion because they were safe, and all that remained of his modest acts of patriotism was that, in the eyes of the bureaucrats, he was compromised. Although he felt no kinship with them whatever, and had been trying to keep them in check all through the war, he now shared the fate of the underground fighters of Amsterdam Harbor: they were called "unreliable" after the liberation, and that was what his colleagues in the Service must call him behind his back. It was the only explanation for the promotion of that colonial inspector over his head. The man had been a prisoner of war and stricken with beriberi in a Japanese labor camp. That was permissible. It had not impaired his sense of good and evil as far as Article 13B was concerned: "The officer shall abide by the letter of the law at all times and leave its interpretation to the authorities in whom such discriminatory powers are vested." It all seemed obvious as he saw Jim Scott briskly stride toward the door of the Golden Pheasant in Chelsea.

The bell tinkled as the door was thrust open authoritatively and the little half-blind dog gave a muted growl.

"Good morning, Commander," the Cypriot waiter said like any shopkeeper welcoming an important customer in the Orient, and he said, quietly, "Hello, Jim."

"Ah, there you are!" Jim cried. "I'm sorry if I'm a little late but your call and your telegram arrived virtually at the same moment and. . . . Coffee please, Oscar."

"Very good, sir. Come along, Sally."

But Sally hopped on a chair at the opposite table with an arthritical leap; there she squatted, one hind leg in the air, staring milkily at the leather patches, the checked suit, the hat on the table, the well-polished brown brogues.

"Well, it's nice to see you again," Jim said with a ready smile that marked time while his alert gray eyes took him in. "How's Susie?"

"She's fine, thank you. Still a little under the weather since the war, of course. Gastric trouble, you know, but otherwise she's just fine." He remembered with a faint nostalgia those early days when Jim and he had had long nightly discussions about women, then about fiancées, then about wives, then about young mothers, and then about women again, in an effort to put their private worries into general terms. Susie was a bitter, dissatisfied woman and Jim knew it, just as Peter knew that Martha was a genteel, sentimental, dowdy *Hausfrau*, who gave the impression of being made of blancmange whereas in reality she was made of drop-forged steel. Martha and he had disliked one another at sight, possibly because, at that time, he had been more intimate with Jim than she. "How's Martha?" he asked.

"Bearing up," Jim said, smiling at the waiter who came with a cup of coffee. "Thank you, Oscar. No, thank you, no sugar. The waistline, you know, ha, ha. She's a bit flustered right now, what with Angela's return, you know. Worried the child won't have any young people to divert her. American college holidays are quite different from the English ones, you know."

"Yes, I suppose so," he said, thinking how fortunate Jim had been to be able to send his daughter to America when the bombing started, and wondering what price he would have to pay for it, in what the law called "alienated affection."

"I can't wait to see her again," he said.

"Well, you will, I hope," Jim said with breezy insincerity. "Next time you're here, let's all have dinner some evening, and take in a show."

"I'd love to," he said, feeling a growing attachment to the little dog that followed the conversation with the envy of a lower species, a canine Homer overhearing a

dialogue of gods in a divine language. Perhaps that was all Venus and Apollo had said, "Let's all have dinner some evening and take in a show," to make Homer smite his lyre.

"Well, what brings you here this time?" Jim asked. "Oh, of course, the white-slave racket. You say you're on to another victim?"

He told him about Thorens, the girl, the ferry, the taxi, the block of flats in Ashburnham Road. As he told the story, he was struck by the casualness with which he referred to the girl, as if his subconscious wanted to protect her from Jim's dehumanizing objectivity. He could not be expected to feel compassion for someone he had never set eyes on. "So there it is," he concluded. "How do you suppose you'll go about it?"

"About what?"

"About arresting him."

"You say the address he gave Immigration is the address he actually went to?"

"Yes."

"And Immigration raised no objection to his entry, or the girl's?"

"No."

"How old is the girl?"

"Twenty-one."

"Then I'm afraid there's little we can do at this stage."

"What?"

"So far, the man hasn't done a thing that would justify arresting him or even searching his flat. His passport is in order, he's been admitted by Immigration, he's traveling in the company of an adult alien whose passport must also be in order or she wouldn't have been admitted either; what do you propose I do about it?"

"Well, there are various possibilities, I would say. To

start with, the name Thorens is an alias, as we all know."

"Do we?"

"Of course we do. We ran his description through Interpol and he turned up under three different names, two in Paris, the other in Barcelona."

"For all we know, Thorens may be his real name, and even if it is not, what is the charge?"

He could not believe his ears. For a moment he thought that Jim was just sparring with him in order to test the arguments for Thorens' arrest, but he was not. He was not going to arrest Thorens. He was going to let him go right ahead and ship that girl to South America. "Do you realize what the man is doing?" he asked. "You know the racket. Here goes another innocent girl, the age of our own daughters, about to be exported as a whore against her will. Are you going to let him?"

"For one thing, we don't know whether it is against her will," Jim said, his patience showing, "and for another thing, what we have to deal with is the law. If this man works within the law . . ."

"Within the law? But, for God's sake . . ."

Jim raised a pale hand. "Please let me finish. Perhaps I formulated it incorrectly. If this man's activities are un-assailable by the law as it stands, then there is only one solution . . ."

"Stop him, regardless," he blurted out, and cursed himself. He should not get emotional over this.

"That's where you and I differ," Jim said pleasantly, but with the alacrity of triumph. "If we want to stop him, we'll have to change the law. The worst that we could do would be to take the law in our own hands. That, in my opinion, was what the war was about, the only justification for the death and the destruction we and the others brought upon ourselves. I am certainly not going to re-linquish that principle now that the war is won."

"Very noble," he said, "but do you know where that principle would have landed you in Holland during the Occupation? In front of the firing squad."

"I don't doubt it," Jim said calmly.

"I see. You think that's where I should have ended up?"

"Don't be ridiculous. I don't think anything of the sort. I realize that you on your side, being occupied, had to break the law during the war to serve our cause. But now you must make a conscious effort to correct the contempt for the law you have developed for the best of reasons during those years. You must realize, as I've just said, that the war was fought to protect the citizen from his government or its civil servants manipulating the law to suit their own aims, and . . ."

"Oh, for heaven's sake," he cried. "I don't want a bloody lecture. Look . . ."

"I think that's exactly what you do need. I . . ."

"Look, we have known one another for twenty-five years. We have worked together, we have been friends, we are friends . . ."

"That's exactly it. That is why, in this case, I have to be more alert than ever. Because we are friends, I am not going to arrest that man without proper justification."

"But what justification do you want? Here's a white-slave trader, leading a victim to her fate across your territory! What else do you want?"

"I want an instance in which this man has broken the law so far. Believe me, Peter, I am not being stubborn or highhanded about this. It is a matter of principle."

"Well, same here. I am not going to let him get away with it."

"I beg your pardon?"

"Look, Jim. After twenty-five years, I am not going to be intimidated by your newly won authority. You sound to me like a man who has not yet recovered from his promotion."

He had said it half jocularly, but the sharpening of Jim's nostrils showed that it had been a stupid thing to say. Jim's adherence to the letter of the law with such religious fervor probably had a personal cause, but it was not his promotion. Whatever its cause, right now he had to count with it. The girl's life depended on it. Should he speak aloud the thought that crossed his mind? He looked at the other's tight, uncompromising face and decided he would. If this was to be a showdown, let it be an adult one. "I hope you're not piqued?" he said. "I would hate to think that a girl's life was to be decided by my treading on your toes."

"I must confess that I find this an unfortunate discussion," Jim said.

"It's a hell of a lot more unfortunate for the girl than it is for you or me."

"I didn't realize you felt so strongly about it. I must say, it dismays me."

"Why?"

"I think it's a bad idea that a police officer should get emotional about a case. You are a servant of the law, not a Paladin."

"Look, Jim, if this were a case of a mug trying to run some diamonds out of the country, or some national treasure, a rolled-up painting or somebody's bust, I'd play with you. But here is a girl, a Jewish girl who's been in a concentration camp, who has lost her parents to the gas chamber, who has not a relative left, and is now being carried off by this hyena. Now, wouldn't it be within the spirit of our victorious law to make that creature open his jaws and drop her, and never mind the means we use to achieve that end?"

"I'd love to have a long debate with you about ends and means, as in the old days," Jim said. "In fact, I think we should, and the sooner the better. But right now I just haven't the time."

"I see." He smiled and felt a silly, pointless satisfaction at seeing the discomfort in Jim's eyes. "Right now you're too busy protecting the law to protect a helpless girl about to be raped in a brothel in South America."

"I don't think I want to argue with you, Peter," Jim said, taking up his hat. "I will contact Immigration, and I'll see whether we can't find something in the man's past to justify a warning which might put him off . . ."

"Look, Jim, I suspect this is pointless, but let me re-mind you that this man is probably a German ex-Nazi. He's of the type that did not heed civilized warnings, re-member? All he understands is force. You have to sling this man into prison, at least, if you want to stop him, and you know it just as well as I do."

"All right, granted. Then, what we can do is interview the girl and tell her the truth. If, after that, she still wants to go, it's up to her."

"And who is going to do the interviewing? When? Where? What effect do you think the appearance of one of your female wardens will have on a girl with her his-tory?"

"What axe have you to grind?"

"I don't get you."

"What is your personal interest in this case?"

"The same as yours, I suppose. It's a test case for what I, as well as you, consider to be the principle we have lived and worked by for most of our adult lives. I maintain that your equivalent of our Article 13B, which tells us to stick to the letter of the law and leave its interpretation to others, is not a principle but an excuse, a loophole for our consciences faced with the gateway of the Old Bailey. Remember what it says there? 'Protect the children of the poor and punish the wrongdoer.' Well, here is your child of the poor, here is your wrongdoer."

"And this is not the Old Bailey. You cannot take the law into your own hands any longer, Peter. The war is over. You must come back to law and order or . . ."

"Or what?"

"Or you'll get into trouble," Jim said with a smile. "You might find yourself forced to resign from the force, if you can no longer adhere to whatever the article is you mentioned."

He had to face it: if he wanted to help the girl he should not antagonize Jim any longer, but treat him as what he was: an adversary. "You're right, Jim," he said, "I'm sorry if I let myself be carried away. As I'm Dutch myself, I wonder whether it would be a good idea if I had a talk with the girl, rather than one of your people."

"By all means. I'm amazed you didn't do so before she left your country. It would have simplified matters."

"I'm sorry to have wasted your time."

"Don't be so damned aggressive. You know jolly well I'm delighted to see you, only I can't help feeling that this matter could have been handled a little closer to its source. But I'm delighted it brought you here. What about dinner tonight? I mean, at the club?"

"I'd love to. So, it's all right with you if I go and see the young lady and have a word with her?"

"But, my dear Peter, surely this is a rhetorical question? You are a free agent, so is the girl, so is the man.

As far as I am concerned, there is no case. Why are you smiling? I mean it."

"I know you do, Jim. Where do you want me to meet you for dinner?"

"Oh, well, I'd say give me a ring some time this afternoon and we'll make it definite. All right?"

"Anything you say."

"That's agreed, then." He got up, picked up his hat; then he looked at Peter with a quizzical expression, half smile, half frown. It was as if the future hung in the balance for a moment, as if he still could choose between sitting down again and working it all out, honestly and sincerely, or washing his hands of the affair. "I had better pay for your taxi, while I think of it," he said. "Oscar!"

"Yes, sir. Yes, Commander, yes, sir."

Peter watched him leave and stride briskly down to the curb where, discreetly, almost magically, the police car came gliding to a stop. "Well, Sally," he said to Homer at the foot of Olympus, "so you don't like sugar, eh? Well, let's try this cookie." While the little dog sat crumbling the biscuit, he remembered that he should have asked Jim for some money, but perhaps it was better this way. He felt enough of an unwanted relative as it was. He pushed back his chair, got up, put on his hat and said, "Be seeing you" to the waiter and, "Bye, Sally" to the dog, then, putting on his coat, he left the Golden Pheasant and its tinkling bell, deep in thought.

As he set out in the direction of Ashburnham Road, he felt something heavy bang against his leg as he walked. It was the captain's gun; he had forgotten to leave it behind as he had planned the night before. Now it might come in handy; when he had decided toward the end of

35

his conversation with Jim to go and see Thorens he had not visualized how their meeting would work out. It was unlikely that Thorens could be intimidated into giving up the girl, except at gunpoint. Even so, he might be hard to convince. Inspectors of the Amsterdam Police did not go about London shooting people whom commanders of Scotland Yard refused to arrest.

He stopped in front of the block of flats and looked up at its mutilated façade. The building had been sheared off along an inner wall, the rubble of the destroyed apartments had been cleared away but on the wall there still were patches of wallpaper, discolored and buckled by rain, and the remains of fireplaces. One of them still had its mantelpiece; on it stood a row of what must have once been books. For some reason the pathetic little row of soaked and grimy books in that inaccessible spot made him think of the girl, staring at her own face reflected in the night, and he was suddenly overcome by a rage that took him completely unawares. He realized at once that he must control it at all costs, or it would trick him into an error of judgment. He must have all his wits about him now. He put his hands in the pockets of his overcoat and, after a quick look up and down the street, he entered the building.

The hall was dark and still smelled of rubble dust. On the gate of the elevator hung a notice that he could not read in the dark, but he understood it was out of order. As he quietly mounted the concrete stairway to the first floor, grit crunched under his shoes. "That's the miserable thing about bombed-out buildings," his next-door neighbor, who was in the building trade, had once said. "Clean them as often as you will, the dust goes on flying." On the first-floor landing he found two doors. By the light of a match he found a visiting card on one of them, attached with a thumbtack: "A. F. Thorens." It was all in the open, no hint of subterfuge, the man must be very sure of himself.

He pressed the bell and waited in the darkness, but nothing happened. He had not heard a bell ring inside, so it must be out of order too. He knocked on the door and put his hand back in the pocket of his overcoat as he heard steps approaching. The door opened.

Thorens did not look surprised. He looked as if he had expected him and dressed for the part. He wore a violet silk dressing gown and carried a long cigarette holder. His blond hair, gray at the temples, was carefully brushed. He stood there like a man who was conscious of the envy he caused in the meek; a man who was utterly sure of himself.

"Hello, Inspector," he said with a smile. "I was expecting you."

"Mind if I come in? I'd like a word with you."

"By all means. Can I take your coat?"

"No, thank you," he said, "I will only take a moment."

Thorens had accompanied his offer with a gesture toward a coat rack in the corner. He did not see the girl's coat on it. He wondered where she was.

Thorens opened the door to a sitting room; he entered. It looked prosperous; the furniture was Portuguese, the arms of the chairs ended in lions' heads, their leather backs were embossed with coats of arms. An oil painting of someone's ancestor hung over a fireplace, flanked by crossed sabers. On the wall was a collection of arms: old-fashioned pistols and daggers and Javanese krisses, a proud show of virility.

"Well, Inspector?" Thorens asked, closing the door. "What can I do for you?"

"I don't think there's any need to beat about the bush," he said matter-of-factly. "You obviously spotted me right at the start and you know what I'm here for."

Thorens inhaled, looked at the tip of his cigarette and blew out a breath of smoke. "It would seem," he replied, "that your friend Commander Scott has enlightened you."

"In what way?"

"If there were any possibility of apprehending me on legal grounds, you would not be here. He would."

"Very true," he said, smiling, feeling calm and clear-minded. "Commander Scott had to admit defeat. He represents British law and, as you know, the British have not known an Occupation. I have. Do you understand what I mean?"

Thorens gave a thoughtful little laugh, and concentrated on the tip of his cigarette again. "Surely you don't mean that as a threat, do you, Inspector? You don't think I am as impressionable as all that?"

"I'll tell you what I think. It is important you should know."

"Ah?"

"I think that you are fit only to be killed, like a rattlesnake."

"This really is a compliment," Thorens said, amused. "You couldn't have formulated the success of our organization any better. Of course, I don't know what you're talking about," he added, hastily. "I just think that, whatever you may have in mind, it implies a defeat of Interpol."

"Look, Thorens," he said, noticing to his dismay a return of the rage he had thought he had under control. "The situation is this: for the moment, you cannot be stopped by the law. There are only two ways of stopping you. One is to talk to your victims and tell them who you are, the other is to kill you. You may choose. Where is she?"

"She is not here," Thorens said with a smile, "and I can't tell you where she is. She is on her way elsewhere, that's all I can say. So, there's only the other thing left, Inspector."

He realized that the man was taunting him and he felt calm again. "All right," he said, "as you wish. Don't let's waste any more words. I have warned you, I can do no more."

"But how crude, Inspector," Thorens said, still with that confident smile. "Suppose you were to kill me? What purpose would that serve? Your friend Commander Scott would realize full well that you had killed me without the slightest provocation. There is no reason for me to provoke you, I have all I want. As far as I know the British, you would find yourself with the law on your tail. Or don't you care?" He scrutinized him for a moment with an odd, mocking sympathy, then he said, "Come, Inspector, wake up. The war is over. Ten years from now your hatred for me will be as quaint as my SS dagger up there. There was a time when to receive such a dagger was a consecration; now every American G. I. wants one, to take home as a souvenir, the demand is such that a factory in Germany has started to manufacture them again. Where would I be if I went on cherishing the memory of the day I received mine, after swearing the oath of allegiance? 'Blood and Honor.' At the time those words filled me with pride; now my only interest in them is that they are engraved on the blades of all SS daggers, and that to a connoisseur they give away whether he is dealing with an authentic one, or with a present-day copy."

"How?"

Thorens smiled. "You see, even you cannot escape the morbid fascination. I'll show you." He took a dagger in a worn sheath from a hook on the wall. "We prevailed upon the factory to make a slight variation in today's inscription." He pulled the dagger out of its sheath. "Look: where it says *'Blut'* . . ." Then he saw the revolver.

He stood for a moment stock still, incredulously; then the color slowly drained from his face. "Well now, Inspec——"

"Don't move!"

He froze. His smile had not faltered, his eyes were cold and bright; the only thing he could not control was the color of his face. It was now ashen. "Very clever, Inspector. This makes it self-defense, of course. How stupid——"

"Stand still!"

He sighed. "All right."

"Where is the girl?"

The muscles in his jaw tautened and slackened; otherwise he stood perfectly still, but his bright eyes became defiant. "Why, Inspector!" he said brazenly. "Don't tell me you are smitten by her!"

Then the fury that Peter had controlled with such self-confidence surged back, with staggering violence. His body stiffened as from an electric shock; with a feeling of panic he realized that he was going to shoot him, that he was at the mercy of a power beyond his control, a pawn in a game that had started underneath the clock in the hall of the station. His finger tightened on the trigger, and he saw in Thorens' eyes the realization that he was in earnest. For a moment it seemed as if the man were going to throw himself on him, then he started to tremble abjectly, still standing motionless in that waxwork attitude, holding the dagger in one hand and its sheath in the other. "But why?" he cried shrilly, with a voice that had shed all pretense. "What for God's sake does she matter? What do any of them matter? They are only Jewish bitches that slipped through the net! This one is from a medical-research camp, she is no good to anybody. She has even been sterilized!"

At those words, Peter felt the blood draw away from his face. He felt sick in his stomach as their full meaning penetrated, and then he was overcome by a strange confusion. Who was he, to stand there threatening this soul in utter damnation with a gun? He did not believe in God, or heavenly justice, but at that moment he realized that to shoot Thorens would be an act of preposterous presumption. He suddenly felt puny, as if the man he faced had flared into a genie of evil, a fallen angel, from whom he could only flee in mortal terror. He put the gun back in his pocket and left the room.

As he crossed the hall, he heard a door squeak but he did not look back. He went out, down the flight of stairs, out into the open. He crossed the road and leaned over the parapet of the Embankment. The barges tied up to the shore were resting on the mud flats, the tide was low. A little sandpiper ran up and down at the water's edge, pecking in the mud.

There he stood, defeated. Whatever his motive might have been, it was the defeat that counted. He had proved to himself what must have been obvious to everyone else for years: he could not cope with his times. He had faced evil, gun in hand, with the chance of stamping it out for ever; instead he had thought about God and meekly turned away when Thorens had revealed the extent of his damnation. He had to face it: he was an old man, unable to cope any longer. It would have taken a member of a younger generation to pull that trigger, someone to whom the memory of the world through which the little patrol boat had sailed with the proud young sub-inspector on its foredeck was not Paradise Lost; someone who had grown into boyhood amid the whispered stories of concentration camps and razzias and extermination furnaces.

He saw a small launch go past, gaily romping with the tide. He remembered Jim telling him, long ago, that up-river, at the lock near Hampton Court, swans on summer nights drifted like ghosts in the moonlight. He remembered the image Jim's words had evoked at the time, an image of unbearable nostalgia, while those words rang out once more in his memory: "She has even been steri-lized!" He covered his face with his hands, overcome once more by confusion. Why had he been unable to pull the trigger? What was it that had kept him from slaying that man as he would a rabid beast? Was it be-cause he had never realized how deep Man had fallen in those years of the war? It seemed as if a mask had been ripped away, not from the face of the enemy alone, but from the face of their generation, his own. He had, dur-ing the war, seen the Nazis and the Quislings do their henchman's work, he had seen the yellow stars of David on the coats of his Jewish neighbors, he had heard them abducted at dead of night, in trucks, heard their thin cries, "Goodbye! Goodbye!" fade away into silence, but only now, on hearing Thorens blurt out those words, had he realized that he who had listened and they who had abducted belonged to the same generation, were members of the same body, part of the same soul. Some time in the past, some sunlit summer's day long ago, Thorens must have bicycled through the dappled light and shade of a German forest with a dog running by his side, a boy on his first bicycle, as innocent of his destiny as he himself had been when he paddled his first canoe into the magic garden of the marshes behind the village where he was born. Two boys had set out in life, one on a bicycle, one in a canoe, and they had finally faced one another in a bombed-out flat in London, over a gun.

As he stood looking at the muddy water and at the little sandpiper busily pacing up and down along the miniature surf, wrapped up in its own world, he felt the sudden urge to do something positive, something that would not solve anything but might absolve something, however infinitesimally small, of what all the boys of his year had done. Then he realized that someone was standing beside him. It was the girl.

He tried to hide his shock as he asked, "Where do you come from?"

"I was in the next room," she said. Her voice sounded very young.

"So you heard?" he asked.

"Yes," she answered. "At one moment, I thought you were going to shoot him."

"Yes," he said, "it looked like that for a while. Then I thought better of it."

"My father couldn't do it either," she said matter-of-factly, and she looked at him with her big dark eyes for the first time.

"What do you mean?"

"He told my mother that if the Germans came to fetch us, he would fight them. I overheard him talking about it. He was going to shoot as many Germans as he could and then he would shoot us and then himself. I was convinced he would do it, for I knew he had a gun, and I planned to crawl under the bed so that he would not find me. They came in broad daylight, we were all in the sitting room. But he must have expected them, for he pulled out the gun and pointed it at them and they stood for a moment in the doorway, afraid to move. Then he lowered the gun, as if he had suddenly seen something, something we couldn't see, a ghost. They snatched the gun away from him and struck him in the face. That's what I remember most clearly. The way he lowered that gun and was struck in the face."

"I see," he said lamely.

"I didn't understand it at the time, I still don't understand it. All I know is that it was not cowardice. I wanted to tell him that, but by the time I got around to realizing it it was too late. He had been transported to another camp, the last one."

"I see," he said.

"Can you tell me why you could not do it?" she asked. "Don't if you don't want to, but it is important to me."

He looked away. He had no right to answer that question for her, knowing that she would interpret it as her father's conclusion at his moment of truth. "Would you have done it?" he asked.

"Oh yes," she answered with the naive callousness of this new generation, to whom all nightmares were a familiar reality. "If I had had a gun."

"Why?"

"To stop him doing the same thing to others," she answered; and then she added, "No, that's not true. I would have done it because that is what I felt like doing, when I realized that he was not planning to smuggle me into Palestine despite the money I gave him."

"Is that what he said he would do?"

"Yes. I knew he was a Nazi, of course, one of the thousands that are still about. I can spot them in a crowd, they don't even have to open their mouths. But I thought that this one might do what he said, if it was only to put one over on the British even after his defeat. I obviously still idealized him."

"I'm afraid so," he said.

"Just as a matter of interest, what was he planning to do with me?"

"White-slave trade. A—er—house in South America."

She stared at him for a moment, incredulously, then, to his alarm, she began to laugh. She laughed whole-heartedly, infectiously; it transformed her completely. For one short moment he saw her as she would have been if there had been no war: a gay, young Jewish girl, full of joy and vitality. But at this moment her laughter was all wrong. It was horrifying.

"Sorry," she said, seeing his face. "You must forgive me. It is very funny but it's a private joke, I'm afraid. It's almost a pity he did not go through with it. Oh well," she added, serious again, "either way, there went my last chance to make something out of my life."

"What do you mean?" he asked.

She shrugged her shoulders. "He was my last hope of getting into Palestine. All that's left for me now is to go back to Holland and enter some sanatorium."

"Why? Are you ill?"

She said, lightly, "Yes."

To change the subject, he asked, "Why can't you get into Palestine?"

She looked at him, surprised. "Haven't you been reading the newspapers? The British won't admit any more immigrants until the state of emergency is lifted."

"Well, that won't last for ever, will it?"

"Even if it is lifted, as long as the British are in Palestine there will never be unrestricted immigration of

Jews. And have you any idea how many there are waiting to be admitted right now? Hundreds of thousands in the camp of La Ciotat in France alone, and millions all over the world. If I were to join the queue, I don't think my turn would come before the state of Israel is founded and, by that time, it will be too late for me."

She had said it calmly, and he realized that she was not only convinced it was true but had accepted its inevitability.

"How else could you get in?" he asked.

"Apparently the gunrunners take on Jews, occasionally," she answered. "Their headquarters seem to be in Tangier. That is where he said he would take me, from London."

"And what were you planning to do in Palestine once you got there?"

"Become a nurse in a mental hospital, for survivors of the camps. It's the only thing that would give me the feeling that everything that has happened to me had a point." Then she added, for the first time with some emotion, "I don't think a Christian can realize what Israel means to us. In the camps, we talked about nothing else. The camps were terrible, but, on the other hand, it was a sort of revelation. I had never lived exclusively among Jews; I found out that all sorts of characteristics I had thought to be personal to me, such as being excitable and talking all the time and being tremendously interested in everything and exhausting everybody else, were in reality not personal characteristics at all, but. . . . I'm sorry, I'm getting carried away."

"Go on," he said.

"Well, I have said it, really. Only among Jews can I be myself. Myself, I, and not a generalization: a Jewess among the goyim. Now that I am one of the few who survived the camps, I feel even more alien. I feel like a —a migrating bird left behind by its flock. But, well, never mind. This is the way it is, and so I suppose this is the way it has to be. When were you planning to go back?"

He tried to suppress the impulse that had forced itself upon him as she talked, and he said, "Whenever it suits you. I should be back tomorrow morning at the latest." Then he gave in to the impulse and added, "What would you say if I offered to take you to Palestine?"

She looked at him, alarmed. "I beg your pardon?"

"What would you say if I offered to take you to Palestine?" he repeated, calmly. He had a curious sensation of unreality and, at the same time, of a tremendous liberation, as if this had been the purpose of all the bewildering moves that had been made with him as a pawn in this mysterious game of destiny. It was a reckless proposal, yet it seemed inescapable, as if he had had the choice between shooting Thorens or taking over from him the promise with which he had tried to lure this lost child to her perdition. At the same time, he wished he had never said it; for, although he could not immediately grasp the consequences his decision would have, he realized at that moment its full magnitude.

"You can't be serious," she said, almost angrily.

"I am," he replied. "If you want me to, I'll take you to Palestine."

"But how much is that going to cost?" she asked, confused. "I mean, I haven't got a penny left. I gave him all I had. There is, of course, the money of my father's business that the Germans confiscated, but. . . ."

"It's not a matter of money," he said. "It's a matter of your really wanting it."

"I—I don't understand," she said, with a sudden weariness that, for some reason, made him feel ashamed and left him at a loss for words.

They stood silently side by side for a few moments, staring at the little sandpiper running busily to and fro along the water's edge. Then she asked, "May I ask you something?" And as he said, "Of course," she continued, "How old are you?"

He looked at her face, her eyes, her desperate effort to prevent herself falling a victim once more to yet another man obsessed by a demon. "Too old," he replied, smiling, and then the corners of her mouth began to tremble and she laughed and her face became once more that of a gay, young Jewish girl; but as she laughed, her eyes filled with tears. "I would have said, too young," she said, foolishly.

He suddenly became conscious, completely, of his responsibility, and a great peace came over him, a certainty that he had never known before. "I'll tell you what," he said. "Down the road there's a little restaurant where we'll have something to eat; then, while you have your coffee, I'll quickly go and change some money, and then we'll go and see the sights. Have you ever been to London before?"

"No," she said. "No, never." She obviously still did not know what to think.

"Well," he said, "we'll go and see the Tower, and Madame Tussaud's and—er—Buckingham Palace. And then there are other things only very few people know about. A few miles up the river for instance is a lock, near a place called Hampton Court, and at the lock there are lots of swans. Would you like to see that?"

"Sounds wonderful," she said, bewildered.

"All right," he said. "Let's go."

48

It was a strange day. He watched the two of them as if he were outside himself, an observer. He saw a middle-aged man and a young girl seeing the sights of London. It was a long time since he had seen them with Susie, long before the war, and everything seemed to have changed. Only the Tower

of London had miraculously escaped the destruction of the part of the city in which it squatted, and for a brief hour Sir Thomas More seemed more important than the nameless dead that were buried around his scaffold, underneath the rubble of their banks and offices.

He rang Jim from the Tower, shown to the booth by a Beefeater. Only in England did a man with a halberd opening the door of a telephone booth not seem an anachronism; Sir Thomas More might have spoken from it to his daughter if it had been there. It did not really matter that it had not, for Man's soul and its conflicts and its momentous moments of choice had remained unchanged. In the cell, where a kind guide in medieval garb said softly, "Here Sir Thomas wrote his last work, 'A Dialogue of Comfort,'" it seemed as if he had just taken the old man his supper and was speaking in hushed tones so as not to disturb him.

From this timeless booth Peter heard a bell ringing at the other end of the line, and then a polite voice, "Scotland Yard." He asked for Commander Scott and was asked his name. After a while the polite voice answered that the Commander was not in his office, but would he like to leave a message? He said he would ring back later.

He rang back an hour or so later from Madame Tussaud's, after first asking a dummy where the telephone was. The girl laughed freely for the first time and they strolled, with a feeling of relaxation, past the kings, the ministers, the writers, the painters and the crooks, the last of whom were in the majority. He cunningly omitted the Chamber of Horrors and thought he had done it very neatly, but her smile made him wonder.

"Scotland Yard."

"Commander Scott, please. This is Inspector Jongman speaking, from the Amsterdam C.I.D." As he waited, he watched her from the little glass box. She stood leafing through Madame Tussaud's catalogue, looking slight and unobtrusive, yet somehow transformed. The girl he had watched as she stood staring at her own reflection the night before now stood idly leafing through Madame Tussaud's past, and that, somehow, was a momentous difference. He wished he knew how to formulate it.

"Are you there, sir?" the polite voice asked.

He said he was.

"I'm sorry, but Mr. Scott is in conference. Would you care to leave a message?"

"No, thank you," he said. "I'll ring him later."

He rang him again from the lock keeper's office near Hampton Court. As he waited for the connection to be made, he gazed out of the low little window at the girl standing on the lock gates, staring down. Behind her were the Dutch garden and the somber house built by the Dutch prince. They had stood in front of his portrait and that of Mary, and strolled through the maze and the shrubs cut to resemble pears and poodles. It had been once more as if time had stood still, and Protestant William were still brooding in the gazebo while Mary cheerfully harassed the gardeners toiling with huge shears to correct nature. "All right," a voice said, with a sound of fatigue. "Put him on."

"Jim?" he asked. "This is Peter."

"Ah, yes," the voice said cheerfully. "Sorry, I've been tied up. What can I do for you?"

"I just wanted to tell you that I talked to the girl and I have her with me now. I'll take her back to Holland by night ferry."

"Splendid!" Jim cried with genuine relief. "Good show! So the case is closed?"

"Pardon?"

"I mean, we still have to devise a means of stopping our friend of course, but for the moment there is no immediate urgency. That right?"

"That's right. I'll send you a summary of my report for your file."

"That'll be fine."

There was a short pause during which Jim did not take up the vague agreement they had made for dinner that night.

"Do you know where I am ringing you from?"

"Er—no. Should I?"

"I'm ringing you from the lock near Hampton Court."

"Ah, yes. Charming spot. What are you doing there?"

"This is the first chance I've had to look at it since you told me about it. Remember?"

"I'm afraid I don't get you."

"On our buoy, twenty-five years ago."

"Our what?"

"Our buoy. You remember, the light buoy in Amsterdam harbor, where we spent those nights watching the freighter with the opium."

"Ah, *buoy!* Of course. I'm sorry, the line is bad. Yes. Well, I'm sorry, but I have someone waiting. Let me know when you're in town again, then we must go and have dinner somewhere."

"Yes," he said. "Let's do that. Goodbye, Jim."

He put the receiver back on the hook and paid the lock keeper for the call. When he came out he joined her on the lock and looked at the river and the trees. There were no swans, but perhaps they came later in the season. She asked, "Is there something wrong?"

"Why, no. What makes you think there is?"

"You look harassed. What happened?"

"Nothing. I just said goodbye to a friend."

He did not tell her of his foolish hope that the three of them might have had dinner together; he touched her shoulder and said, "Let's go back to town and eat something before we catch the train."

"Do you know any other places as nice as that little pheasant thing where we had lunch?" she asked.

"You wait and see," he said, hoping he would be able to find the Chinese restaurant where he and Susie had dined before the war.

He did not, or perhaps he did. There were four Chinese restaurants close together in Soho, the one they entered was huge. It had three balconies overlooking an arena full of tables where foreign sailors and giggling girls juggled clumsily with chopsticks, while a trio in tail coats wheedled "Come to Papa, Do," on a cello, a saxophone and an upright piano, which was made to sound Chinese by a sheet of metal stuck inside. The menu was bilingual; it reduced "Hong Kong Loempia" to "meat balls," but as he was ordering he kept it away from her, she was not interested in the Chinese part anyhow. She gazed enviously over the balustrade during the meal, unable to take her eyes off a table in the arena where, apparently, the staff of a freighter were entertaining new girl friends. If only he had realized she was hungry for that kind of thing he would have taken her to Harwich by an early train and laid on a meal with the captain and the chief engineer. As it was, she ate her food absent-mindedly; when one of the freighter's staff sang a song that should have remained unsung she was the only one in the place who laughed. Even the newly won girl friends were a bit genteel about it and he realized that she had not understood the words. There she was, after going through more horrors and human depravity than anyone in that four-tiered room, and she was the only innocent among them.

As she sat there, covering her mouth with her hands to hide her laughter, her eyes twinkling, a chill went down his spine as he saw what the little blue streak was on her right wrist. He had noticed it before, but had paid no attention to it; now, in the harsh, unromantic light of the Chinese restaurant, he saw that it was a number tattooed into her skin, her registration number of the concentration camp. As he stared at it, horrified, she lowered her hands and her eyes scrutinized his with a sudden suspicion. She ate in silence for a while, no longer paying any attention to the party downstairs, then she asked, "May I ask you something personal?" She had tried to make it sound casual.

"Of course."

"Are you married?"

He could not help smiling. "That is not very personal, is it? I am." Then he realized it was not what she had intended to ask.

"Have you any children?"

"One daughter."

"What age?"

"Your age."

She looked away; then, gathering all her courage, she asked, "Do you really realize what you are risking when you . . . if you should be foolish enough to keep your promise?"

"What do you mean?"

"I mean," she said, showing a strain he did not understand, "are you sure about your motives?"

Then it dawned on him. She had caught his look as he discovered the number on her wrist, and misinterpreted it. He looked at her with deep compassion: there she sat, a child lost in the jungle, and asked him whether he was in love with her. He was about to tell her the truth when he realized he should grant her this. He was her mirror and for once the mirror should lie. "Does it matter?" he asked, trying to sound evasive. "You were willing to be helped into Palestine by a Nazi, why not by an old fool?"

But she looked at his eyes, saw the truth, put her marked hand on his and smiled. "Sorry," she said.

The band below struck up "Roll Out the Barrel," Chinese version. The Merchant Navy in the arena sang it, a ragged chorus, standing solemnly to attention, while the girls giggled and the leathery little headwaiter in the shadows furiously worked his abacus.

As the train sped along through the night, he looked at the landscape growing darker, at his own reflected silhouette and, beyond it, the blurred presence of the girl dozing in the far corner. Poor child, there she went again, another train, another man at whom she clutched like someone drowning, hoping against reason that this one would be different and really carry her to the shore of her promised land. He again felt what he had felt that morning: that, if necessary, he would give all he had to take her to Palestine. He felt it without emotion; it was an undramatic certainty he had discovered at the base of his being. He had reached the bedrock of his soul.

4

The observer's detachment that had been with him all day now pervaded him with a calm serenity he had never experienced before. For the first time in his life he was at peace. In the past, in his conflicts with Susie, in his loyalty during the war, in his being passed by for promotion, he had instinctively assumed that he himself was somehow to blame. He had borne his feeling of guilt as a pilgrim his load, only he had been a pilgrim without a goal.

Now this was changed. Now his goal was to take this desperate girl to Palestine, and he suddenly felt that he understood Susie better, without trying to see things from her point of view as he had done in the past; he understood Jim; he even understood Thorens in his diseased despair. He knew that this serene detachment in which he now moved would be assaulted in the near future, when others began to be affected by the decision he had made. But it did not matter. Right now, during these moments of reflection in the train, it seemed that he would never really lose that peace, whatever the future might bring.

He did not wake her up until the train slowed down for Parkeston Quay, Harwich. She looked at him for a moment with bewilderment, trying to disentangle herself from a dream, then she smiled and said, "Gosh, I really slept. Where are we?"

"Harwich. By the way, where's your luggage?"

"I'm afraid I left it behind in the flat. It wasn't much."

"So you have nothing?"

"No. But it doesn't matter."

"I'll get you a toothbrush and—and that sort of thing on board. Now let's go, quickly; you join the queue for Immigration, I'll nip ahead and book you a good cabin before the crowd comes on. I'll meet you at the gangway."

He passed through the British side of Immigration as quickly as was possible with the charming bald-headed officer, who was delighted to see him. In the past, they had always had polite, sunny little conversations about outdoor life and rationing and what a blessing a sense of humor was because it gave one a sense of proportion; this time Peter excused himself, saying he had an urgent job to arrange on board before the crowd came on, and the bald man said with polite haste, "Well, in that case, I'd better stamp you quickly, hadn't I? Now, let me see, which page are we on? It's time you got another passport, you know. This one is nearly full, isn't it? I think your people are so much more sensible about these passports than we British. Now look at this: a nice, slim, handy volume, flexible, easily slipped in the pocket, whereas those British things . . . hard-bound volumes, not meant to follow the movements of the human body, you can't stick them in your inner pocket because they stop you bending over, you can't carry them in your hip pocket because they stop you sitting down, all you can do is to walk with them in your hand and. . . . Oops! The wrong stamp! So sorry, old man. We've just had the Danes in. Now let me see. Ah, here's our little friend. Righto! Sorry we haven't been able to talk at all this time. On your next visit, when you are not so pressed, we might sit down and have a cup of tea, if that sounds attractive to you?"

Peter said he would be delighted and wondered if he could yank the passport out of the cheerful man's hand.

"I'm awfully interested in your country, you know. Here we are, only—how many?—sixty-odd miles apart, same soil, as far as this region goes, as yours. Now tell me: why are your tulips a blazing glory that stuns the world, whereas the things my wife rears in the garden . . . I mean, when she puts them down on the altar for the Easter service, I find myself praying that God may have a sense of humor."

Peter said, "Haha," and yanked. They parted, waving, shouting melodiously, "Goodbye!" and "See you soon!" while the next passenger, who had been breathing down his neck with increasing vigor, put down his passport with a slam. Before he vanished in the darkness of the quay, he heard the bald man chant, "Now whom have we here? Mr. Holland on his way to Holland! Hahaha. . . ."

The same self-conscious old sailor with the beribboned cap stood at the foot of the gangway and asked Peter apologetically for his boarding card. He knew he would find the chief engineer in the reception hall, because he always sat there as the passengers came on, to look at the girls. There indeed he sat, in portly anticipation, and his face fell a shade when he saw Peter.

"Sorry, Chief. I won't keep you, but I have a girl with me who needs a cabin and I wonder if you . . ."

"You mean to say you don't need one yourself?" the chief asked, eyebrows raised.

"Oh, I'll make out," he said, unfortunately, and the chief cried, "I bet you will. Why, Inspector Jongman! Let's get you the Bridal Suite. This calls for a celebration."

"Sorry to disappoint you," he said, trying to catch the tone of heavy banter in which the chief felt at home. "I wish it were true, but this is the girl I told you about last night. I'm taking her back to Holland."

"You don't say," the chief said, suddenly serious. "You know, I've been thinking about that case all day, off and on. I hope you got him."

"I got her," he said with a smile. "First things first."

"You know," the chief said, "I found today that I am not as harmless as I always thought I was. I found myself thinking: if I laid hands on that guy, God knows what I would do with him. I think . . ."

"Let's get her a cabin," Peter urged as the first passengers came stumbling in with their suitcases, breathless from climbing the gangway.

"Okay." The chief hoisted himself out of his club chair and put his cap on the seat. "Let's go and see the purser."

The purser sat behind the gilded bars of a ticket window and looked sour. "I'm afraid we are full up," he started, but the chief made a rude noise with his lips and said, "Don't give me that, Henk. I know you, remember? We have three meals together every day."

"What has that got to do with it?" the purser asked, unpleasantly. "Full up is full up, and I'll thank you to keep your bathroom noises where they belong."

"Okay," the chief said. "In that case, I suppose I had better introduce you. This gentleman asking for accommodation for a lady is Commissioner Jongman of the

Amsterdam Vice Squad. He'll be around later to ask for your pass key; he has some checking to do on marriage certificates in your double cabins."

The purser smiled like a caged python and wrote out a ticket. Peter thanked him for the chit and the key and paid in Dutch money.

"But that doesn't take care of you, now, does it?" the chief asked as he moved away.

"I think I'll spend the night on the bridge, after seeing you and the captain once we are at sea."

"The Old Man will be on the bridge himself for the first watch," the chief said, "to stand in for the second officer."

"Why? Is he sick?"

"Got hit by a taxi this morning. Maybe he's broken his ankle, maybe it's just twisted. Anyhow, he has to lie with his foot in the air for twenty-four hours and see. Good evening, Miss. Sorry, Inspector, see you later."

Peter waited for her at the foot of the gangway. She took a long time coming through Immigration and Customs; when finally she emerged, she was accompanied by a customs officer. The night air set her coughing, when she reached him she could barely make herself heard. "I told him I had no luggage," she whispered, "but he wanted to check with you."

"All right, officer," he said, showing his card. "The lady is my responsibility."

"Ah, I see. That's all right, sir. Sorry, sir. Thank you very much. Have a nice crossing." The officer saluted and turned away. Anna had recovered her breath and heaved a sigh of relief. "Somehow their politeness is frightening," she said, still hoarse. "Did you manage to get cabins?"

"Yes. I think you'll be quite comfortable. Here's your

key. Now let's go and get you that toothbrush, and then you had better go to bed. You have a nasty cold."

She took his proffered arm and said, "All right."

"The shop doesn't open until we sail," he said, as they climbed the gangway, "but perhaps I can get round the purser again."

"There's no hurry," she said. "You don't really want to send me to bed at once, do you? I would love to see the ship leave. It's only the tail end of a cold, honestly."

"All right," he said. "Maybe I can arrange for you to see it leave from the bridge, as long as you stay inside the wheelhouse. Would you like that?"

"Oh!" she cried. "Could you really?" She looked up at him as if she were ten years old. Then he realized they were standing in the entrance to the reception hall and that the chief was watching them, fascinated.

She registered with the purser, Peter showed her to her cabin and said he would wait for her in the hall. When he got back to the hall he found the chief and asked, "How are you making out?"

"Not nearly as well as you," the chief said.

Surprised at his own equanimity, he smiled and patted the chief on the shoulder.

"Well, you should have seen the way she looked at you," the chief said.

"She needs some toilet things. Do you think we have to wait for the shop to open, or is there a back door?"

"Sorry," the chief said. "If this had been a fortnight ago I could have helped you, but right now the lady in charge is not in favor of me. You know, women always go from one extreme to the other."

"All right," Peter said as he saw her coming along the passage. "I'll be seeing you later on. Captain in his cabin?"

"I suppose so. Don't expect him to be charitable,

though. That second officer certainly isn't going to be popular with the crew."

"Are we?" she asked excitedly when he went to meet her.

"What?"

"Are we going to see the ship leave from the bridge?"

He smiled and took her arm. "Let's go and ask the captain. But don't be disappointed if he says 'no,' he seems to be a little harassed tonight."

"I have never been on a ship's bridge before," she said as they went along the passage to the captain's quarters. "Do you know him?"

"Yes, I do," he answered, trying in the meantime to think of a means of placating the old man. He should have brought something for his dachshund, a rubber bone or a cloth cat.

As they entered the little sitting room with the goddess and the cubic lamp, after timidly knocking without receiving a reply, the old man came out of his bedroom snorting like a lion, followed by the dachshund. He bristled with animosity and was about to shout something explosive, when Peter said, "This is Miss Held, who was your passenger last night. She is going back to Holland."

The change that came over the old captain was miraculous. "Ah," he said with a charm and a politeness that were disturbing. "I'm very happy to have you with us, Miss Held. We worried about you last night. This calls for a celebration." The dachshund turned around and slunk back to the bedroom.

"I think I know what Miss Held would like best," Peter said. "She would like to see the ship leave from the bridge."

The old man hesitated, then he said good-naturedly, "But of course. She'll be most welcome. We leave in ten minutes. You heard about the second, I suppose? Where's that damn steward? Sit down, please, Miss Held." He went to the door and pressed three separate bells. Outside there was an instant scramble; the steward and a sailor appeared in the doorway, joined a moment later by a breathless young man in greasy overalls. Obviously the whole ship knew about the second.

"You there," the captain said to the steward, ignoring the other two. "Have you happened to notice what the time is?"

"Yes, sir . . . no, sir," the steward stammered.

"Well, make up your mind!" the captain roared with relish, "but get the drinks that I have always had at this hour, ever since D-Day! Why, today of all days, have you decided . . ." The steward had fled. The two others faded away clumsily.

The captain did his transformation act again while he turned around. "I'm sorry," he said, like a benevolent old uncle. "I forgot to ask you what you would like to drink. But I suppose you'll find something you like on the tray when it comes."

"You have a lovely cabin," she said with sincere admiration, and Peter realized to his astonishment that she meant it. For someone with her past, this must indeed look like a haven of taste and luxury.

"Yes," the captain said, casually strolling to the corner to sneak the cap off the goddess. "It was designed by the interior decorator who did the 'Home of the Future' at the Colonial Exposition in Paris in 1935—before your time, I suppose. I had to add a few touches of my own, of course, to make it cozy."

"Such as?" Peter asked.

"Well, mainly in the bedroom," the captain answered, fixing him with a baleful eye. Then he asked her, "Did you meet my dog?"

"I thought I saw a dog come in, but he went back in there. Was that him?"

"I suppose so," the captain said, "unless he smuggled in a girl friend while my back was turned. That has happened, you know."

"When?" Peter asked.

"About a month ago," the captain said, beginning to laugh, "a lady came on board with a little bitch that . . . well, they made friends, you know. It was quite a business. . . . I mean . . . ah, there you are!" he cried with relief as the steward staggered in, sideways, carrying a tinkling tray, followed by the chief engineer. While the boy arranged the contents of the tray on the table, Peter introduced the chief to her, and the dachshund peered unobtrusively round the door, at ankle height.

"There he is!" the captain cried. "Come on in, and show the young lady what love and patience can achieve!" He picked up a cheese cube and whispered to the girl, "Now you watch this."

The ship left a quarter of an hour later, after the dachshund had downed four cheese cubes, two frankfurters and a pretzel, and the captain four genevas, leaving the chief choking in the effort to keep up with him.

As they entered the darkened wheelhouse, Peter felt as if he were stepping into another world. By the faint light of binnacle and radarscope, the silhouettes of the pilot and the helmsman could be discerned, black in the darkness. The captain introduced them to the pilot, a Mr. Darling, who had guided more ships into and out of Harwich harbor than anyone alive. "All right, Mr. Darling, she's all yours."

The faceless Mr. Darling mumbled something self-conscious and sounded the foghorn. It roared close over their heads, and she grabbed Peter's sleeve in the darkness. The engine-room telegraph rang, and Mr. Darling mumbled something into a microphone which set a winch hammering on the foredeck and a whistle throbbing ashore. The vessel slowly moved away from the quay, then the engine-room telegraph rang out once more and Mr. Darling muttered, "Hard port, son," to the helmsman.

"Hard port," the helmsman repeated, spinning the small steering wheel.

Peter had witnessed a liner leaving many times, but it still gave him a feeling of pride and regret. At those moments he knew what had gone wrong with his life; he should have remained a ship's officer instead of taking on the tempting job with the harbor police after a year at sea as a mate's apprentice. At the time, it had seemed such a sensible solution. He had had no means of knowing then what he knew now: that by leaving the sea he had left part of himself.

He hoped that this small male world of decency and craftmanship would restore to her some confidence and respect, reassure her that all men were not necessarily sadists and megalomaniacs. She stood quite still in her corner, watching the modest, competent Mr. Darling guiding the big ship through the darkness with gentle commands to the helmsman and an admirable economy of movement; during the whole proceedings he walked only once from one side of the bridge to the other and used his night glasses twice. The captain strolled from radarscope to binnacle and from binnacle to depth recorder, still in command of his ship although the pilot was giving the orders. Yes, Peter thought, this is where I should have been, it would have made all the difference. His marriage would have been different, he himself would have been different; but there was no use regretting the irrevocable past.

The captain showed her the chart room, the radio cabin and the wireless operator, who tried to combine a he-man approach with listening to the weather report from Scheveningen Radio.

"I'll see Miss Held to her cabin," Peter said to the captain, after she had seen everything. "She has to buy one or two things at the shop first. All right if I come back up?"

"Of course," the captain said in the darkness. "I'll be delighted. Goodbye, young lady, get a good rest. It was a privilege to meet you."

Peter took her arm to lead her out, but she said, "Please don't come. I'll find the way. You stay here."

He hesitated, then he said, "As you wish. Don't you need some money?"

"No, thank you. I have enough."

"All right. Sleep well. See you in the morning."

She whispered happily, "Goodnight."

After she was gone, no one spoke on the bridge for some time, except the pilot who muttered his commands and the helmsman who echoed them. Then they rounded the flashing light of the outer buoy and Mr. Darling said, "Well, captain, there she is. Anything else I can do for you?"

"Yes," the captain said. "Go to my cabin, and find yourself a drink. Sorry I can't come with you tonight, but I'm standing in for my second officer."

"So I heard," Mr. Darling said quietly, as, for a reason only known to himself, he put on a pair of gloves. "I hope it's nothing serious."

"It is," the captain said. "His ankle won't bother him, but as soon as we get home, I'll have him certified. Do you know what happened? He backed into a backing taxi. Now where have you ever seen a thing like that, outside the pie-throwing movies? I'll sail this ship with village idiots if it can't be helped, but I draw the line at the missing link."

Mr. Darling, to whom this obviously was too much culture at that time of night, muttered, "Quite," and effaced himself after mumbling " 'Night, son," to the helmsman.

"All right, Karels," the captain said. "We'll have the automatic on, course eighty-seven. Tell me when you're on it."

The helmsman flicked a switch and pulled a lever and after a while he called out, "On eighty-seven now, sir." The captain went to check, his stern old face was for a moment lit theatrically from below by the binnacle light. "All right," he said, "steady as she goes, and stand by."

The helmsman said, "Yes, sir," and stepped back into the darkness; the little wheel moved eerily of its own accord with a clicking noise as the automatic pilot began to operate. The captain's face loomed green and disembodied in the darkness as he cast a look at the radarscope; then he came to the front of the bridge and joined Peter who stood looking out through the revolving window.

Peter waited for him to speak, but as the old man remained silent, he said, "By the way, I'd better give you your gun back before I forget it."

"All right," the captain said. "Throw it on my bed when you pass the cabin. Did you use it?"

"No."

"Good," the captain said. Then he remained silent again for a long while, as they both stared out into the night, at the sea and the bow of the ship slowly rising and falling among the stars. "What's that number she has on her wrist?" the captain asked finally.

"Her registration number from the camp."

"Do you know which camp?"

"I don't know its name, but it was a medical-research camp where the Nazis experimented on human beings."

The captain grunted in the darkness. Peter could not make out whether it signified acknowledgment or indignation. He was not prepared for the quiet statement: "I suppose if I had been in your shoes, I would have shot him."

"I almost did."

"Well, it shows you're a better man than I. But then, you see, I thought about the Jews a lot during the war. I was torpedoed twice, once in the Arctic. It took conviction to keep going after that, the conviction that you were serving a cause that made sense. Well, I found that all I needed to do in moments of doubt was to think of what they did to the Jews. Not that I am particularly fond of Jews, mark you, personally I wouldn't go and seek them out, but I think that if a man is a Jew, that's an act of God like being an Arab or a Chinese or an Eskimo, and if you start torturing people for that, you have to be put in a strait jacket by the sane part of mankind. And that was what we were doing, that's to say, that's what I told myself when I saw my boys dragged out of the water, delirious with frostbite, black with oil. See what I mean?"

"Yes."

"During all that time, I never killed anybody," the captain said. "But I think I would have done it now, faced by your man. I would have done so for private reasons out of my own past: thoughts at night on my bunk, or walking in Trafalgar Square feeding the pigeons, or reading a fiancée's letter to a blinded seaman. And that's not the way justice should be done, is it now? What are you going to do with her?"

"I promised to take her to Palestine."

There was a long silence. Peter tried to discern the captain's face, but he could barely make out his silhouette.

"That's a tall order," the old man said at last. "It's none of my business, but why did you promise that?"

"I don't know. It just seemed the thing to do, at a given moment. I mean, after I had discovered that for some reason I was incapable of shooting him. I—I'm sorry. This can't make much sense to you, I suppose."

"Well," the captain said. "Hats off. But you may well have shot yourself instead. I suppose you realize that."

"I know there'll be difficulties."

"You are putting it damn mildly," the captain said. "Are you really that optimistic, or are you whistling in the dark?"

"Why? You think I overlooked something?"

"For one thing," the captain said, "and all this is none of my business, mind you, you may not be prepared for people misinterpreting your motives. You see, I know that your promise to this girl has nothing to do with her personally—or has it?"

He smiled in the darkness. "Look, captain," he said, "I don't think any of it matters. What does matter is that this girl, after what she went through, shall be taken to her promised land. As far as I am concerned, that's all there is to it and if people around me should want to give it their own interpretation, it's their business."

The captain grunted and then, after a thoughtful silence, said, "Well, it seems all right. All I can do is wish you luck. And, if it's of any interest to you, I wish I could go with you. Boy, a thing like that makes me feel twenty years old, with the wisdom of my grandfather! I suppose if I were worth my salt I'd offer to take over

from you. I am in a better position for this kind of under-
taking than you are, but I'm a coward. I would be
afraid."

"Of what?"

"Of my wife, for one thing. Not that she's difficult,
but all women have a core of granite, or the human race
would never have survived the Stone Age. That's the
core I'd find myself up against."

"Don't you think she would understand?"

"No, sir. The core begins where they refuse to understand. If you want my honest advice, don't even risk an-
tagonizing her."

"What do you mean?"

"If your aim is to get that girl into Palestine and not
to purify your own soul, then you should use your
brains rather than your guts. I mean this: tell your wife
that the trail of these white-slave traders leads to Palestine and that you have to go there. See if you can't sell
your superiors that deal too. Then go to Tangier, with
their official blessing, and start scouting about for a
means of shipping her to Palestine. I am suggesting this
because I have a friend who lives in Tangier and who
writes me a long letter once every three months or so.
We used to be colleagues on convoy duty and now we're
sort of pen pals. He went wrong, if you understand
what I mean; he sits in Tangier in a hotel called 'Tarzan'
and deals in all sorts of contraband: cigarettes, whisky,
arms, Jews. He may take her on, for a consideration. He,
or the like of him, is your only chance. The English have
really sealed Palestine tight."

"Isn't there an organization that arranges for the immigration of people like her?"

"I suppose there are several. But they must have
thousands of displaced Jews lined up, waiting their turn.

I would try my friend Van der Pink. But don't expect to find an idealist. If he took her on, it wouldn't be because he was moved by her past or angry with the Nazis; he has a quarrel on a higher level, with God. You should read his letters. They are religious tracts in mirror writing. He isn't a good guy at heart, he's a bastard. But he may do you a favor if you tell him I sent you. He won't want to risk losing his pen pal. I am God's forwarding address, if you see what I mean."

A telephone buzzed in the darkness, and the captain, with the sureness of a cat, walked toward the instrument and lifted the receiver. "Bridge," he said, then he listened, added, "Thanks, I've seen him," and put the receiver back. "These lookouts will do anything to show you they are awake," he said, close once more in the darkness. "That trawler is at least five miles away. Where are you going to get the money?"

"For what?"

"You don't think you'll get this girl there for nothing, do you? Van der Pink may be willing to wangle her onto one of his gunrunners, but he certainly won't do it for nothing. No, sir. That would be leaving a loophole for God. So where will you get the money?"

"How much do you think I'll need?"

"I don't know, but I'm sure it is expensive. And in dollars, of course. Anything from two to three thousand, I would say. You see, most of the passages for illegal immigrants are paid for by American conscience money."

"I don't get you."

"Well, there are Jews in America who write stuff like, 'every time a British soldier is killed in Palestine, there is a little holiday in my heart.' The least a man can do, after writing that in his study an ocean away, is to collect some money to pay for the passages of illegal immigrants. You know, the people who don't do anything are usually the ones who pay. You might apply for her passage money to one of those organizations. I can't tell you where they are, Van der Pink can. But if I were you, I would forget about telling my wife and the rest of the world that I had crashed off my horse like Saul and got up as Paul. I'd play my cards as close to my chest as I knew how, and try and have my cake and eat it. Lord, this is quite a lecture, isn't it? What's her health like?"

"Why?"

"Might make a difference to those organizations. I don't know which way, though. It depends on whether they work in cooperation with the Palestine underground. Those Jewish boys of Haganah are no sentimentalists, that I can tell you. Anyhow, you go to Tangier and see Van der Pink, and take it from there. He's quite a character. Some sailor, he was. Lives in the wrong century. These private battles with God, they're out of date, you know. There are no more continents to discover, and no more fears beyond the horizon except about whom you might meet there. Where the hell is that boy with the tea?"

The boy came in presently, and they had tea in the chart room and the captain concentrated on yawning and extemporizing on the postwar brand of junior officers.

When the first mate came to relieve him, the captain said to Peter, "You'd better sleep on the couch in my sitting room, if you don't have a cabin. You'll be all right there until dawn, when the Dutch pilot comes in for his drink."

The dachshund sat waiting for them, looking noncommittal by the side of the empty dishes on the tray. They had a nightcap, and prepared for bed. Before he vanished in his quarters, the old man said, "Well, friend Jongman, if you are going through with that plan of yours, these are probably the last hours of peace you'll have for some time. Make the most of them."

Peter smiled and went to bed.

There is, south of the Central Station in Amsterdam, on the busy waterway that leads from the city's canals to the Eastern Dock, a little building called "The Tram Terminal." The name is incongruous, for no trams leave from there. It is the station for the small, fast passenger ferries that cross the port to the northern part of the city, and for the water buses that go to the outlying islands and the old dead towns of the Zuyder Zee.

5

There is a nice little restaurant in the building, with a terrace from where you can watch the ferries coming and going, the tugboats and executive launches racing by, and the sight-seeing boats filled with eager trippers dawdling in everybody's way, while the captain extolls the questionable beauties of the Central Station via a microphone.

"Now, if you'll wait here," Peter said, after finding a quiet corner for Anna out of the wind, "and order some coffee or whatever you like, I won't be long. It'll take me about an hour. My home is across the harbor, so I'll have to take one of the ferries—over there." He pointed at another jetty across the basin, where pugnacious little black motorboats, battered and buckled, raced one another to arrive first at the gap between two of their kind. It was a marvelous sight, he had often sat there for more than an hour, feeling guilty as he was supposed to be on a job. It was surprising, however, how many jobs involved sitting on the terrace of the Tram Terminal, sipping coffee and nibbling shortcake. Anybody with a bad conscience crossing from north to south was bound to arrive at either jetty, as the big car ferries across the harbor were known to be watched by the police.

He hoped she would not feel bored and lost, and, on

an impulse, he went into the hall of the little building to buy her some magazines. The most suitable seemed to be one called *Libelle*, full of sewing patterns and gossip about film stars, and another called *Let's Laugh*, which was a favorite among the crews of the harbor police. She thanked him, surprised and delighted at his attention; after he had fought his way on to one of the little buckled boats he steamed past the terrace amid a tight crowd of fellow passengers, and waved at her over the heads. She waved back, small and forlorn in the masculine crowd on the terrace: big, red-faced farmers from the north trying to talk with cigars in their mouths and speculators of the stock exchange sitting in the sun with their hats tipped over their noses. It was one of the first warm days of spring, a day such as the day of the German invasion had been, when people had gone about their business exactly as they did now; even when the German Panzer columns rolled into the city, girls had stood on stepladders outside the houses with their backs to them, washing windows. Strange that the war and all its horrors should have left so little trace on the face of Amsterdam. Only an unobtrusive girl in a corner of the terrace of the Tram Terminal.

He had at first thought of taking her home with him straight away, for he did not want to keep Susie in the dark about this, despite the captain's advice. He might keep it hidden from his chief, but not from Susie. He should, right from the beginning, make it plain to her that this had nothing to do with their marriage; if anyone should be prevented from misinterpreting his motives right from the start, it was she. The trip across took ten minutes; from the jetty on the north side to his house was a seven-minute walk. If he wanted to be back in an hour, that left him half an hour to explain things to

Susie, which should be ample.

Only after he had let himself into the house did he realize it was the first Friday of the month, for he smelled a strong odor of beeswax and in the hall stood a stepladder with a pail and a ceiling mop. It was Mrs. Dop's day and she was the first to greet him. She looked like one of those women at the foot of the guillotine, with a kerchief around her head, an ageless apron and big, bare arms that looked maternal in an angry way. He had always fled the house on Mrs. Dop's days; she was an honest woman who believed in giving people their money's worth; if they went to the luxury of hiring a charwoman to do the month's cleaning, the least she could do was to turn the house upside down. He greeted Mrs. Dop shiftily as she shot him a steely glance and set her jaw, for to her he was not a man, he was a pair of boots entering her clean hall. He tiptoed across to the sitting room where the furniture stood huddled together disconsolately in the middle of the floor; he thought for a moment that the adjoining dining room was empty too, as the chairs had been upturned on the table and the piano pushed away from the wall, but then he heard a dissonant chord and realized that someone was dusting its back.

"Susie?" he asked.

She rose flushed from behind the piano. She too wore a kerchief around her head and she brought out a broom. It was amazing what little change twenty-five years had wrought; she still looked lithe and young, and her blue eyes flashed as impatiently as ever. She might not be a beautiful woman according to *Libelle* or *Let's Laugh;* to him she was as exciting as on that first day when he had spotted her on the sun deck of the liner arriving from the Dutch East Indies. Pity about her quick temper, but one could not expect one without the other.

"What are you doing here?" she asked, also looking at his feet. "I thought you were in England."

"I'm sorry," he said. "I didn't realize what day it was, but something urgent has come up which I must discuss with you."

"Now?" she asked.

"Now," he said.

She cast her eyes at the ceiling, sighed theatrically and said, "Isn't that just like a man? We haven't had a conversation worth speaking of for ten years, he has to wait until the house is upside down and Mrs. Dop has trouble with her husband again. . . . What is it about?"

He knew he had to nail her down somehow, he tried to by saying, quietly, "I'm going to Palestine."

"Fine," she said. "Anything, as long as you don't upset Mrs. Dop. Go and pack quietly and go out by the kitchen."

"I am not being sent there," he said. "I'm going of my own accord."

She had vanished behind the piano again but this brought her back. "What did you say?" Her face was on the level with the top and she stared at him incredulously between the bowl of imitation fruit and the little bust of Beethoven. The book on the stand said, "Twelve Celebrated Minuets." For the first time since he had made his decision he wished he could spare her this.

"Listen, Susie," he said, "can't we talk this over somewhere quietly for a moment? I know it's awkward for you right now, but it's terribly important."

"But why?" she asked. "What are you going to do there?"

He sighed, and said, with reluctant nonchalance because this was not at all the way he had planned to tell her, "Smuggle in a Jewish girl."

Before she had had a chance to catch her breath, the door was flung open and Mrs. Dop strode in, looking like an invader of some prehistoric tribe with her ceiling mop and her bucket. "Well," she said aggressively, "that was the hall ceiling! You finished here?"

"Er—one minute, Mrs. Dop," Susie said. "Not quite— I mean . . . go ahead, I'll go to the kitchen."

"No point in going if you haven't finished," Mrs. Dop said disdainfully. "I'll do the kitchen, unless you want me to start on the brass."

"No, no," she said. "I had finished here. You go ahead. Come along, Peter."

He followed her past the muttering Mrs. Dop, along the edge of the hall to the kitchen where the morning's breakfast dishes stood drying in their basket on the sink. Mrs. Dop had lined up all the brass on the other side: candlesticks, ashtrays, wall plaques depicting Rembrandt's *Anatomy Lesson* and *The Night Watch*, and a synagogue lamp which had somehow found its way years ago onto the upstairs landing. The pointlessness of the objects, revealed by their standing together on the sink, gave them a strange poignancy, for they somehow spelled home. She closed the door of the kitchen and turned around and asked, "Now will you say that again?"

"You know the job I was on," he said, "trailing that gang of white-slave traders who picked up girls without relatives to take them abroad. The day before yesterday, I followed one of them who was taking a girl out of the country, a Jewish girl who had been in a camp and whose parents and family had been gassed. Did you get my telegram, by the way?"

"But how?" she asked.

"How what?"

"How are you going to smuggle her in?"

"Let me tell you what happened first. I followed them to the man's flat in London after talking it over with Jim. As it turned out . . ."

"How old is she?" she asked, and then, as he looked bewildered, "How old is that girl?"

"About Betty's age. But let me . . ."

"Ha!" she cried, a strange, vicious laugh of despair and fury. "You fool! You . . . you stupid old billy goat!"

He was so taken aback by the suddenness of her attack that all he could say was, "But you don't understand! You don't even know what I am going to do . . ."

"You told me!" she cried. "You're going to smuggle a Jewish girl into Palestine! What else is there to know? The rest. . . ."

She jumped as the door behind her back was pushed open and Mrs. Dop strode in, still brandishing her ceiling mop. "Sorry," Mrs. Dop said unconvincingly, "but I can't do that ceiling with this old thing. It makes streaks. Where did you put that new head you were talking about?"

"Oh, er . . . in the broom cupboard," Susie said with acid sweetness. "It's in the box marked Rags."

"It would be," Mrs. Dop said; then she ripped open the door of a cupboard, bent over inside and started, muttering, to burrow among its clanging and clattering contents. The cupboard struck back at her with broom handles and the snakelike coil of the vacuum cleaner, falling across her powerful shoulders. She emerged victorious, holding an object which looked like a scalp. "Now how do you expect me to fix this thing?" she asked. "It's you who buys them."

"It's very easy," Susie said. "You just untie the knot on the old one, or cut it, take it off and pull the new one over the pad."

Mrs. Dop snorted and muttered, "The things people think of." Then she strode out, dragging the mop and the scalp, leaving the scene of the battle to be cleaned up by her subordinate.

Susie started to put the brooms back in the cupboard automatically, saying, "Don't let's waste any more words on this nonsense. I'm willing to forget about it all on condition that you stop acting like an adolescent, or a madman, which at your age amounts to the same thing."

"But you haven't listened to me at all," he said quietly, feeling once more that strange, tranquil determination which he had experienced for the first time the day before, the immovable, unassailable core of his being. "You are jumping to conclusions. Please let me finish."

She stood for the first time truly amazed. Something in his calm perseverance was alarmingly new. In the past, she had always settled their arguments by nipping them in the bud as she had tried now; it had worked for twenty-five years. He suddenly realized, as he saw her standing there, momentarily at a loss, that he had never been allowed to finish what he was saying if it was not to agree with her. She was a strong, masterful woman; but it was the inevitable counterpart of her honesty and courage. "This man had trapped her with the promise that he would take her to Palestine," he said. "As Jim decided that we could do nothing within the law as it stands to stop him at that particular moment, I went to his flat to shoot him."

She shook her head as if all this were a figment of her imagination, and went to the sink, where she turned the tap on and off, becoming angry with herself when she realized what she was doing.

"I didn't do it," he said, "because at the ultimate moment, I could not. Something inside me made it impossible."

"I should hope so!" she cried. "Am I expected to stand here and listen to you patting yourself on the back because you did not shoot somebody? Am I to understand that you are going to risk your house, your family, your job, everything that I have managed to salvage after all these years of incompetence and weakness and—and failure and—God! What am I going to do with you?"

"You are going to let me finish," he said quietly. "You might as well understand why I am doing it, because I am going to do it, Susie."

"But what? Why? This is ridiculous!"

"After I left the flat, I felt as if I had wasted my life," he said doggedly. "And then the girl caught up with me and I found out who she was and what had happened to her; this had been her last chance to get into Palestine because she was ill. And I suddenly realized that the only way in which I could regain my self-respect, make sense of the war and what had happened to her, and to me, and that man, and all of us, was by doing this: to take her to Palestine myself. It was the only way of—of living up to what I suddenly, at that moment, realized was my standard of decency."

She looked at him long and intently, her big blue eyes harassed and sad. He had never known that the surplus of strength that had always enabled her to come out victorious in their battles of wills in the past was so small. Suddenly, inexplicably, he felt guilty.

"But why you?" she asked. "Isn't there an organization to handle this sort of thing?"

"There is, but it would be too long for her to wait, because of her health."

"Well, shouldn't you try? Rather than just throw everything away on an impulse? Or is that what you want? Is it your way of telling yourself that you're sick of—of the life you have been leading for the last ten years?"

"I don't know," he said honestly, "but that is not the point. The point is that I want to take this girl to Palestine and make sure she gets there, whatever the cost."

"That may be a fine attitude for a bachelor," she said, "if all the cost involved were your own affair. But what about me? You can't do this thing and tell yourself you are paying for it. All you stand to do is gain."

"I don't understand."

"You say you have to do this to regain your self-respect. Fine. But what about me? They'll fling you out of the force, it'll cost all the money we have, you'll find yourself arrested or interned or maybe even shot over there, so who will be doing the paying? I will. This house, that I've kept for you as long as we've been married, that this very morning I and that woman are working for, giving hours of our life for, I'll have to give up."

"You're rushing to conclusions."

"You mean I am facing you with the truth you want to run away from. And what about your daughter? What about Betty? It may not matter that you're about to ruin my life because that you've done anyhow, and let's say that I am at least partly to blame, but I won't let you ruin hers."

She had said it without vehemence, and he realized that it was now her turn to reach the bedrock of her soul. He suddenly felt physically cold, although nothing else inside him seemed to have changed. His hands felt as if he had gone out into an ice-cold night. "How did I ruin your life, Susie?" he asked. "Let's have it out, if that's the way you feel."

She looked at him, his eyes, his mouth, his body and then at his eyes again, and there was no tenderness, not even pity in her look. "By being a failure," she said. "By having no ambition, no firmness, no anger, no religion. Nothing of the things I thought you had when I first met you. The boy I met was gay, dashing, full of life and promise. The man I married. . . . Well, what's the use? That has been my mistake and I'm paying for it. I have been paying for it for twenty-five years. I've paid for it with my life. But not her. I won't let you do the same thing to her. Do you hear me? You shall not ruin Betty's future."

He swallowed and cleared his throat and asked quietly, "How would my saving a child from despair ruin Betty's future?"

"Don't try to make it sound like that," she said. "Stop trying to make me feel that I am preventing you from doing something noble, because you aren't. God only knows what got into you and what brought it about, but you have finally found a way in which to express your bottomless, merciless egotism. Your soul must be saved, so there she goes."

"Answer me, Susie. How?"

"You know just as well as I do that her future is not hers but Albert's. Marrying Albert is her only chance to escape from the mediocrity you have condemned her to by being a failure. Here you are, after twenty-five years: Inspector of the C.I.D. All I beg of you is: stay it, until you are pensioned off. Or, at least, until she is married, although even then it would in all probability still ruin his chances of promotion."

"Why, for heaven's sake?"

"You know what his company is like. It offers a wonderful opportunity for bright young executives, it takes care of their housing, the schooling of their children, their insurance, their club life, everything is taken care of, but they must conform. What do you think the chances of promotion are for Albert when they find out that he has a mad father-in-law, or worse, a tramp? Because that's what you'll turn into if you let go of your job, your house, your world, of me."

"I'm sorry," he said. "I can't have made myself clear. I . . ."

But she would not listen any more. "Then let *me* make myself clear," she said. "I'll do everything in my power to stop you. You hear? Everything, anything, because you are hurting my child. Now go and tell that to your white slave."

He stood facing her for a moment, speechless with grief, anger and a bewildering, giddying surge of physical desire. For as she said those last words she had revealed herself for what she was: a defiant, unconquered woman. Although they now would fight until one of them gave up his very identity, he knew that he loved her and always would, whatever happened. But before he was able to say so, the door to the kitchen was opened once more and Mrs. Dop came in with her mop saying, "Well, I give up. You try to get this damn thing off, I can't. I'm not an engineer."

He changed the head of Mrs. Dop's mop before he left, and Susie went back behind the piano.

He went back by ferry, shaky with the delayed reaction to the clash of their wills and the unexpected, bewildering desire her defiance had aroused in him. For the first time since his decision he was made aware of the volcano of his subconscious on which he lived, his reason tilling its slopes with the naïve self-assurance of a peasant. During the short trip across the sunlit harbor he groped around, half awakened, in the darkness of his soul for something, anything he could cling to in this unexpected realization of the boiling lava underneath the bedrock of his soul.

6

If only he believed in God, if only his sheltered childhood had not been warmed by the setting sun of human self-assurance, that exploded with the First World War! He remembered his father, a gay little grocer who read Marx and Freud and sang "Arise, Ye Chained from your Dungeons" with his fellow members of the Atheist Glee Club. He remembered the noisy meetings to which he had been taken as a boy, where speakers, wildly cheered by unchained businessmen and shopkeepers, pronounced religion to be opium for the oppressed and a fairytale invented by tyrants, a consolation for slaves. Had his father been a member of the Reformed Church of the Netherlands, he would have gone to the meetings on the other side of the street, where similar speakers challenged their opponents to come and meet them on neutral ground, which meant in their own hall, where the atheists were booed as luxuriously as the sky pilots were across the road. His father had died without the aid of clergy and he had died triumphantly, brave little grocer setting sail for interstellar space. Those he left behind were the ones in whom doubt began to gnaw as his body in its plain coffin was lowered without a song, a prayer, any comfort at all except the determination that they were not to be fooled by any mummery, witchcraft or hoopla. The word "hoopla" was uttered by the president of the Atheist Association, and it had somehow summed up the arrogance of it all. Not of his father, who had died in the moving man-made triumph of what he believed to be reason, but of those he left facing life with the weapons he had downed. It had been possible to conquer the peace, the comfort and the security of the nineteenth century with the sword of reason and the voice of truth, but now the twentieth had exploded and revealed man's soul to be that of a beast of prey prowling in the jungle those weapons were as powerless as a peashooter against the horrors of Auschwitz and Hiroshima. Crossing the harbor to meet his fate, Peter wished so fervently that his childhood could have left him some standard, some law other than plain human decency to cling to, that the wish almost turned into a prayer. But there was no one, nothing to which he could pray, for the God of his childhood, irrevocably embedded in his subconscious, was an old man in a nightshirt with a white beard sitting on a cloud, and Jesus was a saccharine human canary that spinsters kept in a cage for the comfort of their barren souls. He had nothing to go by but the single-minded goal he had set himself: to smuggle a girl into Palestine. Beyond that lay nothing but the darkness his father had left behind, as the small sun of his self-assurance set in his grave.

As he saw her sitting in the corner of the terrace, waiting for him, small and unobtrusive among the businessmen and the burghers crowding the terrace, he felt again like a pawn in a game beyond his comprehension. For a fleeting moment he suspected that, despite appearances and his own confident conception of their relationship, she was the one who led the way. But when he faced her and she welcomed him with a nervous smile and a searching look, he settled back in his inner certainty. He realized that she must have feared his telling his wife about her, that she had sat waiting not just for his return but for the verdict. He smiled at her and said, "Well, that's settled. Now let me tell you where we go from here. I'm going to take you to a hotel in town, probably the YWCA if they have a room for you, and then I'll go to see my chief to arrange for leave of absence. In the meantime, I'll get you some money so that you can buy yourself anything you need for a trip of, say, two weeks."

"But I don't want to take your money," she said hastily. "It's wonderful of you to help me get there, but I don't want you to pay for me."

"Well, have you got any money?" he asked kindly. "I mean—available at this moment?"

"Not just now," she said reluctantly, "but my father's business will certainly be given back to me, once they have sorted it all out; I'm his sole heir. I insist that we go to see a lawyer or a notary and that we draw up an agreement by which I pay you back every cent I owe you."

"All right," he said, "if that's the way you want it, but first let's go and see about the hotel, and then I must call on my chief, for already I've left it rather late. After that, we'll do anything you like in the way of notaries."

He beckoned the waiter and paid for the cup of coffee which turned out to be all she had taken during that hour. When he got up and smiled down at her she hesitated and asked, "Was everything all right?"

"How do you mean?"

"Did your wife understand? I mean . . . did she agree to your doing this?"

"Of course," he said. "She is a decent, generous woman who is just as delighted as I am that you give us this chance to undo some of the—well, injustice."

She searched his eyes for the truth and said, uncertainly, "This is wonderful. I—I would love to meet her to thank her."

"We would have liked to have you stay with us," he said, "but she is in the middle of cleaning the house and our daughter is getting ready for her wedding, which means, of course, that everything is upside down."

"I understand," she said. "But please thank her for me. Shall we go?"

They went and he wondered whether she had believed him, then he decided it did not matter. All that mattered was that she was now on her way.

They took a tram to his bank, where she waited in the hall while he went to cash some money. The old ex-Marine who acted as a guard and strutted about importantly, his chest covered with curios from forgotten colonial wars, eyed her with a beetle-browed frown; he saluted with relieved recognition when Peter came back from the teller's window and smiled at her and said, "All right, my dear. Let's go." He had taken a substantial sum out of his savings; luckily Susie and he had separate accounts, as they had been married under agreement of economic independence, as was usual under Dutch law in cases like theirs, where the bride had some property of her own from which she derived a small income.

He found Anna a room in the YWCA, gave her an envelope with some money and hurried off before she opened it, saying he would give her a call after he had seen his chief.

Commissioner Bartels was a huge, sleepy, slow-moving man who sat behind his bare desk rather like a bull alligator sunning himself on a river's bank, blissfully at peace in the security of his somnolent power. To anyone meeting him for the first time he looked like a benign, fatherly figure, who might growl but only to hide a sentimental heart. As a matter of fact, he was one of the most astute, hard-bitten and cunning chiefs the Amsterdam C.I.D. had ever had. The mere fact that he had managed to sit behind that same desk, sleepily blinking, all through the years of the German Occupation meant that he must have a soul cast in concrete. The fact that he still sat there after the upheaval of the Liberation and the shake-down of his department by Quisling-hunters meant that he would survive anything except the age of retirement.

He was in the habit of addressing his inspectors by their first name, so when he welcomed his subordinate with, "Hallo, Pete. Nice to see you," it did not mean anything at all; but the time he had kept him waiting had taken care of that. "Well," he continued affably, "what news have we today?"

"I trailed our main suspect to London," Peter started, but left it at that under the chilling gaze of the Old Man's slate-colored eyes.

"I know," Bartels said cheerfully. "I was talking to your friend Scott this morning on some other matter and he mentioned your visit. You have persuaded the victim to come back with you, I gather."

"That's right," Peter said, with a sinking feeling in his stomach as he realized once more the efficiency of the old alligator's grapevine. "I think it is the only procedure left to us until the British find a formula by which he can be arrested."

"Quite," the commissioner said with a smile. "I plan to borrow a motherly woman sergeant from the Vice Squad for that purpose. In the future, she will intercept the girls in question at the Hook, and tell them what they have let themselves in for, so there will be no need for you boys to go haring off on missions of mercy to England in the future. I trust you found your friends over there well?"

"I did," he said, and suddenly the detachment rose up inside him to sustain him once more. As if touched by a magic wand, the old alligator on his sunny bank melted into a cunning old egomaniac, clinging to his seat in all weather, who did not care a damn about what he was supposed to sit there for. He realized he had no means of making his request of personal concern to his chief, so it would probably be turned down. That was just too bad. It would not change his determination. "I would like three weeks' leave without pay," he said calmly, "and I would appreciate it if you could make it operative as from now."

The commissioner eyed him unblinkingly, as he had eyed German commandants, Gestapo spies and hotheaded leaders of the victorious Resistance. "Why?" he asked kindly.

"For personal reasons."

The Old Man pondered the reply and mused, "Now let me see. You have how many years to go? About twelve, isn't it? Right. You are quite resigned to spending them without promotion, I take it, so it's just a matter of sitting out your time."

"I would hardly put it that way."

"All right," the chief said with the flashlike speed of reaction that never failed to stun his victims. "Let's hear you put it *your* way."

"Well," Peter started, trying to recover his wits in a moment of confusion. "I think that so far I have not given you any reason for complaint. I've done my job as well as could be expected. Now I come up with what is, I grant you, an unusual request for a short leave of absence which won't cost the city anything, I think it might be granted without causing a precedent."

"I am glad you brought this up," his chief said with cheerful casualness, "because I've been thinking about you for some time now."

"Ah?"

"As you know, I am reorganizing my department, let's say streamlining it, a thing that has been postponed far longer than I intended by the war. While reviewing my staff, I found myself thinking about you in particular as an example of, how shall I put it, irreproachable, reliable inefficiency. Now don't take this personally, just look at it for a moment from my point of view. An organization like my department is a living thing, and any living thing is alive by virtue of the fact that its members are growing. Well—what the devil am I talking about? I am not a biologist and so the metaphor is probably way off the mark. What I mean is, why did you join this department in the first place?"

"Commissioner," Peter said calmly, with that strange physical coldness he had experienced when he faced Susie chilling his hands again. "I came here to ask you for three weeks' leave without pay. I have been in this service long enough to justify this request and I don't feel prepared to sit here after twenty-five years and undergo an interrogation on the reasons why I joined this department."

"Quite, quite," the big man said, unaffected. "I like to have your opinion and I am glad you gave it to me. Let's compromise. I'll give you your leave, which of course you'll apply for in writing, and instead of making it three weeks, I'll make it indefinite; the resumption of your service to be discussed on your return from Palestine."

Peter sat for a moment dumbfounded, then he rose, said, "As you wish," and left the room.

As he walked aimlessly along the canals of the city, deep in thought, he was haunted by the question: who told him? Every answer he came up with brought grief and doubt, for the only people who knew of his decision were the captain, Susie and the girl. He had decided firmly to put it out of his mind when he realized that the only possible one was Susie. She had told him frankly that she would use all means at her disposal; she had been as good as her word. What Bartels' amiable compromise boiled down to was that he would be fired if he went to Palestine. And, after all, Bartels was right. However noble his motives might be, by smuggling the girl into Palestine he would come in conflict with the law, and this made it impossible for the service to retain him.

Once he had accepted this, he walked on briskly. He should get to the British Consulate as quickly as possible, for he was certain now that they would try and stop him. He might be an old copper gone soft, but his twenty-five years' experience had at least taught him that two could play the game. He knew they would attempt to stop him and he knew how; the only chance he had to outwit them was by continuing to act as if he were stupid. The challenge filled him with new determination. During the few minutes it took him to get to the consulate, a plan of action had formed in his mind.

The consulate was very English. The moment he crossed the threshold and was received by the smile of the receptionist, he was in another country. She was not pretty, she was not acting on the presumption that she was; she wore her heavy make-up as a mask and her cardigan and string of pearls as a uniform. He told her he wanted to apply for a visitors' visa for Palestine and neither her face nor her manner changed when she asked for his name, although he guessed that they had been alerted. He was let into an office where a young, mousy gentleman sat behind a desk, dwarfed by Queen Victoria in oils and King George VI in colored lithograph, facing one another on opposite walls like millstones momentarily without motion. The young man gave him a squirrellike smile, and said, "Could you tell me, Mr. Jongman, what the nature of your business is over there?"

He told him, solemnly and stupidly, that he was Inspector of the Criminal Investigation Department of the City of Amsterdam, and that his business in Palestine was private.

"It would be," the young man said with a feminine laugh, trying to act as if he understood the hint. "I am sure our people will know about your coming, won't they?"

"They might," he answered stolidly.

"Well, in that case," the young man said, "there won't be any trouble getting your visa. Just fill out this questionnaire, will you? It's a mere formality. And then, if you would be kind enough to come back, say, the day after tomorrow, with your passport, the Consul will deal with it at once."

He repeated, slowly, "The day after tomorrow?" with a worried frown.

"That's the quickest we can make it," the young man said. "Usually it takes much longer, you know. There's a state of emergency in Palestine. Everything has to go via the Foreign Office."

"Are you sure it will be settled by then?"

"I should say so."

"H'm," he said. "Well, if I had to cancel, I am sure KLM are used to that."

"I beg your pardon?"

"Sorry," he said, rising and picking up his hat on the desk. "I was just thinking aloud."

The young man smiled with a trace of excitement in his pale blue eyes that assured him the seed was planted.

His next stop was at the KLM booking office. What he had to do was necessary and he did it reluctantly, because it was going to cost him money that he would not be able to recover till after his return. But if he did not pay in advance for the two seats he booked for Rome on the week-end plane, Bartels might not be convinced. In the past he himself had always believed a man was serious about transportation the moment he paid in advance, and only twice in twenty-five years had he been let down.

The KLM people had obviously not been alerted. They would get their call that afternoon, after the Consul had telephoned the C.I.D. And then, suddenly, an instinct told him that Bartels might know even sooner, a slight feeling of discomfort that he remembered from the war years, when for the first time in his life he had been shadowed instead of the other way around. He was careful not to look, but he knew there was someone on his trail. He even knew who it might be: that young sergeant just promoted from the street force. The others knew him too well.

He entered the barber's shop below the Industrial Club, the only building nearby that had a second exit which a young city sergeant would have no means of knowing about. It led from the Club itself, an old venerable bachelors' institution, into an alley behind the building. The young sergeant would not yet know that even industrialists can have creditors. He bought a small bottle of hair bleach at the counter, then he slipped into the alley, crossed the busy thoroughfare of the Damrak and walked to the Stock Exchange Building, in the basement of which was situated the uniquely Dutch institution of the bargees' exchange.

There, under a vaulted ceiling veiled with clouds of cigar smoke, sat hundreds of identical men in blue seamen's jerseys with blue peaked caps and the type of slippers only bargees wore, waiting for a cargo to be chalked on the board that would suit them and on which they would start bidding. The transport would go to the captain who quoted the lowest price or the fastest voyage, depending on the nature of the cargo which of the two was decisive. The intricate inland waterways of Holland carried thousands of barges of all sizes, speeds and ages, manned by these dour, taciturn men who usually operated them alone with their wives; only when a barge was so huge as to demand a minimum crew by law would there be a deck hand.

The only chance for him and the girl to cross the border unnoticed would be to find a widower looking for a deck hand to go south into Belgium or France. He made his way to a desk at the far end of the dark hall, where sat a huge burly mariner with a boxer's nose and a bowler hat who never lit his cigars but ate them. His name was Hendrik de Kooi, and he was the most powerful man in the business because he knew all the skippers and their barges exactly for what they were worth. Peter had come to know him toward the end of the war, when potatoes were shipped across the Zuyder Zee in an endless string of barges, some of which carried, underneath their innocent loads, a secret compartment for concealing young men trying to escape deportation. He had been able to help Hendrik because the German inspector with whom he was forced to work had trusted him. Those had been unhappy days of soul searching; the German had been a kind, decent man. Now Hendrik de Kooi considered him a hero, because, in the world where he sat eating his cigars, ships and the men who sailed them were either good or bad; you cannot ship a load of eggs with someone who is complicated and deserves a chance to sort himself out in the peace and serenity of the rivers.

"Inspector!" the huge man cried, opening a mouth that was pitch dark because of the cigars. "How are you? Glad to see you!" and he stuck out a hand that felt like an old-fashioned tiller. "I'll be with you in just a second, just let me deal with this neighbor here. Now listen, Hart," he continued to an angry little man with white hair and a brand new cap showing the crossed flags of Holland and Belgium. "You can't take on a load of sugar beets five times within a week. Your wife has to go and see her doctor on Wednesday to get her cast off."

"Well, dammit," the old man cried, "there's no need for a doctor to do that! I'll do it myself, with a hammer."

"Don't be a fool," the big man said kindly. "She's a good woman, she deserves more than having you lam away at her with a hammer, just for a stinking load of sugar beets. What do you want the money for anyhow? You're rich enough. Why don't you cut the top off that barge of yours and turn it into a houseboat and give that woman a chance to plant some beets for a change, instead of making her steer all over the country behind that wicked flat wheel of yours? You're lucky it was only her leg."

"You keep your big nose out of my affairs," the little

man said viciously. "Wait till my son hears about this! Telling me what to do with his mother!"

"I know, I know," de Kooi said resignedly. "You are real men, you two. Go and sit down, I'll see if I can find you a nice, lazy trip north. There's some lumber coming up."

"Lumber?" the old man asked greedily. "I'll take that. You see what you can do, eh? And no offense meant."

"I'll be calling you," Hendrik de Kooi said and he sighed as the old bargee waddled back to a table on rapid bowlegs, lighting a cigar as he ran. "Seventy-three years old," he said, "and he would sock me in the jaw any time I cared to dare him. Boy, some of these oldsters are tougher than you and I ten years ago. What can I do for you, Inspector? Looking for someone?"

"This is a private deal," Peter said. "I mean, it has nothing to do with the service and should be kept between you and me. I am trying to get a man and a girl to North Africa without papers. How would you go about it?"

The big man stopped chewing, took the remnant of his cigar out of his mouth, gazed at it and put it back. "What are they?" he asked. "A couple?"

"No. They might pass as father and daughter, though."

"What's their trouble?"

"I'll tell you if you want me to. I mean, if it makes a difference to you."

"All right. I'll take your word for it. North Africa, eh? I haven't got anyone going that far."

"I didn't think you had. But I'd be content with the north of France. Belgium even, if that's all you've got."

"So it's the Dutch border they are worried about?" The big man scratched his head without removing his hat. "That means they'll have to cross into Belgium at

Loozen; both Maastricht and Terneuzen are too tough, the military police will swarm all over them there. You know, this is Holland: fifteen soldiers with guns and grenades and desert boots on this side of the border, and one sleepy Belgian yawning his head off on the other. Seems we have to keep our younger generation busy. Now, let me think."

While he thought, a worried, fat civilian with a celluloid collar and dark rings under his eyes came to his desk and said in a hoarse whisper, "I've got an offer from *Cornelia*, Captain Huberts. Any good?"

"No," Hendrik said, still thinking, as if he were opening a familiar drawer absent-mindedly. "He can't take that cargo across the delta at this time of year. Try Frank over there. His *Eben Haeser* is a good ship and he's looking for a return load end of next week."

"Too late," the man whispered. "I'll have to take the other man."

"Suit yourself," Hendrik said and, after the man had gone, he continued. "Have a look at that character standing by himself at the second pillar on your port side. See him?"

"The old one, you mean?"

"Old? Hell, he's about our age. His wife died a month ago, and he has scrap iron for Paris. He's looking for a deck hand and might take on the man's daughter too if she'll cook. I may be able to talk him into going via the South Willems Canal and Loozen rather than the delta; I can get him a cent per ton off his insurance for the safer route. He's a miser, so he may bite. It all depends whether your man is of any use on a barge. Is he?"

"Yes."

"How good?"

"Same as me, I'd say."

"That'll do. And what about the daughter? Can she

cook and clean and darn and that kind of thing?"

"That, I wouldn't know. She's the one it's all about. She's a Jewess who has been in a concentration camp. I doubt whether she learned any cooking there."

"I see," the big man said, champing on his cigar. "In that case, I'll get her on, even if all she can do is file her nails. But don't expect him to be a charmer. He's a mean bastard, but one thing I can promise you: even if he finds out they are on the run, he won't hand them over to the police. Not until he gets to Paris, that is. Jan Brandt!" he bellowed with a voice like a foghorn. "Jan Brandt, vessel *Hendrika!*"

The man moved toward them with a slow, rolling gait, his hands in the pockets of his short blue coat, his cap over his eyes.

"I think I've solved your problem for you, neighbor," Hendrik said as Brandt reached the desk. "I've found you a deck hand who wants to take on for Paris and a young woman to look after you."

"Woman?" Brandt asked, sourly. "I don't want any woman."

"Well, that's your funeral," Hendrik said. "It's a man and his daughter and he won't work without her. They are used to sailing together, they lost their ship to the mortgage. So here's your chance to get a good man, a decent man, a man who is reliable and mature. The sacrifice you'll have to make is that you'll have your brass polished and your meals cooked for you."

"Got no room for a woman," Brandt said doggedly. "Got one bunk out for'ard, that's all."

"What about those twin beds you had put in a year ago? You aren't sleeping in both of them, are you? What's wrong with giving the man one of them, and letting the girl use the foc'sle?"

"I'll tell you what's wrong with it," Brandt said. "I don't want a total stranger lying beside me, belching and scratching, where my wife has lain for thirty years."

"Don't tell me any stories. You only got those beds last year. Until then, you lay on top of one another in that rabbit hole underneath your steering gear."

Brandt grunted. "How much do they want?"

"He asks forty guilders and his keep. The girl will come on for her keep only. So you might say that you have a deck hand for twenty a week and his keep. Man, I haven't heard of a deal like that since before the war."

"What is this to you? Are they friends of yours?"

"They are friends of this man here, who happens to be my friend."

"What is he? A man trader?" Brandt asked, looking Peter over with a sneer.

"All right, neighbor," Hendrik said calmly. "Have it your own way." And he bellowed, "Captain Schol of the vessel *Adventure Two!*"

"Hold it," Brandt said. "I'll take them. But I'll pay thirty for the two of them and not a cent more."

"Captain Schol!" the foghorn roared. "*Adventure Two!*"

"All right," Brandt said grimly. "When can they come on?"

"That's another point," Hendrik said. "They want to come on in 's Hertogenbosch, so it depends how soon you can get there. Where are you at the moment?"

"I'm at Duurstee lock," Brandt answered, "and I'm not taking them on in 's Hertogenbosch. I'm going the other way."

"Why? If I were you I'd take the South Willems Canal and cross the border at Loozen."

"With all those slow locks? No, thank you. Why the

hell can't they come to me? Must I go and fetch them? What is this?"

"Look, neighbor," Hendrik said, with strained patience. "I get you a crew, I give you good advice. If your nature tells you to stand there and snarl, live and let live. Captain Schol!"

"But it'll cost me a day extra to go to Antwerp via Loozen!" Brandt cried. "Those locks are the slowest in the south!"

"So what? You are not on a time charter. And what's more, I'll get you a cent per ton off your premium if you take the inland route. If you go now and lock through by yourself and make that short run alone, you'll be in 's Hertogenbosch at eight thirty tomorrow morning."

Brandt shrugged his shoulders and turned away, without saying goodbye to either of them.

"You see?" Hendrik asked. "Your party is not going on a vacation. By the way, I assume they can be there?" Then he roared once more at the top of his lungs, "Last call for Captain Schol of the vessel *Adventure Two!*" and muttered, "The Frisians over there will think I'm off my rocker, because Schol is in the Baltic right now. So you see, Inspector, anything to help you."

"Thank you, Hendrik," he said. "I appreciate it. I'll tell you about it some other time, but you have probably saved a girl's life there."

"Oh, well," Hendrik said, with unexpected embarrassment, "it's all in a day's work."

As Peter passed the pillar where Brandt stood, the man said sourly, "Tell your party to join me in 's Hertogenbosch," and as Peter smiled and tipped his hat, he wondered how he was going to explain his presence the next morning.

He left the building, and as he walked past the busy waterfront toward the ferry station he was suddenly overcome by a feeling of despondency. How was that man Brandt, who had eyed him with such cold distrust, going to take it? How was Anna going to take the work, the cramped quarters, the coarse food? He would not have worried if it had been a matter of days, but a trip from Holland to Paris by barge was going to take weeks. And what would they do after Paris? How would they get to Tangier? The captain of the Harwich ferry had given him the address of his friend Van der Pink in Tangier and said he would write him a letter, but would he? Where were they heading, what had he brought upon her, and upon Susie and Betty?

7

He stood still and looked at the traffic of the sightseeing boats, the little passenger ferries, the crew launches from the shipyards across the harbor, the tugboats. It was the rush hour; the water of the turning basin in front of the Central Station could barely be seen for boats, while the big thoroughfare overhead was a solid stream of bicycles through which trams ground their way, clanging incessantly. No one stopped to marvel at the dexterity of the helmsmen below, who drove their boats at full speed through one another's ranks without scraping, though the tolerance between the rubbing strakes was less than a hand's width. How would he make out, once he was expected to take the helm of a barge and sail it through narrow bridges, into locks that left a finger's width to spare on each side, through tunnels where he would have to steer lying down, through hectic ports like Antwerp, mazes like Ghent, winding rivers like the Scheldt, the Oise, the Seine? He had not steered a boat for years and then only the patrol boat at odd moments when the old helmsman was making tea. He thought of the old man humming "Daisy" in the little foc'sle, his light blue eyes full of joy and kindness. He had died long ago, before the war, in that other world that seemed to have gone forever, a world of innocence and kindliness and decency.

He looked up at the skyline of the city across the water, the old warehouses with their honorable names like "Concord," "Brotherhood" and "The Four Gospels." The spire of the Saint Nicholas Catholic church with its neon-lit cross seemed to drift among the clouds; on the façade of the Salvation Army Headquarters beside it another neon sign switched on and off: "God Calls You." It looked impersonal and urgent, as if someone were wanted on the telephone. He heard screams and giggles as a crowd of girls spilled onto the jetty from one of the passenger ferries: factory girls from the chocolate plant across the harbor. They took the double stairway to the road above by storm and caused a brake-squealing, bell-clanging, shouting confusion among the steady stream of bicycles as they boarded a streetcar that drove off looking like a beehive, with swarms of them clinging perilously to the handrails. One boatful of nameless girls, just a few score of the millions of their generation, and all this for just one of them. But then, who was he? He joined the crowd waiting for the ferry and vanished in it.

A quarter of an hour later he emerged from it on the other side of the harbor and started to walk home past the sleepy waterfront of fishermen's houses with the wooden gables that Monet had painted. Night was falling underneath the boughs of the elms that lined the seawall on which tanned eel nets were spread out to dry, their green glass floats reflecting the setting sun like convex mirrors. Beyond, on the misty water, the day lingered among the stakes and the small dark buoys of the fishermen's channel. Ducks were quacking their last massive chat before the night came to cover them with silence; at the far end of the wall, where it turned toward the drawbridge, three old men sat close together smoking pipes, chatting like the ducks; their yellow clogs looked like big webbed feet. There could not be much difference in the monologues of the ducks and the old men: fish, the weather, the encroaching night. Peter mumbled a greeting as he passed and they grunted in reply.

When he crossed the drawbridge, he stopped to gaze at the harbor beyond. The horizon had now vanished in the evening mist that rose from the water like smoke; somewhere to the west the mournful foghorn of a steamer hooted, a drawn-out warning answered by the perfunctory toot of a harbor tug. He could picture the scene as clearly as if he were watching it: the freighter, the tug, the car ferries wallowing clumsily in the wakes of the scores of crew launches scurrying across, loaded to capacity with workmen and engineers from the yards, and over it all the restless gulls wheeling against the yellow sky. It was his world, it was part of him, and as he stood gazing at the evening haze he realized that that part was larger than he had suspected. The thought of leaving it behind filled him with apprehension. What had he taken on?

During the short walk home he seemed to wake up to reality, the reality of the man that Bartels and Susie knew as Peter Jongman. His great decision the day before had been made by the boy who had once sailed this harbor full of self-confidence and joy, it was to be carried out by the plodding copper Bartels had fired, and he could not think of a more unsuitable person. This momentous mission called for a soaring eagle, not a clipped middle-aged duck, tied to his little patch of water, his dumb urge for security, his monologue quacked at nightfall. He did not doubt the rightness of his decision; he woke up to the fact that he had been the wrong man to make it. It did not shake his determination, but it dispelled the detachment that had so far pervaded him with peace.

When he got home, he opened the door quietly, to postpone meeting Susie. He knew exactly how she would behave, how her voice would sound and her eyes would look, and he foresaw his own meekness with a faint nausea. As he stood in the hall he noticed the Eden hat and stylish overcoat of Albert and Betty's little flowered hat. One thing you had to say for Susie: she had managed, against overwhelming odds, to push her daughter up one rung on the steep ladder that led through the middle class. But for her, Betty would have screamed and giggled with the girls spilling out of the ferry and stormed the steps to the street.

The door to the kitchen opened and he hitched up his smile; but as he faced Susie he saw that she was not as he had expected her to be. She was charming, flashing at him the huge smile that he had missed for so long, and she said "Oh, there you are, darling. Ab and Betty are here. They've got some very exciting news about his job. Go in quickly. I'll fix you a drink."

He hesitated, then he followed her into the kitchen. She turned around as she heard his steps behind her and seemed surprised; then, suddenly, her façade crumbled and she looked weary and haggard and terribly worried. She turned away from him and filled a kettle and put it on the gas ring and struck a match and said, "I've been thinking. I think I'd like to meet that girl. I think it's important. Do you think she could come here tonight?"

She took him by surprise; his first reaction was that it was too late now; she had done something irrevocable when she picked up the telephone and rang Bartels. But on second thought, it might make all the difference. Susie was, despite appearances, a warm-hearted woman. Seeing the girl might well have the same effect on her as it had had on him. Yes, it was an excellent idea.

"If you like," he said.

"Why don't you ask her to come for a cup of tea after supper? Unless you think that the night air will hurt her?"

"Why?"

"Well, she's ill, isn't she? Or so you told me."

"Yes, that's right."

"All right then, go and ask her. I assume she can be reached by telephone?"

"I'll try," he said, "if you're sure that's what you want."

She started to say something, but changed her mind; instead she gave an exasperated sigh and said, "What on earth did I put that kettle on for? Get out of the kitchen. Go and do your telephoning. Go on."

He turned, opened the door to the sitting room, said, "Hello, Albert," and "Hello, Betty," and went to the telephone. He dialed the number of the YWCA, asked for Miss Held; as he stood waiting for them to find her he glanced at the young couple sitting close together on the sofa, leafing through the French *Illustration*. Susie found the turtledove way in which they behaved charming and touching; he was irritated by it. He rarely admitted it to himself, but he disliked the smug fat boy on the sofa, and was not taken in by his sentimental nuzzling as Susie was. To Susie, this was the rapturous romance she herself had missed and which she now saw enacted by her own child. To come home these days was like visiting a home for the blind, each of them in love to the exclusion of everything else: the boy with himself, the girl with love and Susie with her daughter. There Betty sat, flushed, innocent and entranced, a kitten playing with a bobbin. As he stood watching her, waiting for his call to be answered, he was struck by a strange thought: suddenly he pitied her for her sheltered life, her innocence. The tattooed number on Anna's wrist seemed at that moment a credential of her humanity.

"Yes, hello," a soft voice said on the telephone.

"This is Peter Jongman," he said. "My family would like to meet you. Have you any plans for this evening?"

"No . . ."

"Well, then, my wife suggested that you might like to drop in for a cup of tea after dinner. I'll meet you at the ferry if you think you can get that far by yourself. Otherwise . . ."

"Oh, I can get there," she said. "But are you sure this is all right?"

"Yes," he answered. "I'll meet you at, say, the eight-fifteen ferry which leaves at eight o'clock opposite the station. You remember the one I took?"

"Yes."

"It goes as far as the William the Third lock. You go all the way. I'll meet you there. Goodbye for now."

"Goodbye."

Susie came in with a tray as he put down the receiver. She looked as flushed and entranced as her daughter. He had never known her to make so many titbits and cookies and innocuous cocktails as she did these days; the sight of her so happily fussing always made him feel ill at ease, as he realized that he had failed to bring out that side of her himself in the past. In a way he was to blame for the fact that she now smothered these two youngsters with an excess of affection that was bound to end in horrible loneliness, for her. The boy's smile was already growing thin as he thanked her for her attentions; soon he would be cracking jokes with his fellow executives at stag parties about mothers-in-law. But there might be a baby for Susie to fuss over by then, unless the company judged it unwise to start a family at this stage.

"They may be a little warm still," Susie said breathlessly as she put the tray on the low table in front of them. "Just let them be for a moment. They're much better when cold."

"How delicious," the boy said with alarm in his eyes as he looked at the tall glasses filled with a poisonous green liquid, slightly sweating. "What is it?"

"Try it," Susie said delightedly. "Something Indian we used to make at home."

"Ah," the boy said.

Betty laughed. "Don't look so worried, darling," she said. "It's a tamarind cocktail. You'll love it."

"I'm sure I will," the boy said insincerely and hugged her with a smile that Peter could no longer bear to watch. "Anybody know where my cigars are?" he asked.

"Where do you think?" Susie answered without looking around.

"Well, they aren't."

"Nonsense." She looked at the mantelpiece and said, "Must be Mrs. Dop. Look in the hall."

"Why would a woman put a man's cigars in the hall?" he asked. But no one paid any attention. He went to look for his cigars, rummaged futilely in the glove drawer and among the stack of old magazines underneath, looked under the hats and even inside the hollow elephant's foot an uncle of Susie's had given them for a wedding present as an umbrella stand, then he heard her voice behind him. "Is she coming?"

"Yes."

"When?"

"The eight fifteen."

"Are you still looking for your cigars?"

"Yes."

"Well, do that later. Go and wash your hands now, it's dinner time."

"All right." He heaved himself up from his knees and went to the kitchen.

"Don't go in there," she said. "I have something cooling off in the sink. Go upstairs."

He went upstairs.

As he stood washing his hands he started to plan Anna's moves for that night, after she had been to see them. It was a good thing after all that she was coming. He had a lot of instructions to give her. He worried for a moment about her crossing the harbor alone after dark, but then he remembered that she was sure to have a shadow, so that was one worry less. It depended on who the shadow was whether she would have to go to great lengths of make-believe that night or whether she could just go to bed. The identity of the shadow would also tell him whether old Bartels suspected any trickery on his part or not. Chances were he did; he probably had thought the whole thing out while sipping his glass of geneva on the terrace of the Red Lion, watching the rush-hour traffic struggle by. It would have taken Bartels about five minutes to get to the point in his planning where he was now; five minutes more and a second glass of gin would have taken him out of sight. There was only one chance of escape from his somnolent gaze, and that was to convince him he was right about his subordinate's stupidity. He obviously did not believe that men could rise above themselves.

The meal was exactly as it had always been on Friday nights for the last year, ever since Susie had first invited that charming young man she had met at Mrs. Haanstra's. They had not seen Mrs. Haanstra since, for Mrs. Haanstra had a daughter herself. Now the charming young man sat modestly at the head of the table, his collar spotless underneath the premature double chin, his gray eyes slightly preoccupied with something he seemed to discern behind his future father-in-law's insubstantial silhouette. His left hand dutifully held Betty's, but his right, which wore a big signet ring, toyed impatiently with a fruit knife while a pianola roll in his brain produced a mechanical monologue about the stock market and the unlikelihood of a German industrial resurrection. Betty pretended to listen to what he said while she looked at his lips; Susie followed every bite he took with worried interest, as if his very presence were the outcome of the alchemy of her cooking.

Peter leafed through a picture book of memories as he watched Betty sitting there, lost in her love. He remembered her in her cradle, screaming blue murder whenever he bent over her to tickle her chin. He remembered playing horsey for her and taking her on his shoulders to gallop around while she squealed with delicious terror, until he felt the alarming warmth of the result of her excitement trickle down his back. They were both punished and giggled secretly together in the bath; at that time Susie had been very stern with the two of them, as if they were in league against her, which had often bewildered the child. Then, a few years later, there she was: coming home from school with pigtails, one bow missing, eyes flashing, hissing through the gap in her teeth, "He'th a thtinker! A mean thtinker! Look! He thtuck my plait in the inkpot!" and she showed the back of her dress with a dark smear on it and Susie cried, "Scandalous! It's ruined!" and they both vanished, fuming and lisping, into the same bathroom where he and she had once giggled in secret defiance. Still later, they would turn up for the Thursday night concert in party dresses after taking more than an hour primping in the bathroom, covering the black lino with powder and shouting at one another to hurry up from various rooms of the house. They would have a hasty snack standing up at the kitchen table and then wind one another in wraps and put their coats around their shoulders and grab their sequined purses and voyage across the stormy waters of the harbor to the *Concertgebouw*, where they would look daggers at other dresses and smile at other smiles while Tchaikovsky downed his glass of cholera-infected Neva water and died with heart-breaking, melodious sobs. For Peter Thursday night had been sandwich night, a delightful evening of yawning and scrutinizing the newspaper and scratching his head and humming loudly and puffing blissfully at his cigar, feet up on the sofa, until they came home and they all had rolls and cheese and bouillon together while Betty asked whether her mother had seen that ridiculous skirt Mrs. Flabbinga was wearing, she was sure it was a bustle, and Susie said, "Don't be catty. That was *all* Mrs. Flabbinga." He had sat sipping his bouillon and looking at the child through the steam and wondering which man would in the end make off with this innocent gaiety, this guileless trust, and hating him before he had a face. Now there he sat, opposite him; and he could have been worse. If they were lucky they would be so busy living that they would never wake up to the fact that each sat facing a total stranger at the breakfast table. And then, suddenly, for no reason at all, he knew that this was a farewell.

He sat through the rest of the meal absent-mindedly, listening to Albert and to Susie and to their great surprise: Albert was going to be promoted to assistant manager of their third Amsterdam production center, the one for fluorescent bulbs, so they could not only marry much sooner than they had expected, but live very near indeed, probably this side of the harbor too, because the plant was going to be built on the northern outskirts. Now it might be difficult to get a house, so they had been thinking about a houseboat and that's where you come in, Daddy. You know the harbor so well. Where do you think would be the best place to put a houseboat?

He talked over the possibilities with them, which were not many, because the narrow channels branching off the harbor were slums and on the waterfront itself there would be too much wash, but they might go and have a look at the fishermen's harbor to the east or the yacht basin beside the ferry landing. Then Susie said, "If you have to meet that ferry, darling, you had better hurry," and he saw to his surprise that it was eight o'clock.

As he walked along the dimly lit quay toward the lock on the edge of the dark void of the harbor, he was overcome by a feeling of unreality. This could not be he, Peter Jongman, walking there, planning to desert his wife, his child, his job; it could not be true that he was about to disappear without a trace. He remembered one moment, long ago, when he had stood in front of the door to his parents' house the morning before his transfer from the harbor police to the C.I.D. He remembered feeling the urge to put the key back in his pocket, get on his bicycle and vanish without a trace. The impulse had seemed inexplicable and foolish at the time; he had shrugged his shoulders and turned the key in the lock and entered the corridor—the long, dark corridor at the end of which he now walked, hands thrust deep in the pockets of his overcoat, shoulders hunched, a middle-aged man planning to elope with a girl. That was what it would look like to others, and he was no longer sure that it was not true. He considered the possibility calmly as he walked along. His motives might, unknown to himself, be as simple as that. For all he knew, he might be escaping from Susie, his job, the lovers on the sofa, the specter of old age. Yet he could not shake the certainty underlying it all: whatever his motives might be, here was a martyred Jewish child yearning for the promised land, and he would take her there.

As he reached the dock he saw the green and white light of the ferry bear down upon him, changing to white and red as it swung around to its mooring. Then there she was: slight, self-effacing; if he had not been looking for her he would not have noticed her in the small crowd. He could not have helped noticing, however, the burly man in a bowler hat, who stood elaborately trying to look at his wrist watch in the darkness to give his hanging around a pretext. He could not see the man's face, but he suspected him to be a recruit from the city desk, brought in to avoid recognition. Judging by his clumsy acting he should be easy, but perhaps it was better not to take any chances.

"Hello," she said. "How kind of your wife to invite me."

He said, "Yes," uncomfortably, and added, "Did you have a nice trip?"

"Oh yes, it's lovely crossing the harbor at night."

"This way."

They did not say much as they walked along the edge of the night. There was no wind, the mist magnified the sound of their footsteps. Their shadow wore rubber soles, yet he was following them much too closely in his anxiety not to be shaken off. Where did the man expect them to go? Peter toyed for a moment with the thought of leading him up the garden by taking her into the fishermen's poolroom where he always had a game of billiards on Saturday nights, and where there was also a convenient back door as in the Industrial Club; but he decided to stick to his plan and appear more stupid than those who trailed him. He had not expected it to be so difficult.

Until they reached the house, he still thought that her visit was a good idea; the moment Susie took the girl into the sitting room after meeting them in the hall he knew it was a mistake. He knew by the way in which she said, "This, Miss Held, is our daughter, Betty." She was not moved by what she saw as he had been, she wanted to show Betty to the girl and then turn around and ask her not to ruin the child's future. She must be confident of the outcome, as only a mother could be. He found himself hoping she would not be hurt, which seemed ridiculous. There she stood, the indomitable woman who had overshadowed all the years of his manhood, facing a sick, shy girl; and there he stood, hoping she would be spared.

"This is her fiancé, Mr. Hendriks. They are going to be married in two months' time. Mr. Hendriks has just been made assistant manager of a new branch of his firm."

"Congratulations," Anna said. He noticed for the first time that she looked shabby and uncared for; but it seemed unimportant, she behaved with great composure.

They talked a little; Susie inquired after her parents, when she realized her error she changed it into "family" which only made it worse. Albert came to the rescue unwittingly by talking about the new trend in electric fittings for road use, after someone had mentioned the darkness outside. His plant was going to concentrate on fluorescent street lighting, an absolute must now that all the new highways were planned with overpasses and cloverleaves. Everyone listened with a great show of interest and when Albert finally rose after looking at the clock, saying, "I'm afraid we have to go, sweetie, if we want to be in time for the second show," they all protested. But off they went, after Susie had embraced Betty as if she were leaving for the Far East. Peter and Anna stayed behind for a few minutes, while Susie saw the others to the door. They avoided looking at one another; Anna must know by now why she had been brought here. There was about her unobtrusive presence an atmosphere of grief and loneliness. He did not see how Susie and she could ever reach one another.

Susie came in, flushed from her last farewell in the night air, her eyes ablaze with love and determination, her mouth set in a confident smile. He wished he had the courage to take her in his arms now and kiss her and say, "Don't." But he said nothing.

"Well," she said, "They're off. Now, Miss Held, if that's all right with you, I think we should have a talk. Peter, would you mind?"

Here was his last chance to head her off; he let it go by. He went out into the hall obediently and closed the door behind him. His instinct was to flee upstairs and let things take their own course, but he decided to stay in the hall to listen without actually eavesdropping. He would know by the sound of Susie's voice when it was necessary to join them. As he stood there, leaning against the wall among the coats, he was again beset by a feeling of unreality. What was he doing, standing here in the darkness, waiting for two women to start a fight? What had he done or omitted to do in the past, to bring this about as the outcome of the dreams and hopes of the eager young man on a patrol boat tied to a buoy underneath the starry sky? He felt as if this were a dream; any moment now he would wake up to the gentle snoring of the old helmsman and the buoy light blinking green among the stars, and decide to stay with the harbor police, never mind the promotion. Then he heard Susie's voice say, "I am very sorry," in an aggressive tone; "I would have thought that anyone with a trace of decency would not have hesitated."

He could not hear the girl's reply. He did not even hear her voice.

"I see now that I could have saved myself the trouble," Susie said with rising scorn, "but perhaps you understand that I wanted at least to try to appeal to your sense of decency and compassion. I know that you have suffered a great deal, and without any doubt totally without justification, but that you should think this gives you the right to ruin the life of someone your own age who has been more fortunate, that is a sad and nasty outcome of your own suffering."

The girl obviously did not reply, for Susie snapped, "All right! If that's the way you want it, let's see if your Good Samaritan has something to say for himself!" Her steps came to the door, she pulled it open and called, "Peter!"

She did not wait for him; he hung back a moment to create the impression that he came down the stairs, then he entered and closed the door behind him. The girl sat quietly in her chair as if she had not moved at all, her hands folded in her lap, her face calm, but her eyes were somehow unfocused, as if she were completely turned in upon herself. Susie stood with her back to him, her hands on the mantelpiece; she looked up in the mirror when she heard the door. They exchanged a look before she turned around and faced him and said, "I have appealed to Miss Held's charity after letting her see Betty and her happiness. I realize it was a foolish thing to do. As she seems to have lost her tongue, I assume that you are the one who came up with this whole idea and that it is up to you to decide whether you are going through with it or not. Is that correct?"

He said, "Yes," almost absent-mindedly, alarmed by the strange self-hypnosis of the girl, who sat motionless in her chair, her face as white as a sheet, her lips fixed in a meaningless smile, her eyes unseeing. If only she had answered, even in anger, broken out of her self-control to shout at Susie, shout the truth. To sit there like that, as if her soul had escaped from her body, was terrible to see. He realized that, to her, Susie was just another sadist brutally clawing at her, as others had done in the past. Susie must be stopped at all costs; she was, in her self-righteous, heartbreaking mother love, taking up the torture where the henchmen had left off.

"I would like to hear it from you," Susie concluded, with a beginning of the same self-hypnosis showing in her eyes. If only she knew how lucky she was, how innocent, how young. Only yesterday she had stood on the sun deck of the liner in her white dress, smiling down at him; she was still playing with the fire of unexplored emotions, blithely oblivious of the good fortune that had protected her from reaching their limits. "Well?" she urged.

"I think that is a matter between you and me, Susie," he said quietly. "I think Miss Held should go home now."

"You may think so," Susie said belligerently, "but I don't! I want to get at the bottom of this. I want you to realize exactly what you are doing, and why, and I want her to be there so that she may know too. Go ahead!"

"I'm sorry, Susie," he said kindly, "but I am going to take Miss Held to the ferry. You and I will talk later."

"You are not!" Susie cried, her eyes blazing. "If you have the so-called courage to do this thing, you should also have the guts to face the consequences. You've been ratting all your life, this time you're going to stay put and face the music!"

"I will, Susie," he said, "after I have taken Miss Held to the ferry. Come along, child." He stretched out his hand toward the girl.

"You'll stay here!" Susie cried. "If you go now, you need never come back!"

"Come along," he said, putting his hand on the girl's shoulder. "I'm sorry about this. Let's go."

"So you're sorry!" Susie cried, ugly with despair and rage. "You're sorry for what life did to a total stranger, but not a thought for what you're doing to your own child!"

"Come, Anna," he said, saying her name in an effort to reach her across the no man's land behind which she had retired. "It's time to go. Please."

"All right, go!" Susie shouted. "Get out of here, both of you, and may God punish you!"

"Don't, Susie," he said, trying to comfort her without giving in to her violence.

But she shouted, "That's right! 'Don't mention God!' I'm sorry! I forgot! Well, let me tell you this, you lecherous old coward, if there is a God in heaven, he'll break you, you and that—that zombie of yours, or I'll lose every scrap of faith I possess!"

He tried to calm her with a sound that came out, surprisingly, as a laugh. She did not know what she was saying; it was all so ridiculous and wrong and inadequate that if there were a God who listened to prayers and He had a trace of mercy, He would stop her. Just stop, be still, and let the anger pass.

"Come on, Anna," he said and pulled her up gently, but with determination. She did not obey, she submitted, and followed him to the door as if in a trance.

"Don't think you'll ever get out of the country!" Susie shouted. "Don't think I'll let you get away with this! I'll fight for my husband with everything I have! Do you hear?"

They crossed the hall.

"Do you hear, you slut?" Susie screamed pathetically from the lighted room. "You haven't a ghost of a chance, you'll be sorry, you're ruining your own chances of ever getting . . ."

He closed the front door on her voice and, at that moment, all his pity was for her. The girl was beyond pity, beyond reach.

He did not notice the man with the bowler hat until they arrived at the small waiting room on the lock. He had to give her instructions, he had to shake her out of her trance if they were to succeed in what he had so carefully planned. The man would overhear them if they stayed inside, so he took her to the gates of the lock and they stood leaning over the guardrail, with underneath them the steady gurgle of the little waterfall tumbling through the crack between the doors into the pit of darkness below. "Listen, Anna," he said urgently, "this is very important. Are you listening to me? Anna, please."

"Yes," she said, "I'm listening." Her voice sounded calm.

"I am sorry I had to submit you to this," he said, "but I had no choice, I had to play the game. She telephoned my chief this morning, and told him what I was planning to do, so now we are being shadowed."

"I think we had better call the whole thing off," she said.

"Don't worry, honestly. It is all going to work out. All you've got to do now is listen and follow instructions. Here they are. You are being followed by a man in a bowler hat, gray overcoat, smoking a cigar. My chief thinks we are planning to leave by plane for Rome the day after tomorrow, because I have made the bookings, but he is not going to take any chances, that's why he has you watched. Can you follow me?"

"Yes," she said, "but I think . . ."

"I'm sorry, there's no time for that," he said. "The truth is we are leaving early tomorrow morning. I want you to make the man think that you have time on your hands, and won't get up tomorrow morning till late. So go back to your hotel and book for two more nights, then go to a café. There's one near your hotel called "Américain"; it has a reading table. Order a cup of coffee, read newspapers and magazines for as long as you can stand it—at least an hour. Then go out, go to another café across the square, called "Moderne." It has a reading table too. Do the same thing as you did before, and stay till closing time. Now listen carefully. Are you listening?"

"Yes."

"Here is a bottle of hair bleach. At closing time, go back to your hotel and bleach your hair. Tomorrow morning, at half past five, go down to the swimming pool which is in the same building, take a shower, and go out by the street entrance. Lots of people from outside go there in the morning. By the time you come out, the rush hour will have started; take the tram to the Central Station, you'll have to fight to get on at that hour, get out at the station, take a train to 's Hertogenbosch, and wait for me there in the waiting room."

"The third-class one?"

"Yes, if there are two of them, which I don't know. I'll join you there around ten o'clock; if I should be a little later . . ."

He stopped because she was suddenly seized by a coughing fit. It was the same cough he had noticed the night before, dry and wheezing. It reminded him of Betty as a child. She would not calm down until he carried her. "Papa carry," she would croak between sobs and choked by coughing, and only after he had walked up and down the passage a dozen times, humming, stroking her little back, feeling the hot blast of her coughs die down in his neck. . . .

"You should really nurse that cold," he said. "On second thought, you'd perhaps better not take a shower tomorrow morning. Just go down to the swimming pool from the hotel, and out into the street."

The ferry was swinging into its moorings; he took her by the arm and led her to the gangway.

As she stepped on board, he patted her shoulder and said, "See you tomorrow. Goodnight."

He watched the ferry leave, its white stern light dwindled in the darkness. Overhead, invisible seagulls screeched; the fog had lifted, the lighthouse swept the low clouds with its beam.

He walked home along the waterfront; as he turned the corner beyond the drawbridge, he saw the light was on in their bedroom. Before letting himself in he looked at his watch by the light of the street lamp; it was only a quarter to ten. They never went to bed so early. He felt like turning around and spending the night in town, but he could not bring himself to do it. He could not leave Susie alone after the things she had said and which, he knew, she was now regretting bitterly.

But, once again, she surprised him. She sat up in bed, her hair in curlers, sipping a cup of soup, charming, light-hearted, alarming. What had she been up to? Something had happened during the short time he had been away.

He undressed slowly, thinking, while she chatted about the children and their houseboat. She must have telephoned Bartels again, and been reassured that the girl and he were under constant surveillance and she was not to worry. There could be no other reason for her behavior.

After they had turned out the light and he lay staring at the faint flash of the lighthouse behind the curtains, silent in that common world they had shared for so long, he felt her self-assurance falter in the darkness. She lay quite still; he could not see her eyes, but he was sure she too lay staring at the twitching light. How many nights had they lain like this? It had always been the time when the conflicts of the day had seemed to dissolve in the wordless security of being together, the time in which they had best understood one another. Gazing at the scythe of light swinging behind the curtains he foresaw, with chilling clarity, the sorrow and loneliness waiting for her. He took her hand in the darkness, as he had done so often before, and pressed it reassuringly; she did not respond. His heart went out to her and he said, "Don't worry. Whatever happens, I love you."

She did not answer, but he knew she had heard; a moment later he realized that she was quietly weeping.

At that moment his mission almost failed. He was suddenly overwhelmed by the desire to spare her, to do anything she asked, to prove to her that he loved her more than he loved himself. But then he saw the girl's face, her eyes as she had sat there, her soul withdrawn behind the no man's land of her tortured body, and suddenly he knew that the only chance for Susie and him to recapture the happiness they had lost was for him to carry out this mission. He wanted to tell her this, but he could not find the words; soon afterwards he heard from her breathing that she had fallen asleep.

The railway station of 's Hertogenbosch had been heavily damaged during the war; its temporary waiting room looked like a stage set made of three-ply and laths, with a makeshift coffee counter and flimsy tables. It had no ceiling, the walls ended in midair, overhead curved the dark, smoky roof of the station itself. It was a scene of desolation, unrelieved by the gay checkered tablecloths and the jug of flowers on the counter.

8

She sat waiting behind one of the tables in the far corner, and the sight of her brought home to him with a shock the irrevocability of what he had done. She had bleached her hair to a shrill, unnatural color, and looked heartbreakingly helpless and vulnerable with that straw-blond wig, like a baby chick dyed purple for Easter. She welcomed him with a smile of relief; but when she saw the expression on his face she asked, "Is there something wrong?"

"No, no," he said hastily, "so far everything is going as planned. You all right?"

"Fine," she said. "Everything went just as you said it would. How do you like my hair?" She laughed and touched it with a coquettish gesture. "I rather like it." Then she looked at his eyes searchingly, and her face fell, and she asked, "Is—is it cancelled?" She asked it like a child, set for an outing.

He said, "Of course not. We are over the hump now. The rest should be easy."

She went on looking at him with her face set in the fixed smile of self-defense that he had come to know; he tried to think how he could convince her that all that had happened was that her hair had taken him unawares; all he could do was to tell her about the barge they were going to board, and how they would be able to cross the border unnoticed, by water.

"Is that what is worrying you?" she asked.

"No," he said. "Believe me, I'm not worried at all. We are going to be all right." He put his hand on hers reassuringly; then he realized how they must look to others. He glanced around and his heart stood still. Leaning against the counter stood Detective Sergeant Wolters.

He sat for a moment in a numb emptiness. Then he said, "I'll go and pay. I'll be right back."

She said, "I have paid."

"All right," he said. "I'll get some cigars before we go." He strolled to the counter, asked the waiter for five Charles the Firsts; then he said to the back of the man who had turned away as he approached, "Hello, Wolters. How are you today?"

The man looked around, and his expressionless gray eyes tried to feign surprise. "Well now, Inspector, that's a coincidence."

"What are you doing here?"

"It's my day off," Wolters said easily. "I'm looking up my aunt in town. Are you on a job?"

"A private one," he said, "like yours. Well, I'll be seeing you. Give my regards to your aunt."

"I will," Wolters said. "Be seeing you, Inspector."

He went back to her, and took her arm as they made their way out of the waiting room. His thoughts raced with great lucidity. Wolters being there must be one of those coincidences that occasionally fouled up even the cleverest of plans. It was humanly impossible for Bartels to have foreseen all this; also Wolters had deliberately shown himself. Wolters was a tough old bird, as wily as they came, he would never have given himself away if he were supposed to shadow them.

He put Wolters out of his mind with determination and faced his next barrier: Skipper Jan Brandt of the vessel *Hendrika*.

"Can you cook?" he asked as they walked toward the canal.

"No," she said. "Not really. I mean, I can boil an egg and so on, but not a whole meal. Why?"

"It might be nice if you could cook us something occasionally on the way," he said lightly. "We'll have to shop anyhow, so let's get you a cookbook."

"Oh, will you really?" she cried, preposterously young again. "Do you think he would let me try? Has he got a kitchen?"

"We'll see," he said. "I think you are in for a pleasant surprise."

It was a reckless thing to say, but he managed to make it sound reasonable. The next half hour was going to be tricky, but if he refused to let himself be rattled he might bring it off.

He had expected to have to search for the *Hendrika*, but when they reached the canal, there she was, the only vessel moored to the prim provincial quayside lined with the ruins of neat little houses that looked scrubbed and clean even in death. The young poplars lining the canal had been scorched and blasted, but each one was still surrounded by a small protective fence of chicken wire. There were breaches in the stone bank of the canal, but what was left of the quay looked solid, neat and Dutch. Nothing could look more Dutch than the barge, tied up between two of the gaps. A clean flag fluttered from the staff over its stern, its deckhouse was painted in imitation wood grain, the shutters of the little windows red and yellow. The carved nameboard, brightly varnished, stated in letters inlaid with gold leaf: "M. V. Hendrika,

Amsterdam, 146 tons, Captain J. Brandt." The hatch cover was spotless, as if it were freshly scrubbed, the deck was oiled, and the bollards painted silver and red. The anchor winch was an intricate composition of different colors; obviously the ship had often waited for hours on end in front of locks on sleepy summer days. They were about to step on board when a tiny demon came screeching toward them. It was a little black dog, yapping, hoarse with rage. Despite its size it kept them ashore. The door of the deckhouse slid open, and the head of Captain Brandt appeared. He growled, "Shut up, Coba!" and the little dog stopped for a second. Then Brandt recognized him, and frowned. Coba started up again and screamed blue murder, prancing up and down on the gunwhale.

"What are you doing here?" Brandt asked at last, over the yells of the dog.

"Let me tell you inside," Peter said.

"Shut up, Coba. All right. Come on in."

Peter helped Anna down while the little dog, growling, drooled over his ankles. As she stooped and entered the deckhouse, she gasped with surprise.

The inside of the deckhouse, which the bargees called "the pavilion," looked like a miniature parlor fitted out by an elderly spinster. There were mottoes on the wall with Biblical quotations, a calendar of Doctor Schweitzer's mission post in Africa, a carpet on the table and crocheted place mats underneath everything. In one corner stood a potted palm on a tripod, in another a brass birdcage, also on a tripod, with a canary inside that looked as if it were made of brass too. A door led into a small galley apparently full of copper pans, and over the table hung an ornate, majestic oil lamp, suspended from three brass chains to prevent its swinging. There was a smell of beeswax, lavender and coffee. Brandt with his dark jersey and his tanned face looked incongruous as he sat down at the table with an open book on it and a pair of spectacles. The book lay open at an illustration, an old-fashioned drawing of an Indian with a headful of feathers facing a Quaker with a wide-brimmed hat.

"What are you doing here?" Brandt repeated with hostility. "I thought I was going to get a deck hand and his daughter."

"I know," Peter replied. "I'm sorry about that. It was the only way we could arrange this. As a matter of fact, we want to come as passengers, the young lady and I, and you can name your own price. We'll help as much as we can, I am familiar enough with boats to make a fair deck hand."

"Why the secrecy?" Brandt asked, his eyes narrow. "What's all this about?"

"I am on a special mission."

"What mission?"

He hesitated, then he said, "I am an inspector of the Amsterdam Police, Criminal Investigation Department."

"Show me."

He showed his card. Brandt looked at it, with a frown. "Who's she?"

"Miss Anna Held. Her passport is in order."

"What is all this? What's the idea?"

"That I can't tell you, or we would not have gone to all this trouble to keep you in the dark. I know that it must seem humiliating to you, but we cannot take any risks. All I can tell you is that no harm will come to you or your ship, and that my mission has nothing to do with you. So name your price."

Brandt looked from one to the other, speechless, taut with rage. He obviously would like nothing better than to throw them off, and rightly too; but there he was, off his route, without a deck hand, he had no choice unless he were willing to spend another week at these moorings, trying to find help, and lose both time and money.

"Well?"

Brandt set his jaw and said, "I don't like it. I don't like it one bit. But all I can do, I suppose, is shut up and take it. All right. It'll be two hundred guilders—each, and you'll have to work."

It was a scandalous price, a railway ticket to Paris cost fifty guilders, a plane ticket seventy-five. "I think that's steep," he said.

"All right!" Brandt replied. "Get off!"

"Look. A train ticket costs . . ."

"Then why didn't you take the train? I have to feed you, it may take two weeks, three weeks, if we get snarled up in front of the tunnel in the north of France, it may take four. What do you take me for? A sucker?"

"All right, we won't haggle about it." He took out his wallet and counted out two hundred guilders on the carpet underneath the lamp. "There you are," he said.

"I said two hundred each."

"I know. The other half will be paid in Paris."

"No, sir. You pay now, or you get off."

"I'm sorry, but that's the way it's going to be. Take it or leave it."

Brandt looked from one to the other, while the canary shrilled a high mechanical song. "All right," he said, "but let me tell you: I'm not the kind that likes being taken for a ride. Police or no police, this is a swindle. Let's get going."

"I have no working clothes with me."

"That's your worry. Go to the foredeck."

"Could we do some shopping first?"

"No, I've been waiting long enough as it is. If you want to shop, shop at the next lock if we are held up. I'm not going to slow down for either of you."

"As you like."

"All right," Brandt said with a hostile look at Anna. "You get on your knees and do the floor. You'll find what you need under the sink."

"Listen," Peter started, but Brandt cut him short. "If you don't like it, get off," he said, "and don't think you've got me at gun point, it wouldn't be the first time I have sailed this barge alone. So, get moving."

He went out onto the deck. After he had left, Peter patted her shoulder reassuringly and said, "Don't worry. He'll come around. He's angry just now and so would I be in his place. Let's give him a chance to get over it."

"What a lovely room!" she said admiringly. "I never expected to find something like this on board a barge. Do you think I could have a look at the bedroom?"

"Of course," he said gently, "go ahead," and went out on deck.

Coba haunted his ankles all the way to the front of the ship, rabid with rage. The engine started after a series of explosions, belching black smoke until it ran smoothly. Brandt climbed out of the engine room, went into the wheelhouse and wound down the window. "All right," he called. "Let go there."

Peter cast off the forward mooring rope and started to coil it, while Brandt backed the barge into the aft spring line and swung the bow away from the quay. It was a neat maneuver; obviously he had spoken the truth when he said that he could sail his barge alone.

They headed for the bridge and Peter knew a moment of relief, almost exhilaration. They were on their way; his plan had worked. He felt a deep, wordless gratitude and looked up at the bridge keeper with a smile. But it was not the bridge keeper. It was Wolters.

There was no doubt about it this time: Wolters' being here was not a coincidence. Commissioner Bartels had thought of everything. As the chill shadow of the bridge slid over him, he knew that the only sensible thing to do now was to turn back. They would be stopped at the border; Wolters had shown himself so plainly because he wanted to warn him. It was as obvious as if he had called, "Please, Inspector, don't do this to me; take a hint and turn back."

The bow of the barge glided into the sunlight again and he was suddenly overcome by an utter weariness. There was no point in being stubborn; if they wanted to pass that border, they had to get off the ship and try another way. But if Bartels had been ahead of him in this instance, he would foresee their next move too.

"We moor over starboard," Brandt's voice called from the wheelhouse.

Peter saw the lock ahead, the pilings in front of it, and picked up the loop of the mooring cable. He should have gloves to handle it, or there would be no skin left on his hands by tomorrow. Then he smiled wryly; there would be no tomorrow. They would probably reach the border that night.

While they lay waiting for the lock to open, he tried not to think about the future. It seemed as if time had slowed down, as if the moments of that morning had become endowed with a nostalgic fullness. As he sat on the foredeck, his aching hands open on his knees, the ship under his feet seemed to radiate peace and assurance. There was not a speck of rust on her, the paintwork would have graced a yacht; on the hatch to the foc'sle a three-colored star had been painted, with rigid symmetry, a self-portrait of the captain's soul. In the center of the star was a little porthole, all the light the foc'sle had unless the hatch was left open. She was supposed to sleep there. He went to have a look.

As he opened the hatch and peered down into the dark vault he noticed a strong smell of rope and Stockholm tar. To sleep there must feel like suffocating. It was impossible for her; they had to find another solution. Then he smiled at himself once more, and closed the hatch.

The doors of the lock opened slowly, revealing the bows of two heavily loaded barges. On their foredecks two men stood chatting, two little dogs sniffed at one another from ship to ship. In the wheelhouses, revealed as the lock doors opened wider, the skippers' wives stood, chatting over the window sills. On the edge of the lock a big tomcat came strolling toward a brace of cooing pigeons. Overhead, a string of sparrows sat perched on a power line that crossed the canal; in the blue sky sailed proud white clouds like heavenly barges. It was a moment full of hope and promise; Peter slowly lifted his hand in salute to the first of the skippers who came gliding past on his way to the bridge. Coba and her opposite number engaged in a barking match, running along the gunwhales of the barges as they passed. After they had gone by there was a smell of coffee, and of weeds stirred up by the wake.

After the second barge had glided past with chugging engine and rattling rudder chain, the *Hendrika* moved slowly into the lock.

"Where are you bound for, skipper?" the lock keeper called down from the high quayside.

"Paris," Brandt answered from the wheelhouse.

"What's your cargo?"

"Scrap iron."

"All right. Take the last cleat but one."

"Right!"

Peter made fast; as he looked around he saw that the lock doors were already closing. They were the only barge inside. He stood by to pay out the mooring cable as the ship was lowered; the tomcat came to have a look at him, regally indifferent to Coba's frenzied yapping. The pigeons planed to a landing on the roof of the lock keeper's office with a swish of wings. He heard the rumble of clogs and a man in a short white coat appeared above him, carrying a basket.

"Eggs, butter, milk?"

"Ask at the wheelhouse," he said.

"You think the missus would like some extra-special chocolate pudding, freshly bottled?" the man asked. "Why don't you surprise her with a treat?"

"You'll have to ask the captain," he said. "I'm the deck hand."

"Oh," the man said. "Nice day, isn't it?" and he moved off without waiting for the confirmation.

Peter saw the milkman talk to Brandt, who held the aft hawser, and he saw Brandt call down the pavilion steps. Anna appeared with a scarf around her head, wearing an apron that was several sizes too large, and ordered something from the milkman, calling between her hands as the ship went steadily down. The milkman put her order in his basket and lowered it with a line. She carried it inside and came back; Brandt pulled out an old-fashioned purse and counted out some money into her outstretched hand. She put it in the basket and the milkman hauled it up. The lock keeper appeared high up on the wall again and called down, "Here she comes!"

"All right," Peter answered.

The loop of the cable came whistling down and

barely missed him as it lashed the tarpaulin. Brandt's voice screamed from the wheelhouse, "What the devil do you mean, dropping that hawser on my clean hatches? What are you doing on a lock?"

The lock keeper strolled toward him and said a few quiet words that made Brandt splutter with rage; he darted back into the wheelhouse and started up the engine with echoing reverberations in the cavern of the empty lock. Then he called at the foredeck, "Take a bucket, wash that tarpaulin!"

Peter found the bucket, its rope neatly wound around it, behind the anchor winch. He took the end of the rope in his left hand and threw the bucket overboard to scoop some water. It fell with a splash and, before he knew what had happened, the rope was yanked out of his hand by the speed of the ship. He called futilely "Hey, stop!" and started to run along the deck to keep up with the vanishing rope. By the time he had reached the wheelhouse, it was gone.

Brandt glowered at him from the window. "That'll be five guilders and twenty cents," he said grimly. "Go and get another bucket from the galley."

He obeyed, feeling like a fool, and went down into the pavilion. The canary was singing at the top of its voice, the lamp over the table clattered rhythmically with the pulsating of the engine and there was a smell of beeswax. He found her kneeling on the floor, panting with exertion, her cheeks flushed, a wisp of her blond hair over one eye. She looked a picture of subjugation, but her eyes were radiant.

"Look at the floor," she said panting. "Do you see the difference?"

"Yes," he said, "wonderful," and went into the galley feeling as if all this were a dream from which he would soon wake up. He found the bucket and went upstairs.

"You'll find a line in the foc'sle," Brandt said as he passed. "Don't cut it, tie the slack into a coil."

The foc'sle, as Peter lowered himself into it, turned out to be hot and dark. His eyes took a minute before they discerned anything at all. Then he saw a cavernous bunk, covered with what looked like an old tablecloth, three hooks on the wall with a broken mirror over them and, pinned up on the wainscoting, three picture post-cards, left by a previous deck hand. One showed a stiff bouquet, held together by a gilded ribbon, with the legend, "For Thy Birthday." He found the rope underneath the bunk and climbed back into the sunlight. Even the foc'sle now seemed tinged with the nostalgic beauty of what might have been.

The hours passed slowly. They went through three more locks, which were separated by stretches of straight canal shaded by poplars. At noon Anna brought him a plate of sandwiches and a mug of coffee, and sat down for a moment on a bollard to look at the trees and the straight canal ahead. She looked pale and fragile, but it seemed as if everything she set eyes on were a delight to behold.

"Is my room down there?" she asked, seeing the hatch with the painted star.

"Yes," he said.

"May I have a look?"

"Of course."

He opened the hatch for her and warned her to go down backwards as the stairs were steep. She vanished in the darkness; after a while he could smell the Stockholm tar from where he sat.

She took so long to come back that in the end he bent

over the square of darkness and called, "Are you all right?"

She came back into the light, her eyes blinking. As she stood on deck, she said, "I think it's very snug. Do you know that there's a little porthole, behind a newspaper?"

"Where?"

"In the wall. I can't get it open. Will you try?"

"I don't think you can sleep there," he said. "It's much too stuffy."

"Not with the porthole open. I can make something very cozy out of it, you'll see."

"But what about that smell?"

"Oh, that's nothing," she said. "I like it. It smells like my father's tackle box, the one he used to take along when he went fishing."

"Are you people going to get some work done today?" Brandt called angrily from the wheelhouse.

"Coming," she answered, and before he could tell her not to let herself be bullied she was gone, leaving some of her exhilaration in the air. He would have to tell her about Wolters soon.

As the day drew to its close, he had still not found the courage to do so. At nightfall they tied up in a turning basin where another canal branched off to the border and Belgium. There was a little village nearby, huddled under a cluster of trees in the gathering dusk. Brandt said, after they had moored, "Lay the table, tell her to get on with the supper, I'll be back." He jumped ashore, leaving Coba whimpering after him.

This was the moment to tell her. He went to join her in the pavilion and found her talking to the canary, who answered with questioning peeps. She was so delighted with her big doll's house that he could not bring himself to tell her. After all, they had a respite until the next morning, he might as well leave her these few hours of lightheartedness. He forced himself to forget about the next day, helped her peel the potatoes that were the Dutch bargees' staple diet, and showed her how to fry some sausages he found in the food cupboard. They laid the table together; when they had finished she stepped back, looked at it as if it were a drawing she had made, and asked, "Do you think he'll be away long?"

"Why?"

"I noticed some wild flowers on the bank a little way back. Would there be time for me to go and pick them?"

"I think so. Shall I come with you?"

"No, you go and wash," she said. "You must feel very uncomfortable after working like that in your city clothes."

"I'm all right," he said. "I'll come with you."

When the dour skipper came back, he found the table laid and the lamp lit and, underneath it, a bunch of wild flowers in a jam jar. His eyebrows rose and then he frowned, looking from one to the other with suspicion. "Let's eat," he said surlily. They sat down and he asked, "Where is the Bible? Where are my glasses?"

She hurried to get him the book and his spectacles, which she had put on the sideboard. He put on the spectacles, scowled at the book and said, "That's not the Bible, that's my library book. It's over there, beside the birdcage."

She brought it to him. He waited, peevishly, until she sat down, then he opened the book and took off his peaked cap. The top of his head was startling in its bald whiteness, in the lamplight it looked as if he wore a skull-cap.

He must have opened the Bible at random, for he read, "And when they arose early on the morrow morning, behold, Dagon was fallen upon his face to the ground before the ark of the Lord; and the head of Dagon and both the palms of his hands were cut off upon the threshold; only the stump of Dagon was left to him. Amen." He put a ribbon on the page, closed his eyes, folded his hands on the book and prayed, "For what we are about to receive, oh Lord, make us truly thankful. Bless our moorings tonight and protect us from thieves, wash and the weather. For Jesus Christ's sake, Amen." Then he opened his eyes, glowered at her over his spectacles and asked, "Did you make the dog's dinner?"

"No," she said. "Doesn't she eat the leftovers?"

"On board this ship, there are no leftovers. She gets the bone that's in the newspaper on the top shelf, and three slices of bread, and gravy."

"I'll do it now." She got up.

"Sit down," he grunted. "Let's eat in peace." He lifted the lid of the tureen and frowned at the soup. "Give me your plate," he said, and started to ladle it out while the steam rose past the lamp like smoke.

They ate without speaking but not in silence; Brandt drinking his soup set the canary warbling in its corner. Outside, Coba's claws made tiny ticking noises as she paced up and down the steel deck, a little sentry on her beat. The alarm clock in the kitchen ticked louder.

When she had brought in the potatoes, the sausages and the spinach, Brandt served them again and continued to eat with grim concentration.

"If we pass a shop tomorrow or the day after, do you think I could buy some cretonne to make curtains for—for my room?" she asked.

Both men looked up.

"Why?" Brandt asked.

She looked away and said, "People look in." It obviously was not the real reason.

"Let them look in," Brandt said, and continued eating.

It was such a callous thing to say that Peter forgot about the next morning and said, "Of course you can. How much would you need?"

"Oh, very little. A remnant would do. If there is any left over I could use it to make a frill for the counterpane. Have you got a sewing machine?"

Brandt did not deign to answer.

"We'll talk about it tomorrow," Peter said gently. "When we get there."

They finished their meal in silence, then Brandt looked up and asked nastily, "What's for afters?"

"I—I didn't make any," she said. "Did you want some?"

"I want semolina," he said, "or rice pudding or custard."

She looked pleadingly at Peter, and started to get up.

"Sit down," Peter said. "It's too late now. We'll gladly do without it for today."

Brandt looked at him with disgust. Then he closed his eyes and startled them by saying, "We thank thee, O Lord, for Thy bounteous blessings, Amen."

"Cigar?" Peter asked, proffering one in the lamplight.

"No smoking on board this ship," Brandt said, pleased. "If you want to smoke, you'll have to go outside."

He thought of the morrow, and said, "I'm sorry. Well, I suppose you had better turn in, Anna. You've done a good job, but you've had a busy day."

"She's going to do the washing up," Brandt said, "and I give the orders around here."

"If it's all right with you, I'll do the washing up," he

replied calmly. "She should go to bed now. Come on, I'll take you there."

"No," Brandt said, "she can find it herself. I won't have you hanging around that foc'sle."

"I beg your pardon?"

"You're not married, are you? So let her go alone. We've got a watchdog."

He felt like punching the man's nose, but it was important that she should enjoy the few hours left to her. "Do you think you can make it in the dark?" he asked.

"Of course," she said. "Goodnight, Captain, and thank you for letting us come. You—you have a lovely home here."

Brandt looked up over his glasses, but said nothing. They listened to Coba barking as she came out and to her steps going away on the steel deck, followed by the dotted line of the little dog's claws. Neither of them spoke and they avoided looking at one another. Peter got up and said, "Well, I'd better get started. Excuse me." He started to stack the plates.

Brandt sat stolidly reading his library book in the lamplight, letting him clear away and do the dishes in the galley. He turned the pages slowly and read without glancing at the illustrations of war dances, covered wagons exploding and herds of buffalo stampeding. The canary warbled, squealed and throbbed in its cage and Coba whined softly at the top of the steps.

"Shall I let her in?" he asked.

"No," Brandt answered without looking up. "Give her her meal up there. She sleeps on deck."

They themselves slept in the bedroom, a low-ceilinged cabin panelled with varnished three-ply and containing twin beds, a wardrobe and a dressing table, which left room for little else. They undressed self-consciously, bumping into one another and muttering apologies. It was a relief when the light was turned out by a nut-brown hand looking like a glove on a stark white arm; neither of them wished the other a good night.

It was very stuffy in the little room; the porthole stood ajar but gave no ventilation. The reflection of a light ashore rippled on the ceiling and Peter lay looking at it, thinking of Susie. He soon fell asleep.

He was woken up in the middle of the night by a gnashing noise that grated on his nerves. It was Brandt, grinding his teeth in his sleep.

He could not fall asleep again; in the end he got up quietly, dressed in the dark, went out on deck and jumped as he set the little dog screaming at his feet in the darkness. Brandt was out in a flash, calling angrily, "What the devil is going on here?"

9

He explained sheepishly and the skipper growled, "Now we might as well get moving and make up for some of the lost time."

They left. Peter, on the foredeck of the barge, scanned the night nervously. They seemed to be going faster than they had during the daytime, and he had to face reality now. In a few hours they would be at the border where Wolters would be waiting. All he could do was to avoid a scene, and make it as easy for her as possible. They would find another way, eventually. But even as he thought that, he knew they would not. It was now or never.

He knew Sergeant Wolters well. He could not remember a single occasion when he had seen him ruffled, or uncertain. It depended on what Wolters' orders were, whether he had been told to avoid using force or to stop them by any means. It would be pointless to resist Wolters physically; the customs officers would come to his aid. All he could do was to hope for a miracle.

He balked at the thought with unexpected vehemence. He did not believe in miracles and never would, it was weakness and cowardice to rely on them. Yet he did not see how he could get away from that final conclusion: nothing but a miracle could save them that morning.

Day broke as they glided up to the dock of a lonely

customs station in the fields. In the blue light of the dawn a sleepy officer came, yawning, out of a lighted room to meet them. As the man climbed on board and vanished inside with Brandt, Peter thought for a moment, with a flash of foolish hope, that no one else was about. But when he had finished belaying the mooring cable and looked up, he saw the familiar silhouette of Sergeant Wolters outlined against the sky.

" 'Morning," he said.

" 'Morning, Inspector," Wolters said. "It's going to be a nice day, I think."

"Yes," he said, wearily. It came as a surprise that Wolters, despite his toughness, should be so awkward. But he was not going to help him, he was not going to take the noose from his executioner's hand to put it around his own neck. Or was he? Wolters was a simple man who must be more upset by this than he had foreseen. They had always got on well together; Peter even discovered at that moment that, over the years, he had come to like him. He sighed and said, "All right, Wolters. Let's get this over with. You have orders to arrest us, I suppose?"

"No, sir!" Wolters said quickly, with obvious relief. "All I have to do is hand you this letter and wait for an answer."

He took the envelope that was held out to him, and asked, "Why did you wait with that till now?"

"My orders were to hand it to you on the border," Wolters replied. "I thought. . . ." Whatever it was, he could not bring himself to say it. "Could you please read it now, sir, and sign one? I believe there are two copies in there, one is for your files."

Peter tore open the envelope and tried to read the letter by the light of the dawn. It was too dark; he climbed on to the quay and took it to the office window. Wolters followed him at a discreet distance.

It was a letter from the Office of the Commissioner, Criminal Investigation Department. "Dear Jongman," it read, "Now that you are about to leave my jurisdiction, it is my duty to warn you that you are about to commit an irrevocable act, the consequences of which may not be fully apparent to you. Should you indeed aid and abet your party in entering Palestine illegally as is your intention, you will be breaking the law. It is evident that, under those circumstances, you can no longer be retained as an officer of this service and your dishonorable discharge will be effective immediately. I presume that you are fully cognizant of the effects of this measure on yourself and your family, which include the forfeiture of your retirement pension. It is also my duty to advise you that the British authorities are aware of your intention and will do everything in their power to prevent your carrying it out. The mere fact that you have been handed this letter in your present location should help you to determine your chances of success. It would be appreciated if, after due consideration, you would sign the enclosed copy of this letter and return it with bearer, as confirmation that you are proceeding in full awareness of the consequences. Yours truly, J. F. M. Bartels, Commissioner."

He looked up with mixed feelings of relief and despondency. Relief, because they were not going to be stopped; despondency, because this letter brought home to him irrefutably that he was incapable of coping with a mission of this magnitude. For the last twenty-four hours he had been haunted by visions of himself and the girl trying to sneak across the border unnoticed; he had gone to elaborate pains to conceal their movements; he had forced her to dye her hair so that now she looked like a cheap tart; he simply had not possessed the intelligence to conclude that no one could prevent their crossing the border, because their passports were in order. The only border where they could be stopped was that of Palestine.

"Have you got a pen on you?" he asked.

"Certainly, sir," Wolters said, unbuttoning his coat.

He signed the letter on the wall and handed it back to Wolters. "There you are," he said. "Give the Old Man my regards."

"I will," Wolters said. "Is there anything else I can do for you?"

"No," he said. "Thanks."

Wolters hesitated; he wanted to say something, but did not know how to start. Then the customs officer came out of the pavilion and Brandt's voice called, "All right, there! Let go, for'ard!"

" 'Bye, now," he said.

"Good luck, Inspector," Wolters replied. "Good luck, sir, good luck." He tried to put into those words everything he had been unable to say as he shook Peter's hand.

"Get a move on there!" Brandt called.

Peter hurried back on board and cast off. The engine throbbed, the bow swung out; the ship trembled, gathered speed, and they glided into Belgium.

After they had passed through the Belgian customs and cast off again, the sun had risen and they sailed into the delicate beauty of a radiant spring day. There was a smell of early flowers in the air, wafted across the moors by the breeze that had cleared the morning mist, and birds started to sing and warble around them as they glided down the motionless canal that stretched ahead into infinity. The young green of budding trees behind the banks of reeds billowed slowly in the breeze; everything ashore seemed to ripple and quiver and shimmer, as if the whole world consisted of water except the canal.

10

Peter felt a giddying sense of liberation, as if he were waking up together with the birds, the reeds and the trees into this great new day; then Brandt called from the wheelhouse, "Where's that woman? Am I going to get some coffee, or what?"

He lifted his hand in acknowledgment and tapped on the hatch of the foc'sle.

As there was no answer, he tapped again and opened it a crack. The smell of tar and rope was pungent like smoke.

"Anna?" he called.

"Yes?" her voice answered, far away.

"It's time to get up. The skipper wants his coffee."

"Oh," her voice answered, startled. "All right, I'm coming. What time is it? Where are we?"

"It's still early," he answered, "but it's a lovely day. We are in Belgium."

"What?" Her voice sounded incredulous.

"Yes," he said. "You crossed the border in your sleep."

She remained silent for so long that he called, worried, "Anna?" He tried to peer through the crack of the hatch; then it was suddenly opened from the inside. Her head appeared in the sunlight, her blond hair looking more like a wig than ever, her eyes blinking in the daylight.

"Sorry," he said. "I didn't mean to rush you."

She gazed at the reeds, the budding trees, the white mare's-tails in the sky. "Is this Belgium?" she asked.

"Yes," he said.

She looked at him as if only now she began to believe it, then she said, "I think you are wonderful."

She took him completely by surprise; he stood there, at a loss for words, then Brandt called, "Hey! Dammit! Did you hear me?"

"Yes," he called back. "She's coming!"

"Come aft yourself!" Brandt called. "I want you to hold the wheel for a moment."

"You'd better hurry," he said to her. "He seems to be in a vile mood."

"I'm coming," she said hastily. "I'll just comb my hair."

He hurried aft, growled at by Coba.

"Sounds as if the gear is kicking up again," Brandt said as he entered the wheelhouse. "Hold the wheel for a moment, while I go and have a look. Tell her to make some coffee," he added. Then he vanished down the engine-room hatch.

It had been years since Peter had last steered a ship, and he felt a flutter of panic. He did not know where the controls were, or how she responded to the wheel, and whether right wheel would swing her to starboard or to port. He swallowed, his hands gripped the spokes tightly.

But the canal was straight and empty; the moors and the reeds seen from the wheelhouse looked serene and peaceful; in the distance, on the horizon ahead, the weather vane on a church spire flashed in the sunlight. The ship slowly pulled to port; he gave a shade of starboard wheel. The bow seemed to hover for an instant, then it calmly swung back. That was one thing settled: she had a normal wheel. Now, where were the controls? He looked at the dashboard and saw that nothing could be plainer. Brandt must have waited many hours in front of locks in bad weather and spent them painting the interior, lonely widower in the rain. Underneath every switch and dial its function was painted in stiff italics: *Anchor Light*, *Running Lights*, *Oil Pressure*, *Water Temp.*, and, touchingly, *Clock*. The metal sparkled and gleamed, the varnish looked as if it had been applied only yesterday, the woodwork had been polished to a luster. As Peter looked up, he saw overhead, in a small frame, a motto: "I am with thee and will keep thee in all places whither thou goest."

The bow swung slowly toward the other bank and, again, the ship obeyed the wheel. A kingfisher flitted across the canal ahead of them; the wave of their wake made the reeds bend down to the water and straighten up again, as if the wave were not confined to the canal but rolled on, across the banks, the trees, the moors shimmering in the sun. Peter's confidence grew; he patted the big steering wheel with a boyish gesture, then, suddenly, a voice said, "Here's your coffee."

He had not seen her come in, he had not even heard the door slide open. "Thanks," he said. "We had better put it on something, or it'll make a ring on the varnish."

"I'll get one of those little mats," she said. "That's what they must be for. Where is he? I have his coffee here."

"In the engine room, checking the gears."

"Anything wrong?"

He shrugged his shoulders. "Can't be very serious. He is a perfectionist, I think." He sipped his coffee.

"Isn't it beautiful?" she asked, looking out. "I didn't know Belgium looked like this."

"It looks different seen from the water," he said. "Everything does."

"I still can't believe it," she said. "There I was, last night, worrying about where we would be today. It's —it's a miracle."

He glanced at her, startled, then he asked, "How did you sleep in that rope cupboard?"

"Wonderfully well."

"I have to speak to him about it. You can't live in that stench. We'll have to find another solution."

"Oh, no, please don't," she said, urgently. "Please; I like it there. I know exactly what I want to do to it, to make it cozy. Please let me stay there."

"But you can't breathe! When I opened that hatch this morning, it was stifling."

"It wasn't, where I was," she said, with moving obstinacy. "I was very comfortable." She hesitated, then she concluded, "So that's settled. I think I had better take his coffee down to him."

He heard the door roll behind him; there was silence for a moment, then her voice asked, shyly, "It is, isn't it?"

"Eh?" He turned around and saw she was still standing in the doorway.

"You will let me stay there, won't you?"

"Of course," he said. "You told me what you wanted, so that's settled."

She looked at him for a moment, uncertain, then she

said, "Yes. . . . Of course," and rolled the door shut behind her.

A few minutes later the door rolled back again and she appeared at his side, smelling of diesel oil. "Phew, it's hot down there," she said, "but it's a lovely engine. Have you seen it?"

"No, not yet."

"Everything is polished, even the iron. You know, he has pot holders down there, specially for the handles, so that he won't leave marks on them."

"He certainly keeps his ship in top shape."

"He's a strange man," she said. "He must have been very lonely."

He glanced at her and said, "I suppose so."

"The one I find difficult to get on with is the dog. She nearly bit me this morning when I went to give her some milk. Do you think she'll come to trust me?"

"Did she drink the milk?"

"Yes."

"Then I wouldn't worry. Any more coffee?"

"Oh yes," she said, "and then I had better go and make the beds."

He wondered whether he should mention that no one had had any breakfast except Coba, but he just said, "Do that," and turned the wheel.

The bow, after a moment's consideration, obeyed.

They moored in the village he had seen on the horizon because Brandt wanted to do something to the gears.

11 Peter went ashore with Anna to do the shopping. The village street looked as if it had missed a century. A farmer's buggy stood parked at the curb in front of an old-fashioned pharmacy, the horse dozing over its nose bag. There was not a modern house in the street, yet they all looked as if they had been built yesterday; even the cobbles looked scrubbed and the trunks of the elms lining the sidewalk were whitewashed. Outside the general store stood a row of clogs neatly lined up against the wall. "Let's get ourselves some clothes," he said. "I feel uncomfortable in these. So must you."

"Oh, all I need is an apron that fits me," she said. "His wife must have been enormous."

A little bell tinkled as he opened the door. Inside it was dark and there was a strong smell of cloth and fresh wood; this, they discovered, came from a small alcove filled with wooden shoes.

"We should get some," he said. "They are the best things on board a barge."

"But I couldn't possibly walk in them. I've never worn them before."

"We'll get you a pair with leather uppers," he said, "and you'll be wearing soft slippers inside them anyhow. That's the secret."

A wizened old man came toward them from among the dark rows of coats in the background, bringing a smell of Brussels sprouts with him.

"Good morning, good morning," he croaked, brainlessly gay like a tame crow. "What are you going to spend your money on this morning?"

"Grandpa!" a shrill voice called from behind the coats. "Come back here at once!"

The old man grinned, showing toothless gums and giggled, "She thinks I'll warn you, and I will." Then he whispered hurriedly, "Take off ten per cent," as slippers came swishing toward them; an angry woman with bleakly glinting spectacles appeared, caught him by the arm and pushed him back among the coats. She came back a little breathless and asked, her eyes invisible behind her mirroring glasses, "Well now, what can I do for you? Isn't it a lovely day?"

"To start with, we'd like some clogs. Leather-topped ones for the young lady."

"In here," the woman said, preceding them to the alcove. "He's a real handful, you know. Eighty-seven, but you can forget about the eighty. I had to give up my line of toys; he crept out of his bed at dead of night to play with all the little cars. What's your size, dearie? High instep?" She looked at Anna's foot and said, "My, that's a child's size. Let me see—I may not have those with full leathers, only with a strip. Would you mind?"

"Anything, as long as it doesn't hurt."

"These here are extra-special," the woman said, showing a pair of brightly painted monstrosities, on the noses of which little leather flowers were nailed. "They are the so-called Ballroom Specials. I've only a few of them left."

"I think they're a bit ornate," Anna said kindly.

"The purpose of anything a woman wears is to make her look pretty. You just ask your pa."

He smiled stiffly and said, "I think she should try a pair of ordinary ones first, to wash the deck in."

They ended up with the Ballroom Specials, the flowers

separate in a little paper bag, a pair of slippers, two aprons, two gingham dresses for the price of one, two red kerchiefs, a pair of bloomer-shaped slacks for wear around the ship and a small remnant of flowered cretonne. The woman said, "Your turn now," sizing Peter up.

He bought clogs, slippers, shirts, socks, a matched set of short jacket and trousers in smelly but indestructible corduroy and a French beret, which was the uniform of all Dutch deck hands. They were both given an ounce of caramels with the compliments of the management; when they finally went out with their parcels Anna said, "How wonderful of you to let me take so long over those dresses. I think I really got the nicest of the lot, don't you? I'm not sure about the slacks, but I suppose they're practical." She sighed happily and looked around at the freshly painted day outside.

"I think we deserve a breather," he said. "Let's have a cup of coffee. This way."

"Those kerchiefs are awfully pretty. I know they're just farmer's hankies, but I'm sure if I sold them in Amsterdam, I'd get twice the price."

"You mean, if you bought them in Amsterdam, you'd pay twice as much," he said with a smile.

She frowned and looked at him quizzically, then her face broke into a smile. "Yes," she said. "I am really Jewish."

"Of course you are," he said, taking her arm. "That's why we are on our way to Palestine."

"I still can't believe it. Did they ask for your passport at the border?"

"No, nobody cared. All they worried about was what was in the holds."

"I think you are so clever," she said. "What a wonderful idea to go by boat."

He was glad to hear her say so, for it settled something in his mind. They were now free to take the train, and he had been toying with the thought of leaving, feeling at the same time that he could not desert Brandt now that he was dependent on them. Obviously there was, as far as she was concerned, more to this than just a matter of expediency.

"This looks good," he said. "Let's go in here."

It was a small café; a stoop with wrought-iron railings in the shape of two swans led to a glass door; blue fly screens in ornate ebony frames masked the lower half of the high windows, on which was painted in two mathematical halves, *"Grand Caf"* on one side and *"é Du Sport"* on the other.

"I wonder what the 'sport' stands for," he said as he opened the door for her. They entered a dark mahogany-paneled room with a billiard table, a monumental counter and a few marble-topped round tables. The sport turned out to be a mechanical football game in a flat glass case which looked antique, with ivory knobs and a scoreboard as worn as a kissing stone.

A bald man in shirt sleeves and a black silk waistcoat came to take their order and vanished again through a door behind the counter, without having said a word. They looked around at the racks of billiard cues, the cuckoo clock, the big old-fashioned lithos on the walls; then the clock clanged out ten strokes and ten cuckoos, ending with the slam of a door. "It seems as if the war never got here," Anna said. "This is how the world of my grandparents must have looked. They had a shop in Zutphen."

"The Belgians knew how to cope with an occupation," he said. "For them it was the second time."

"My grandparents would not have believed what happened to the Jews during the war," she said musingly. "To them, Israel meant a mystical country, a sort of legend. I don't think they ever dreamed of it as a nation, with real people, to which they belonged. I know I didn't, until I saw it."

"When was that?" he asked.

She glanced at him, and seemed to hesitate. He held his breath; he knew this was a very important moment. If she talked on, consciously this time, it would mean that the first part of his mission had succeeded.

"When we were herded out of the death-camp," she said, "and driven along country roads toward the center of Germany, we knew that liberation was near, but no one believed we would make it. People died like flies; anyone who fell down was shot. A friend of my parents, a lawyer, who had one son left, walked just ahead of me. His son fainted and he carried him on his shoulders for hours. He did not know he was dead. When he found out, he fell. All of a sudden we were stopped on the edge of a forest, and the Germans disappeared. They just vanished, none of us saw them go. At least, I didn't. I ran into the forest and . . ." she wavered, withdrew behind a smile and said, "You won't believe it if I tell you. It sounds as if I made it up. I didn't believe it myself."

"What?"

"Well, I . . . I ran through that forest, stumbling, tripping, getting into a terrible panic, thinking they were following me, and then I came to a road, just a track through the trees. As I stood there, terribly afraid, completely at a loss, I heard the sound of a heavy engine approaching. A rattling, like a wagon of some sort. I lay down, terrified, behind a tree and saw it coming down the road, waddling, like a big toy. It didn't look as if it were driven by humans at all."

"What was it?"

"It was a tank. I was sure they had seen me. I was completely crazy with panic. I thought that they were heading straight for me, that they were going to crush me. I tried to jump up and run away, but I couldn't, not any more. I couldn't even look away. I knew my luck had run out. My turn had come."

"And then?"

She smiled. "Then it rattled past, and as it went by I saw, painted on its side, a big star of David. I found out later that it was the only Israeli tank in the Allied Army. Seems unbelievable, doesn't it?"

"Yes," he said.

"I couldn't believe it either. I lay there paralyzed for a moment, then I jumped up and shouted in Hebrew and started to run after it." She smiled and said, "I've been running after it ever since."

The bald man in the silk waistcoat came, carrying a tray with two cups of coffee and two pieces of cake and put it between them among the parcels.

"Nice morning, isn't it?" he whispered.

"Yes," Peter said.

Brandt found them half an hour later, playing football, with their coffee cold on the table and two little piles of coins among the cups. He looked wrathful in his blue overalls smeared with oil. "What the devil do you think you're doing?" he asked angrily. "I've been looking for you everywhere."

"How's the engine?" Peter asked.

"It's been running for hours. Hurry up. We've lost enough time as it is." He slammed the door and was gone.

"All right," Peter said. "I suppose we had better go. Don't let yourself be intimidated, though. His bark is worse than his bite."

"Oh, he doesn't worry me," she said. "I'm used to being shouted at."

"Yes," he said, "I suppose you are. Shall we go?"

They gathered their parcels and went out into the tranquil street and walked underneath the elms toward the waterfront.

As they walked along, he reflected how their relationship had changed that afternoon; out of the cowed girl trying to blend into the background a different person was slowly emerging. There must be a different person behind this mask of submission or she would never have survived the concentration camp, the medical experiments, the death march she had told him about. Walking silently with her under the elms, he wondered what that other person was like and whether he would ever come to know her.

It started to rain after sunset. They had left Loozen, and tied up at the intersection of their rustic canal with the huge waterway that skirted the border from Antwerp to the river Meuse. Brandt decided to stop before entering it, otherwise they would be worrying about their moorings all night, for there was a constant traffic on the big canal of tankers churning past at full speed, dragging a wave like the surf.

12

After Peter had tied up for the night and Brandt had lit the mooring light, they came down into the pavilion smelling of rain. The table was laid, the lamp was lit, the canary sang in its cage; it was like entering another world, a cottage of peace and snugness hidden in the vast woods of the night. Anna stood in the galley, a red kerchief around her head, flushed with the heat of the stove; when she saw the silver glistening in their clothes, she asked, "Is it raining?"

"Yes," Peter said. "We're just in time."

"Would it be all right if I let Coba in?"

"Why?" Brandt asked.

"Because of the rain. She'll get wet."

"That's her job," Brandt said. "If I let her in every time it rains, I'd need another dog to watch while she takes shelter."

"What do you need a watchdog for right now?" Peter asked. "We are tied up away from the shore. Nobody can get on board."

"That's what you think," Brandt said. "But water thieves never come from the shore, they sneak about in rowboats at night and. . . ." He looked at the girl as she stood there in the doorway, flushed, spoon in hand, worrying about a little dog in the rain, and he grunted, "Go ahead."

She hurried up the steps, opened the door to the deck,

called, "Coba! Coba!" and tried to whistle. The little dog's claws came scampering along the gunwale, then a grizzled muzzle, glistening with rain, peeped over the threshold. The little eyes took it all in with an incredulous glance: the table, the lamplight, the riches and the warmth of it all; then it growled.

"Don't be silly," the girl said. "Nobody believes that. Come here." She picked up the little dog, tucked it under her arm, closed the door and came into the room. As she put Coba down, she said, "There now. You make yourself at home." The little animal stood there, shivering, legs spread as if to hold on to the spot, dripping rain water.

"You see?" Brandt said. "She doesn't want to come in. She feels cooped up."

"Nonsense," said the girl with surprising firmness. "She just can't believe her eyes. Give her time. I know exactly how she feels," and she went back to the galley. "Come here, Coba," she said. "I've got something for you."

The little dog looked around for a moment, bewildered, then scurried hastily after her, its claws slipping on the linoleum.

Brandt sighed and shook his head and sat down at the table. He found his Bible and his glasses waiting for him, a paper napkin beside his plate; the flowers she had picked the night before still looked fresh and festive. Peter sat down opposite him, and they glanced at one another across the flowers, waiting. They could hear her voice in the galley; it sounded as if there were two women there, chatting. Brandt listened for a while, then he cried, "Hey, there! Are we going to get something to eat?"

She replied, gaily, "Coming!" and there were some more whispers as if the women hastily finished their conversation. Then she came out, carrying the soup tureen; after a moment Coba peered cautiously around the door, her muzzle white with milk.

"All right," Brandt said, "let's read."

He opened the Bible at random and read, "Whither shall I go from Thy spirit? Whither shall I flee from Thy presence? If I ascend up into heaven, Thou art there. If I make my bed in hell, behold, Thou art there. If I take the wings of the morning and dwell in the uttermost parts of the sea, even there shall Thy hand lead me, and Thy right hand shall hold me." He put the ribbon in the page, and said grace.

They started their meal in silence, pretending not to notice Coba who crept in cautiously, her claws ticking on the lino. She first hid under the girl's chair, from where she peered up at Brandt in suspicion, then the canary started to sound off with ear-splitting joy and she growled.

"Now, listen!" Brandt cried, exasperated. Coba fell silent; the canary warbled on, blissfully out of tune, stretching its neck in a long, sustained trill. "If he carries on like that, I'll have to cover him up," Brandt said.

"Why?" she asked. "I think it's lovely."

Brandt grunted, then asked, "What's next? Or isn't there any?"

"You know very well there is," she said, and collected their plates. Brandt looked after her dumbfounded as she vanished into the galley. Coba made a dash after her, her claws slithering; the canary started as low as possible and slowly ground its way up until it squealed as high as possible, each note sounding out of tune with the next.

"I wonder how long the rain will last," Peter began, cheerfully. Brandt did not reply.

She came back with a steaming dish of potatoes, followed by Coba, then she went to get the rest, and Coba slithered after her once more.

"Stop it!" Brandt cried. "Down! Under the chair!"

Coba leaped into the galley like a frog. The canary sounded as if it were etching glass. Brandt, after clenching his fists, put his glasses back on and grabbed the Bible. What he read seemed to alarm him, for he frowned, glanced furtively at Peter, took his glasses off again and put them aside with the Bible. She came back with another dish, and Coba. As she sat down, Coba sheltered under her chair; then she got up again, saying, "The salt!"

"No!" Brandt cried. "Sit down! I'll do without!"

The canary, jubilant, went on warbling, delirious with its own sound. Coba panted under her chair. Their spoons scraped on their plates, and the flame in the oil lamp purred. Outside, the rain streaked past in swishing waves. Somewhere in the night a ship called, forlorn, across the water. Despite the fact that no one said a word, a feeling of security and snugness grew around them.

When they had finished their meal and she had brought out the coffee, they settled down in silence, each within his own little world. Brandt, his glasses on the tip of his nose, read about the Indians, Anna sewed little curtains that seemed intended for a doll's house. Coba lay blissfully stretched out under her chair, and the canary was busy about his cage, settling down for the night. Peter looked through the *Bargees' Weekly*, but his mind was not on it. He began to realize fully that the miracle had indeed happened, and was filled with an inarticulate gratitude that made him wish there were someone, something, to thank. There came a moment, as they sat there quietly together, when he felt as if there were with them in the small, low room a light, a joy, an almost tangible presence. He read the motto over the pipe-rack, "Where Two or Three are gathered together in My Name, There will I be."

How simple and relaxed life would be if only he could accept that. How stubborn and stupid he was to cling so doggedly to his reason, the reason that had not even managed to conclude that no one would stop them at the border. He thought of the letter he had signed; what it meant was that he had signed away Susie's income. Except for the pittance she received from her securities, there would be no more money coming to her. He thought of writing her a long letter; he finally wrote her a postcard, saying, "Well on our way. Won't be long now. Paid for two tickets to Rome in my name at KLM. Please cancel and collect the money. Writing. Love. P." Rereading it, it seemed to express nothing of what he felt, it didn't express anything at all. He knew that she was facing what might well be the greatest crisis in her life, because of him; he knew that he should feel guilty and tried to formulate the reason why he did not. It had to do with the horror of the father carrying his dead son, the child who fled into a forest and saw a tank with the star of David rumble past. The horror was that the father, the son and the girl had lived in the same city as Susie and Betty and he; it was the collapse of their own world into madness and evil. He looked at Anna, sitting there in the lamplight, sewing, the little dog asleep under her chair; it seemed incredible that people like Susie and he and Wolters and Bartels had just quietly gone on living after the war was over, as if these things had never happened. The whole of his generation, not only in Holland, in Germany, but all over the world, seemed to be united in the tacit determination to pretend it had never happened. Yet they would have to face it, and somehow cope with it, for the sake of Betty, and her future children. He knew that this was what he was trying to do; but he knew at the same time that he would never be able to explain it to anyone else.

"If I take the wings of the morning and dwell in the uttermost parts of the sea. . . ." That was wonderful poetry Brandt had read before the meal. He stretched his hand out toward the Bible and Brandt looked up, his eyes large behind his glasses. "I'd like to have a look at the Bible, if you don't mind."

"Eh? Oh, yes. Here you are."

The girl looked up from her sewing; then she smiled at him and bent her head again in concentration.

Brandt had put the page-marker in the Bible at the spot where he had opened it, Psalm 139. "O Lord, Thou hast searched me, and known me. Thou knowest my down-sitting and mine uprising, Thou understandest my thought afar off. Thou compassest my path and my lying down, and art acquainted with all my ways. For there is not a word in my tongue, but lo, o Lord, thou knowest it altogether. Thou has beset me behind and before, and laid thine hand upon me. Such knowledge is too wonderful for me; it is high, I cannot attain unto it." As he read, the ancient poet, yearning for God, seemed very close, as if his own thoughts at that moment had been given voice five thousand years ago. "Whither shall I go from thy spirit? Or whither shall I flee from thy presence? If I ascend up into heaven, thou art there: if I make my bed in hell, behold, thou art there. If I take the wings of the morning, and dwell in the uttermost parts of the sea; even there shall thy hand lead me, and thy right hand shall hold me. If I say, Surely the darkness shall cover me; even then the night shall be light about me." Reading those words, at that moment, gave him an eerie sense of near-revelation; but as he read on, he sank back into reality. For then the poet cried, "Surely thou wilt slay the wicked, o God! Depart from me therefore, ye bloody men. . . . Do I not hate them, o Lord, that hate thee? And am I not grieved with those that rise up against thee? I hate them with perfect hatred: I count them mine enemies." His father had been right: the Bible was only a tribal history book composed of war songs, family records and fairy tales. If western man, after the industrial revolution, wanted to take up the contact with infinity again that was humanity's eternal quest, then he would have to forget about this prehistoric monument of lust, hatred and exaltation. Then he thought of David, who had written the psalm when he had been in exile like the Jews of today. He looked at Anna as she sat there, sewing, and was haunted once more by the image of the straggling column, the father carrying his dead son, the child fleeing into the forest. He read the psalm again, trying to identify himself with her, walking among the barracks of the extermination camp while the chimneys of the incinerators smoked overhead. "Surely thou wilt slay the wicked, o God! Depart from me, ye bloody men. . . ." He thought of all the Jews persecuted, tortured and slain since the time of David, to whom this had been a real prayer. "I hate them with perfect hatred, I count them mine enemies." Perhaps to be free of hate was a state of grace, not a moral achievement. The psalm ended in innocent humility, "Search me, O God, and know my heart: try me and know my thoughts: and see if there be any wicked way in me, and lead me in the way everlasting." He, who had lived in security all his life, had no right to conclude that their perfect hatred was a regression.

He closed the book and put it aside and closed his eyes

in weariness. Again he felt himself surrounded by a radiant joy, a light, a hope. He opened his eyes and looked at them: Anna, Brandt, Coba, the canary; and he felt that what the ancients had called "god" was the most elusive of all human experiences. God seemed to evaporate the moment man approached Him, cautiously, to catch Him with a word.

Brandt yawned, closed his book, took off his glasses and rubbed his eyes.

"Finished?" Peter asked.

"No, no. I've still a long way to go, but at least that horse thief is lynched. What's the time?" He peered at the clock and said, "We'd better break it up, neighbors. Tomorrow is going to be an early day. We must try and get through Antwerp before nightfall. Maybe we can make Rupelmonde."

"All right," Anna said, gathering up her sewing. "Anything you want before you turn in?"

"No, no," said Brandt. He turned to Peter and said, "You take her for'ard, I'll clear away."

Peter did not show his surprise at the suggestion; neither did Anna. He took her to the foredeck through the windy darkness, Coba hugging their heels. He opened the hatch for her; as she was about to go down the narrow Jacob's ladder, she said, "You can't know what you've done for me today. I can't ever begin to tell you."

"But this was just the first hurdle," he said, embarrassed. "This was nothing."

"Oh, yes, it was," she said. "I . . . I . . ." She could not go on, her voice seemed choked with emotion. She hurried down the ladder and closed the hatch. He heard the strangled sound of sobs coming from below; he went back to the wheelhouse, followed by Coba, only when it had ceased.

They slowly crossed the intricate maze of narrow canals, low bridges, locks and right-angle bends of the medieval city of Ghent. They slowly sailed up the narrowing river Scheldt, waiting at each bend to listen for the horns of ships coming downstream who had to be given priority. First, they seemed to make their placid way through all the paintings of Breughel, seen from the water. Then they crossed the stark, somber landscape of the coal mines, where slag heaps looked like black pyramids erected by a forgotten civilization and the sunlight was hazy with dust. Then they sailed through the sinister world of caves and quarries that lined the canal as they penetrated into France. Finally they tied up with hundreds of other barges in the *"Bassin Rond"* where two large waterways narrowed down into the canal of St. Quentin, the only way of access to Paris. Ahead lay the great tunnel.

13

Brandt had mentioned the tunnel as far back as 's Hertogenbosch; during the long domestic evenings in the lamplight with Anna sewing, Coba snoring and the canary warbling in his cage, he had told them more about it, and even drawn its plan on a piece of paper. It started at the highest lock of the canal, where the hills rose abruptly. It had been dug by the engineers of Napoleon, through to the Oise valley on the other side. In reality, there were two tunnels, one five miles long and the other two miles, separated from each other by a small artificial lake in an uninhabited valley. No one was allowed to navigate the tunnels under his own power; ships were towed through in convoys of sixteen at a time by an ancient electric towboat, called a "ram." Two convoys a day left from opposite ends, one at noon and one at midnight; they met in the little artificial lake in the center, where the tows passed one another.

The *Hendrika* arrived in time for the midnight convoy, the last barge to be locked through that day, and Brandt said, "It's a pity, now we'll have to ship our anchor on board and pass out a length of chain before we start moving."

"What for?" Peter asked.

"When the ram stops in the shunting basin, the ships would pile up unless the last barge passes out enough chain to create a drag to stop them. You'd better start shipping that anchor now."

"All right," Peter said, and he opened the door of the wheelhouse; then Brandt added, "One more thing. Being last, we'll have to stay at the wheel. The others can go to sleep and let themselves be towed."

"In other words, it will be my watch," Peter said good-naturedly.

"We'll take turns, if you like."

"I don't mind. I want to see that tunnel."

"You won't see much," Brandt said. "Whatever light bulbs there were have been picked off by French barge kids with their peashooters. All the light there'll be will come from the portholes and the skylights of the barges ahead of you, and those lights will be going out pretty soon."

"I may give you a call toward morning," Peter said and he closed the door behind him. Coba followed him to the foredeck and watched him ship the anchor.

They moored at the starting place just before darkness. The tunnel was not in sight, but overhead were the spidery wires for the electric towboat. Peter strained his eyes to discern it in the dusk, but it had not yet arrived, the ships moored to the bank were all barges. On the bank small groups of men were silhouetted against the yellow skyline; ahead of them, where the night began, a mountain rose toward a pale harvest moon. Peter was belaying the towlines on the foredeck when he thought he saw lightning twitch in the distance; he looked toward the mountain and saw a green, flickering light shimmer among the trees. Then there came around the bend a huge angular monster, showering sparks. He watched it incredulously as it drew near, it looked like a machine conjured up by Jules Verne: a long, low colossus with thin tentacles on its head, approaching with a whining, clanking sound that was unlike any noise he had ever heard. As the monster passed, he saw the clanking was caused by a huge disk wheel winding in a chain that rose dripping from the water; the whining came from an engine room, the door of which stood open. Further aft were small windows with tasseled curtains, showing an Edwardian parlor with a red plush sofa, teak table, potted aspidistra and a bronze standard lamp, the shade of which was missing. In the shrill light he saw two men, who also looked like characters out of a novel by Jules Verne, with handlebar moustaches and old-fashioned peaked caps; one of them was smoking a meerschaum pipe. It seemed as if the monster, emerging from its subterranean hiding place only at dead of night, had managed to elude time, floating in darkness for fifty years without its crew growing a day older. The ram passed them, then it went through an intricate maneuver of changing tentacles amid a fireworks of crackling sparks, after which it came whining and clanking past once more on its way toward the head of the row of barges, leaving an acrid stench of short circuits. Coba, hoarse with fury, barked until it had vanished around the bend.

The ram was not seen or heard of again until midnight, when it warned the bargees that it was about to move with a long, unearthly squeal of its old-fashioned siren.

Brandt had by then gone to bed; Peter and Anna sat waiting in the wheelhouse where they had gone to accustom their eyes to the darkness. Peter had tried to send her to bed, but she had refused; he had seen her point, he himself was curious about the tunnel. He went outside to cast off and stayed on the foredeck to watch the towropes that tied them to the barge ahead. They strained very slowly; the tow got under way almost imperceptibly. Then the anchor chain he had passed out began to uncoil underneath the ship with a clinking noise, a soft, pebbly rattle that sounded louder as he came back to the wheelhouse; the bottom of the canal was solid rock.

It took the tow an hour to reach the entrance of the tunnel. The ram, flashing blue lightning in the distance, pulled them slowly through the transparent darkness. A thin moon drifted on its back among the stars, over the silhouettes of the trees that lined the canal. There was a smell of wood fires; somewhere a farm dog barked, a low, disconsolate baying that sounded primeval in the night. As they approached the mountainside a nightingale filled the melancholy night with its thin innocent gladness. Then, slowly, they entered the tunnel.

There was nothing impressive about the entrance; it looked small and unsafe, the entrance to a rabbit warren. The first thing that struck them was the echoing sound. So far, the barges ahead of them had glided silently through the darkness; the only sound caused by man in that transparent night had been the soft clinking of their anchor chain as it was dragged over the rocky bottom underneath the ship. The moment they entered the tunnel however, the sounds of the barges ahead increased a hundredfold. Iron screamed and shrieked as the flanks of ships scraped the walls; voices bellowed in the cavernous vault; hatches were opened and shut with a sound of trains shunting; children's questions rang out as if they called right outside the wheelhouse, "*Maman! C'est le tunnel?*" and "*Jean-Pierre! Jean-Pierre, reveille-toi! Nous sommes dedans!*" A gruff male voice thundered, "*Silence!*" with rolling reverberations. Then one little dog far ahead started to bark, and it set off all the others, until the man bellowed, "*Silence! Nom de Dieu!*"

The darkness was complete. Peter and Anna could not see their hands in front of their faces until they began to discern, somewhere ahead, the feeble light of a lantern sliding with the ships. Then someone started to shine a flashlight at a towpath that ran alongside them; men laughed with echoing guffaws, wooden shoes stumbled and a woman screamed, "Rats!"

Peter switched on their flashlight, revealing a dripping vault of stone, blackened by soot and grime, dusty cables along the ceiling, loose ends dangling, empty light sockets. On their left was a narrow towpath, with an iron handrail alongside. As the beam of the flashlight played on it, Coba started to scream and run up and down the deck in a frenzy; a gray shape flitted past.

"Did you see that?" Anna asked.

"A rat," Peter said. "Brandt told me about them. They come as big as cats here. They live in the caves."

"Which caves?"

"It seems there are big caves leading off the tunnel where tools and equipment are kept, or were kept in the past. We should see the entrances if we keep the light on."

"Not for me," she said. "If we keep it dark, the dogs and the children may calm down."

They did calm down, after another hour or so. The faintly reflected lights ahead went out, one by one, until the last shimmer was gone, and they traveled through a ghostly subterranean world in which there were only small sounds, immensely magnified. The sleeping ships screeched and squealed, scraped and gnashed; the clinking of the anchor chain over the rocks below sounded like a distant smithy. The smell of mold and stale air became heavier, a cellarlike chill seeped into the wheelhouse.

"Strange atmosphere, isn't it?" he asked.

Her voice, disembodied in the darkness, said, "I remember going into Granny's cellar when I was quite small. It was full of preserves and dusty bottles of wine and jars of pickles, and a mangle, and an old bicycle with a funny saddle. I was fascinated by it, but I didn't dare go there alone. I always asked her for pickles, hoping that she would eat some too, and then the jar would be empty and we would go down together for a new one, and I'd see the cellar again and ring the bell of the bicycle before going back up the cold stairs on hands and feet. The cat stood waiting for us at the top of the stairs. The cat was just as fascinated as I was but she didn't dare to go down at all. It made me feel very superior, and I pulled a face at her and said, 'Boo,' as if I lived down there, and came up to frighten her. Funny thing was, that was the only time I managed to frighten her. Usually she lay stretched out on the sofa or in my chair, and wouldn't move for me. Granny had to chase her."

Listening to her voice in the darkness, he had the feeling of having entered another world, where time had come to a stop. She told him about the rest of her grandmother's house; the garden with the arbor and its rusty wrought-iron chairs and the iron table, the top of which used to spring back unexpectedly and make the teacups leap on their saucers. While listening to her attentively, he saw images from his own memory: Betty as a little girl, visiting his mother. He heard her shrill little voice ringing out in the marble hall, her terrorizing howls when Susie wanted to close the bathroom door on her. The image of the pouting little child sitting at the far end of that marble corridor, her feet way off the ground, clutching the edges of the seat, came back as if it were not an image from the past but real, alive, the present.

Anna told him about her youth, her family, the holidays that were the highlights of those years, the Feast of Tabernacles when they made exciting little huts of leaves and sticks on the roof, the matzos at Passover, the meal when they would raise their glasses and say solemnly, "Next year in Jerusalem." While she told him this, he saw Betty playing Indians underneath the table in the parlor, looking for Easter eggs among the little shrubs in the back yard, opening her parcels, angry with tension, on Saint Nicholas Eve. He felt as if he were drifting through a dream that was a higher stage of awareness, a fourth dimension in which there was no past, no future, only this timeless present; then he heard her say, "I could sail like this forever."

Even as she said it he realized that this was dream talk, that she too was caught in the spell thrown over them by the tunnel. Like the blind, slowly sliding barges, sailing in their sleep, they would wake up the next morning on the other side of the mountain; this night was a respite from reality, in which they paused in darkness and looked around and saw their lives, past and future, from a point outside time. He felt a joy and a hope he had never before experienced; then he thought of Susie and her loneliness and the failure of their life together, and he hoped that he could bring some of this serenity, this peace of mind with him out of this unearthly night to her when he came back. But whatever might happen in the future, during this one night, this miraculous night on a barge inside a mountain, he had known happiness.

After a while the darkness slowly became transparent. He could not discern anything as yet, but the blackness relented. The noises of the barges scraping and screeching ahead of them faded away; there came a breath of spring through the open window of the wheelhouse, a smell of blossoms and young grass; they emerged from their rabbit warren in the mountainside into the giddying expanse of the starry night, and he was struck by a new sound, so full and joyous and incredible that for a moment he thought it was a trick of his eardrums after the magnified noises of the tunnel. But it was no trick; what he heard, struck with wonder, were nightingales—hundreds, thousands of nightingales, as if all the nightingales of France bred here in this lonely valley.

His happiness reached a still, ecstatic climax of peace and hope and an infinite love for all creation; then he saw, in the light of the thin, cold moon, that the girl by his side had covered her ears with her hands. While the nightingales sang in jubilant confusion, as if all the hopes and joys of creation were given voice, she was sobbing.

After a moment of shocked surprise, he put his hand on her shoulder, moved by a deep compassion, and he asked, "Tell me. What is it?"

But she shook off his hand, opened the door and hurried out. He saw her stoop, open the hatch and vanish from sight.

He wanted to go after her to see if she was all right, but he could not leave the wheel. The nightingales sang around him in boundless, merciless joy, the first flush of the dawn began to lighten the darkness among the stars, they approached the shores of the lake and slowly floated to a stop. As he opened the door of the wheelhouse to go to the foredeck, Brandt came out, yawning.

"This the lake?" he asked.

"Yes."

"This is where the tows pass one another. The others should be down soon. Want me to take over?"

"No, I'm all right. I'll be right back."

"Where are you going?"

"To see if she is all right."

"I'd leave her be," Brandt said, surprisingly. "She usually calms down in about quarter of an hour."

"What do you mean?" he asked, astounded.

"I've heard her every night, at about the same time. She coughs for half an hour, then she calms down. I don't like that cough, I must say. What's the matter with her?"

"Nothing," he said. "A bad cold." He said it absent-mindedly, for he realized that she had not been sobbing at all, nor had she been sobbing that other night on the foredeck when she thanked him for what he had done, just before she went down. "How on earth could you hear it?" he asked.

"Oh, I hear everything," Brandt said, proudly. "Everything that happens on board this ship. Well, if you're sure you're all right, I think I'll turn in again. See you in the morning. Goodnight."

"Goodnight."

He sat in the wheelhouse, watching the morning grow. He saw the uncanny procession of an electric monster like theirs towing a long train of sleeping barges pass by and vanish in the tunnel behind him. Then the eerie wail of the ram's siren undulated once more in the distance, the hawsers tautened and strained, the anchor

173

chain resumed its tinkling on the bottom of the canal, while the nightingales' jubilant choir slowly fell silent before the marvel of the new day.

The ships ahead vanished once more in a mountain, and darkness was about to envelop him again. The last of the nightingales still warbled in the wilderness overhead; he looked up and noticed, over the entrance to the tunnel, an overgrown, mossy plaque. He lit it up with his flashlight. It said, *"Napoléon, Emp . . ."* The rest had turned back into mountainside.

When they emerged from the hillside into the valley of the River Oise, they entered a different world, a world of wild skies with sheaves of slanting sunlight sweeping across treeless plains. On the banks of the river below, thin silvery forests of birches and poplars billowed in the wind like reeds.

14

A spring gale raged over them as they slowly worked their way through the series of locks that separated them from the river; their peaceful journey of somnolent drifting through the delicate green of spring changed into a voyage through the clouds, with wild rain lashing faceless shapes in dripping oilskins on the high walls of locks, and barges blown helplessly across the channel with small bands of midgets powerlessly pulling at them to bring them back under control. After the storm there came two days of steady melancholy rain that drummed on the roof of the wheelhouse, splattered on the deck, gurgled in the scuppers; Coba spent those days inside, sitting on the ledge near the accelerator handle, breathing patches of steam on the windowpane and growling at the swaying trees as they passed.

On the third day, when they entered the river itself and joined the large fleet of barges chugging down the romantic, winding waterway, suddenly something happened outside. One moment there was a wide peaceful river, dotted with ships, a bridge in the distance; a long string of barges was being towed toward them by a low-slung tugboat, the engine of which could be heard over their own. Peter, at the wheel, picked up the binoculars to look at the tugboat and was reading its name, *Guèpe V*, when the lenses steamed over. He pulled out his handkerchief to wipe them when he saw that it was not the lenses, but the world outside. Within a matter of seconds everything around them was wiped out; all that remained was the roaring of the engine of the tugboat, somewhere close in the fog. The sudden change caused him to lose all sense of direction. He pulled down the accelerator, put the gear lever into neutral and sounded the horn. From all sides there came answering blasts in bewildering confusion.

Brandt stumbled into the wheelhouse from the engine room; his hand looked as if it were bleeding but it was red paint. "Where are we?" he asked.

"Last thing I knew we were heading south, for the bridge."

An angry growl sounded close by, over the port side. "What the devil is that?" Brandt asked.

"A tow, pulled by a tugboat called *Guêpe*."

"Damn," Brandt muttered, "one of those brutes. They won't. . . ." Although his lips went on moving, the rest was unintelligible, for he pressed the button of the horn and provoked a chorus of squeals, growls and hoots all around them. Coba, out on the deck, started to bark angrily over the port bow and Peter gave fast starboard wheel. The only indication that the ship was obeying her rudder came from the compass rose, slowly swinging in its binnacle. Then Coba came prancing aft, barking furiously as she ran; Brandt opened the port door of the wheelhouse and they heard another dog answering in the fog. They could not see a thing, the head of their own ship was barely discernible; somewhere inside the cloud another ship was passing. When Coba reached the wheelhouse, she sprinted forward once more on her little bow legs, and started another barking match with an invisible partner.

"That must be the tow," Brandt said. "We'd better watch what she's doing. In a fog like this, the dogs take over the navigation."

Anna came out of the pavilion and asked, "What's happening?" She looked around and said, "Good heavens. . . . Where are we?"

"On the Oise," Peter answered. "It came down a few moments ago."

"What's the matter with Coba?"

"Don't disturb her," Brandt said. "She's busy sailing the ship."

"She's what?"

"Listen."

Coba came prancing aft once more, hoarsely screaming at a high-yapping puppy who was taunting her with baby barks that rose to inexperienced yelps.

"That's the third vessel of the tow," Peter said. Then Coba stopped, panting, and her head jerked forward once more as she tried to cock her floppy ears. "And there comes the fourth one."

Brandt pressed the horn again and said, "Go for'ard, you two, and keep a sharp lookout. Point if you see anything."

They hurried to the foredeck; Coba leaped on to the hatch, crossed to the other side and started to bark at a challenger over starboard. This time it was a deep, throaty bark, sounding forlorn and sad in the grayness, not a match for her venomous, high-pitched abuse. They both strained their eyes to see what was coming, Peter cupped his hands behind his ears and tried to determine the direction from which the sound came; then, suddenly, they were right on top of it: a rowboat with the shapes of a man and a big dog. Peter pointed at them and waved Brandt over to the port side; as they slowly glided past, they saw that the rowboat was tied up to two stakes and that the motionless man inside was an angler, who did not even lift his fishing rod as they scraped past behind him. "How far is the shore?" Brandt called in his private French. The man slowly turned his head, removed what looked like his nose but proved to be a pipe, and answered, "You're on it."

So they were. A shrub floated toward them from nowhere, there was a crunching underneath, a rustling alongside and a smell of grass and animals. Peter wondered what animals, then there came out of nowhere a low moo and the sound of slow applause. Coba and the hazy dog, immobilized in the midst of their contest, were now overcome with embarrassment and tried to save face by growling at one another; he who managed to express the deepest contempt could turn away first.

"Where are we?" Brandt asked the hazy shape in the boat.

"The bridge is about a kilometer down," the man replied. "But you'd better stay where you are until I go."

"Go where?"

"I'll be rowing back to the village this afternoon; if the fog hasn't lifted by then, you can follow me. Plenty of water as long as you keep me inshore of you."

"Thanks," Brandt said, "but I'd like to move on before."

"Suit yourself," the man said, and stuck his nose back on his face.

He turned out to be right. The fog, instead of lifting, became thicker; through it wandered melancholy, coughing shapes that drove Coba frantic before they retreated, mooing, into the clouds. The fisherman vanished from sight; first the top of his body disappeared, then his dog, until at last only the low, dark blur of his boat remained visible from the wheelhouse. A deep silence descended on the river and its banks; somewhere in the fog someone rang a bell at regular intervals, a barge at anchor, warning those who floated silently downstream.

Hours later there came a call from the water, "Skipper! Are you ready to go?" The angler, standing in his boat, glided alongside, poling himself along.

"How far is it to the village?" Brandt asked.

"It's on the other side of the bridge."

"Will we make it before nightfall?"

"If you don't lose me."

"Go out for'ard again, you two," Brandt said to Anna and Peter. "Keep an eye on him and, if you lose him, call out to him to wait." As they went to the foredeck he called after them, "And watch out for neighbors that have stuck their bows ashore! Tell that man to move out as far into the channel as he can!"

But the angler seemed to be quite unruffled by the fog. He had sat down and rowed steadily along, without looking around. They passed four barges tied up to the bank; they did not see them but Coba and the ships' dogs had it out while they strained their eyes to find out where the barking was coming from. Then, suddenly, they found themselves in the center of a low archway; Peter's heart beat in his throat and Anna cried, "Stop! Stop!" to the wheelhouse, but it was the bridge.

They tied up alongside a large Belgian barge and when they had made fast Brandt said, "Well, it won't be for long; at this time of the year there is rarely any fog and, if there is, it won't last."

Peter and Anna went ashore to do the shopping, and Brandt called after them, "Better be nippy about it! If the fog hasn't lifted when it gets dark, you won't be able to find your way back!"

They groped their way across the Belgian's foredeck, Peter helped her down onto a rickety little dock, then they cautiously made their way through the grayness from landmark to landmark: a tree, a pump, a handcart, an ashcan, a flight of wooden steps, a door. When they opened it, they found themselves in a little café, like the scores of others they had seen since that first one in Belgium. There was the billiard table, the counter with its array of bottles behind it, the marble-topped tables and the glass-covered case with the football game. The man who came to serve them looked like all the other innkeepers had looked, except that he wore a different wig, and they ordered two coffees which came, as always, in little individual filters on two cups.

"Let's forget about the shopping, and have a game," he said. "We have enough till tomorrow, haven't we?"

She answered, delighted, "Oh, yes!"

She had won three bars of chocolate when Brandt came in, his eyebrows full of droplets, asking angrily, "Where the devil have you been? I thought you'd got lost."

Peter knew him well enough by now to say, "Your turn. She's won enough."

Brandt grunted, "Kid stuff. I'll give you a game of billiards though."

"All right."

They got the proprietor to open the padlock that chained the cues and Brandt said, as he chalked his, "Only one match, mind you. We have to be back before dark."

"Of course," said Peter, and they started.

Half an hour later two other customers came in, covered with silver, smelling of fog: a man and his wife. When they heard the two men at the billiard table speaking Dutch, the woman cried, "Hollanders!" and started to chatter in Flemish; they were off the other barge. "Fancy meeting neighbors here! What will you have, friend? You can't live on that thin beer. Let's split a bottle of wine."

They did; the man joined them at billiards while the woman sat down opposite Anna at one of the little tables and talked. Peter watched them out of the corner of his eye while he stood waiting for his turn. Anna looked flushed and happy; she was talking with great pride about their ship and their stove and their dog and, oh yes, we have a canary. Have you?

The woman gesticulated as she talked; Peter could not understand much of her rapid Flemish, but her hands interpreted what she was saying: a long monologue about polishing, scrubbing, birds, something square and small that he could not determine. She ended with hats; the gestures her hands made over her tight curls were so descriptive that he saw five different hats before his attention was called back to the game.

They played and chatted for over an hour, then they made their way back to the ships in Indian file, holding hands. The Belgian led them twice around the handcart before he cried, "Got it!" and started to follow a mooring rope. They filed on board, the woman insisted they have a cup of coffee and Brandt did not know how to refuse. They filed into the pavilion; Anna clasped her hands in amazement as she looked around at the carved woodwork, the mirrors set into the paneling, the countless trinkets, scrolls and flowerpots of brass polished like gold, the ornate oil lamp with three tiers of stringed beads and a painted shade depicting Jesus walking the waves. A dog, bowlegged and voiceless, looking like an overstuffed sausage, came waddling toward them, gasping for breath, and was given another lump of sugar to hasten its end.

"Sit down, neighbors, sit down," the Belgian said, pulling up chairs with orange plush seats and tasseled armrests; they sat down at a table, covered like theirs with a Persian rug, but this one had a picture instead of a pattern woven into it: a camel trotting past a pyramid with, in the foreground, a praying Arab. There was a strong smell of wax and coffee; the woman came out of the galley, carrying a steaming pot.

They sat and talked for another hour, then Anna said, "Good heavens, I've forgotten all about supper! Please excuse me, I'll have to go."

The woman tried to make them stay for supper, but Brandt said, awkwardly, "Oh no! I mean, thank you very much, ma'am, but let's do that some other time."

Anna left; the moment she had closed the door the woman said to Brandt and Peter, "What's the matter with you people, dragging that girl through the north in a barge? Are you blind, or what?"

Brandt was the first to recover from his amazement.

"What do you mean?" he asked, aggressively.

"Don't tell me you haven't noticed!" the woman cried. "How like a man! Bringing a girl all that way and living with her all day and not seeing that she is ill!"

"Ill?"

"Of course! Look at her eyes! Haven't you felt her hands? They are burning; that child must be running a temperature of at least a hundred and three."

"Nonsense," Brandt said. "She just got excited after talking to you and drinking too much wine."

"Look, neighbor," the woman said kindly, but settling her elbows on the table, "I know you don't mean that the way it sounds, but I would take that child to a doctor if I were you, and as quick as you can. I wouldn't care to have your responsibility, that's a fact."

"Then what do you think is the matter with her?" Brandt asked.

"I don't know," the woman replied frankly. "I'm not a doctor, but I've spent all my life on the water and I know a sick girl when I see one. I also know that we women would rather die on our feet in our own galley than own up how we feel and watch you men make off with our ship."

"Nonsense," Brandt grumbled. "It's my ship, she's got nothing to do with it."

The woman smiled with judicious kindness and said, "Come on, neighbor, you know better than that."

They left soon after. As Brandt and Peter groped their way back to the foredeck of their barge, through the fog now turned blue, Brandt said, "Don't mind that woman. She was exaggerating. My wife was just the same: no children, so the rest of the world was always ill, for her to mother whenever she saw a chance. Even so, I'd have that cough looked at if I were you."

Peter agreed, deeply alarmed. For suddenly it all made sense; she was a consumptive. But even as the word formed in his thoughts, he rejected it. A nagging bronchitis perhaps; it was even possible that she indeed ran a temperature, as the woman said, they should perhaps not let her do the housework any more, or less of it. But he should under no circumstances dramatize her condition. It was serious enough as it was.

Their meal that night was awkward and full of silences which the canary filled with ravished dissonances. Brandt started to talk to Coba in a false voice which made her hide under the girl's chair, to peer up at him with somber suspicion. Looking at Anna stealthily in the lamplight, Peter could not discern anything new or alarming, but he would feel better when she had seen a doctor, and as they sat quietly reading in the lamplight after supper, the idea of leaving the ship and taking the train to Paris occurred to him once more.

He mentioned it to Brandt after she had gone to bed, taking Coba with her. He started by asking how long the fog would last; when Brandt answered that it might last for days, he asked him if he could sail the barge from here to Paris alone. There were only a few large locks left on the Oise, and two on the river Seine.

Brandt looked at him warily underneath the beads of the lamp, then he said, "I suppose the best thing is to ask her. Why don't you go now and ask her how she feels? If she thinks she should see a doctor, go ahead and take her to Paris. I'll make out."

Peter thought for a moment, then he said, "All right," pushed back his chair, got up and climbed the steps to the deck.

Outside, it was pitch dark; he had to grope his way to the foredeck. A beam of light slanted upward into the fog from the round skylight in her hatch. He bent over to knock but before he did so he looked through the skylight and saw her, huddled on the floor at the bottom of the stairs. For a breathless moment he thought she had collapsed; then he saw Coba sitting by her side, peering up at the hatch, and he realized that she was praying. He got up, furtively, and tiptoed back the way he had come.

"Well?" Brandt asked. He stood in the bedroom in his long underwear, about to put his trousers underneath the mattress.

"She was asleep," Peter said.

They undressed and got into bed; Brandt turned out the light and they lay side by side in the darkness, looking at the ceiling.

"Tell you what," Brandt said. "If it's at all possible, let's push on tomorrow. Without fog, we're only three days from Paris. If we sail through the night, which we can on the river, we can make it in two. What's your next step when you reach Paris?"

"Take a plane to Tangier."

"Not see a doctor first?"

"Not unless it's absolutely necessary. I'll take her to one as soon as we arrive in Tangier."

"Why Tangier?" Brandt asked, and he told him.

"All that's going to cost a pretty penny. Who's doing the paying? You?"

"No, no. Headquarters."

"Headquarters yourself," Brandt said calmly. "I know this isn't official. The customs bloke in Loozen told me. Are you footing the bill?"

"Eventually she'll be paying for it herself. We have an arrangement by which I keep track of all the expenses; her father's business was confiscated by the Germans, and as soon as it is returned to her she'll pay me back."

Brandt snorted in the darkness. "You're not going to see a cent," he said, "and you know it. What are you doing it for?"

"I don't really know," he answered. "I just made up my mind that I would take her to Palestine, even if it cost me. . . ."

"Well?" Brandt's voice urged, sternly.

"Well, a lot of money."

"You can say that again. By the time she's through with you, you won't have much left to call your own."

"Come, come," he said.

"Well," Brandt concluded, "we live in a free country. As the Bible says: let each man work out his own salvation. And that, I suppose, is what you're doing."

He fell silent, and Peter thought over what he had said. It was an astute observation for an uneducated man to make. Then Brandt's voice came out of the darkness once more. "If you should find yourself at a loss after you've taken her there, get in touch with me via de Kooi at the Exchange. I want a partner, because I hate deck hands. And we seem to get along well enough."

"Thank you," he said, astounded.

"I won't need the rest of the money, by the way, until you come back. We'll work out something by which you pay me back as we go along. Also, partnership would mean, of course, that you'd put some money in the business."

Peter smiled and said, "I'll certainly consider it." It was reassuring to find out that a man could rise above himself and yet remain the same; whatever had happened to Brandt, he had not gone through a conversion. Peter waited for him to speak again but that was all. With an abruptness that was almost comical he fell asleep, his breathing became slow and regular.

Peter lay in the darkness, wondering what the future would bring. He was not afraid, he was ready to face anything; all he hoped for was that she might be spared more suffering, more pain, more horror. He wondered what he could do to shield her from harm, other than merely being there and watching over her.

And then, as he hovered on the brink of sleep, it seemed as if their roles were slowly being reversed. It no longer seemed to be he who guided her and tried to protect her from harm; she had taken him by the hand and now guided him and Susie through the fog. Then, all at once, he was Susie, staring at the twitching light on the ceiling; he felt, with bewildered suspicion, a faint plaintive yearning underneath the bitterness, the self-pity, the deeply injured pride. He felt her bewilderment, her indignant surprise; he tried to hold on to her, to urge her to heed that feeling, to cherish it; but the light on the ceiling faded, the fog closed in, and he fell asleep, his hand stretched out toward the man beside him.

Seen from the air at dusk, Tangier looked like a city of the future: a crescent-shaped settlement of white domes, cubes and chimneys. The first lights twinkled on the edge of the surf and in the narrow streets milled the white-coated workers of this vast, mysterious laboratory. The sight of it heightened the feeling of unreality that had caught Peter in its spell ever since he left the barge opposite the towers of Notre Dame in Paris. It seemed as if, after he had shaken Brandt by the hand, patted Coba on the head and helped Anna up the ancient quayside, he had entered a dream.

15

For here he sat, his feet hurting him in the unaccustomed shoes, his eyes smarting with dryness, next to an athletic young English curate who talked about the cruelty of the Arabs toward their donkeys; the dreamlike feeling was not alleviated by the fact that the paperbacked book the curate had been reading at the beginning of the trip, marking passages with pencil in the margin, revealed itself, by falling off his lap, as *The Case of the Spread-Eagled Blonde*. Anna, on his other side, sat looking out of the window at the clouds for most of the time, resigned and a little sad. When he had gone to the foc'sle to fetch her he had caught a glimpse of her standing in her poky cabin, one hand on the counterpane she had made, looking around for the last time. He had called softly, "Anna?" and she had looked up at him and smiled. It was that smile that haunted him as they were carried through the clouds toward their destiny.

When finally they circled over the city and the deep blue sea fringed with the crescent of surf, night had started to fall on earth and they planed down into it. It was hot when the door of the plane was opened, the twilight outside was studded with flitting fireflies; as they walked across the tarmac to the terminal building there came, from one of the spires that had looked like the white chimneys of a power plant of the future, the medieval wail of a muezzin, chanting the prayers of nightfall in an alien harmony. Peter had no idea where they would stay for the night; as they were checked through customs he spotted a row of Arab hotel porters waiting outside, dressed in baroque uniforms that looked as if they came from the wardrobe of a traveling operetta.

He chose the one most floridly decked out, with the word "Royale" emblazoned on his peaked cap; they were guided by the flashing ivory of his smile to what seemed to be a small historical omnibus. When they were helped inside with Oriental flourish, they found it smelled of popcorn. They sat waiting in the smelly darkness for their guide to come back; after a long interval he returned with another passenger, the athletic curate, who beamed as he climbed in and cried, "Ah! You are at the same hotel as I? Jolly Dee. It's the only one, really. The others are frightfully primitive. Are you here for the conference too?"

Peter said, "No."

While the curate mulled over this reply, their guide, now perched on the driver's seat, seemed to go berserk; he screamed at someone outside as if losing all control of his emotions, the door was slammed and the old bus began its journey with a shuddering leap.

The city of the future revealed itself as a relic of the past as they slowly drove, rattling and squeaking, through its alleys and its smells. The white-coated laboratory attendants Peter had spotted from above turned out to be Arabs in white burnooses milling about noisily in the streets and in the squares in such excited multitudes that, after a while, the feeling of all this being a dream was heightened to a point where it turned into a nightmare. After the short respite of a provincial shopping street with lighted windows, displaying mannequins and geometrical arrays of bottles, they were deposited underneath the canopy of an hotel where an Arab flunkey dressed as Louis XV only managed to open the door of their conveyance by putting his foot against the side of it and pulling at the knob with his full weight. The smell of popcorn was replaced by that of mothballs as they entered the hall of the hotel; it came as a surprise to see a white-skinned receptionist appear behind the ornate counter.

The three of them were given adjoining rooms, with hers in the middle. When Peter saw her standing forlornly in her room, in the center of a crowd of reflections, looking about her at the mirrors, he knew she was pining for the foc'sle and Coba and the smell of hemp and Stockholm tar. "It's quite a change, isn't it?" he said.

She looked at him with a strange serenity and smiled.

"I'd like to go out and see if I can find Van der Pink's hotel," he went on, "just to see if he's there and if so, make an appointment. Or shall we have supper first?"

"I'm not hungry. I'll wait for you here."

"But I don't know how long I'll be. I have no idea where it is."

"There's no hurry. I'll be here."

"Order something to eat. The telephone is right there."

"I will."

"I mean it. Don't just sit here and wait. Order something. Make yourself at home."

She smiled again and said, "I will."

He mumbled, "I won't be long," feeling foolish, and closed the door gently behind him.

The only fellow earthling in this Oriental playhouse in outer space was the pallid clerk behind the counter who, in his striped trousers and stylish black cutaway, looked as lost and preposterous as he in his thick tweed suit. "Could you tell me how to get to the Hotel Tarzan?" he asked.

The clerk answered politely, "I don't seem to recollect that name, sir. Tarzan, you said?"

"I'm afraid so," he answered.

The clerk's tired gray eyes seemed to come alive for a moment with a twinkle of amusement. "I'll look it up for you, sir," he said. "Wherever it is, I think it'll be easier if you take a taxi."

"All right. Could you order one?"

"Certainly, sir." The clerk struck a bell on the counter with the flat of his hand and opened a reference book, through which he started to leaf expertly like a gambler shuffling cards. Louis XV was thrust into the hall by the centrifugal force of the revolving door and asked, breathlessly, "Yes, please?"

"Taxi," the clerk said without looking up; it transformed the Arab into a dervish. He whipped out a whistle and started to blow it, throwing himself on the revolving door as if it were a live adversary. He vanished in a swirl of reflected lamplight and flashing brass. "Here it is," the clerk said, with a trace of surprise. "Must be a residential hotel."

"An unusual name, isn't it?"

The clerk smiled. "In this town only the normal is unusual, you'll find. Tell your driver it is north of Bab El Marsa, near the port." The flunkey came spinning back into the hall, coattails flying, and announced that the taxi was waiting.

The majestic Rolls-Royce came as a surprise. The driver sat outside, underneath a tasseled canopy; when

Peter got in he smelled perfume and old leather and saw fresh flowers in a little crystal vase suspended underneath the partition. An enamelled notice beside it said, in four languages, "Do Not Expectorate." He tried to decipher the Arabic version as they drove along. It was very hot.

Hotel Tarzan was a narrow, ancient building in the corner of a square that looked like a film set for a tale of espionage. Peter made his way between a double row of leather chairs and little tables that made the place look like a second-hand furniture shop. At the far end he found two elderly Europeans leaning on opposite sides of the reception counter. They obviously were the day and the night porter, about to change shifts; both of them wore crumpled white suits, the door to a poky lift was standing open.

"Good evening. Could you tell me whether Captain Van der Pink still lives here?"

"Sure," one of the porters said, after what seemed a hostile pause. "Why?"

"I'd like to talk to him."

"Is he expecting you?"

"He is. Just mention to him that Captain Vos of the Harwich night ferry has written to him about me."

"All right," the porter said with equanimity. "I'll take you up. So, if she comes," he continued to his colleague, "just give her the message."

The old man behind the counter said, "You bet."

"This way. We'll take the lift."

The porter hummed an unmelodious tune as he watched the floors crawl past. The cage squeaked and rattled and shuddered; he tried three times to level it up with the fourth floor. "Watch your step," he said finally, opening the grille to a step of a foot high. "This way." He preceded him, humming, into a low dark corridor, then he opened a door and said, "Come in."

It was a low-ceilinged room in bewildering disorder; clothes on a desk, papers on a sofa, books on a bed and, beside a window open to the stars, a tennis racquet.

"That's for the bats," the old man said, following Peter's look of surprise. "In about an hour or so they start flying in and I serve them right back into the night."

"I see," Peter said calmly. It took some self-control, for the old man had spoken in Dutch.

"So you finally got here. What took you so long?"

"We came part of the way by barge, to avoid being followed."

"By whom?"

"How much did Vos tell you?"

The old man shrugged his shoulders. "Enough to make me curious. I gather you gave up your job and your pension to take a Jewish girl to Palestine, who was about to be shipped off to South America. He asked me to help you."

"Will you?"

"I don't often run immigrants," the old man replied. "The Jews in Palestine take care of most of that traffic themselves. They buy boats, man them with their own crews, and abandon them on the beach. I can't afford that. But sit down. Where are you staying?"

"At the Royale."

"She there?"

"Yes."

"You want her to go as soon as possible, I take it?"

"Yes. Will it be difficult to get her in?"

"It hasn't got any easier. For the odd load I do take, I have been forced to change my tactics. I parcel them out now into small lots and beach them over a long stretch of the coast simultaneously, rather than unloading the whole cargo in one place."

"I'm talking about immigrants," Peter said, at a loss.

"So am I," the old man said. Then he added, "Ah, I see, a humanist. Do you drink?"

"Certainly."

"Let's have a pastis. It's the only sensible drink in this climate. Let me sit there if you will, so I can keep an eye on the bats."

They changed chairs; as he prepared the drinks the old man said, "The one to see about her is a Mr. Cohen, an American, who sits in the office of a watch company near your hotel. He is the representative of a group in the States who finances passages for illegal immigrants. Each case is judged on its merits, I gather. I don't rightly know. All I know is that in the past he has been the one who paid me, and I assume he'll want to make sure that his money is spent the way it was intended. You can't expect them to shell out a thousand dollars a head without checking that they aren't importing any Arabs."

"Is that the price?"

"Once you get there, you'll have found out it's a bargain. You want to see her there yourself, I take it?"

"I want to make sure she gets there, that's all."

"I see. Cheers." The old man lifted his glass and stared at him unsmilingly with his light-blue eyes. He looked frail and harmless in his baggy white suit, with thin yellowish hair and delicately veined old hands. There was nothing in his appearance that suggested power or strength; he might be any old man living in a world of memories, monotonous menus and pigeons. His voice was gruff; that and the color of his eyes were the only things that betrayed the sailor. He wore Arab slippers and rumpled socks, above which a band of varicose white skin showed as he leaned back and crossed his legs. "I can't take you on as a passenger unless you pay the fare," he continued. "If you don't have the money, we'll have to make a deal."

"What kind of a deal?"

"From what Vos told me, I gather that you know something about handling boats, as an ex-member of the harbor police. That so?"

"Why?"

"I have a fleet of small craft, and I'm hard up for skippers. I could use you."

"I'm afraid . . ."

"Don't decide now!" He raised a thin white hand. "Think it over. You could make the trip with her to get familiar with the job, all I would ask in return would be two trips as a mate on one of my launches. If you'd care to stay on after that as a captain, you'd be welcome, but that's up to you. My guess is you will. You'll earn at least five times as much as you did as an inspector, it will be payable in dollars, and you'll be able to send most of it to your family, for all your expenses will be taken care of. On our usual cargo you would be paid a bonus for each load delivered, on top of your salary."

"What cargo?"

"We'll cross that bridge when we get to it," the old man said with quiet authority. "Drink your pastis before it gets hot. Cheers again."

"Cheers."

They drank. Captain Van der Pink smacked his lips. "Well, how's Amsterdam these days? Haven't seen it for years."

"It was all right when I last saw it," Peter replied lamely.

"Grand old town," the captain said with foxy bon-homie, stretching his thin legs with a clicking of joints. "Still got that old square-rigger in the East Dock?"

"The *Pollux?* Certainly. Boys on the yardarms every morning."

"That's where I got my training," the old man said fondly. "She has really stood up well."

"I'm afraid she hasn't. The old ship was broken up years ago. The present thing is a flat-bottomed copy of her, made of thin-gauge steel."

"You mean to say she couldn't carry any sails?"

"I'm afraid not. She'd turn turtle."

"Bah!" the captain said with disgust, filling his glass again. "What has happened to our country over the last twenty-five years? Everything is a worthless copy of what was once our national strength. True or false?" His bright blue eyes began to swim a little. He obviously did not hold his liquor as well as his friend on the Har-wich ferry.

"Oh, I don't know about that," Peter said, sipping the pastis. It tasted innocuous, of aniseed. "I think it was a nice thought, to keep the memory of the old windjam-mer alive that way. They could just as well have built a square houseboat for the boys' classes. It would have served the purpose."

"I don't think the young people of today know how exceptional we are as a nation," the old man said, lec-turing the stars. "My favorite story about the Dutch is the one about Admiral de Ruyter, when he was still the young skipper of a merchantman of the West African Company. His tussle with the Arabian sheik. Know that one?"

"I don't think I do." Peter suddenly felt tired and wanted to leave. He thought of Anna, sitting all alone in that room full of mirrors, waiting. He should have sent up some magazines, or a box of chocolates. Pity he always thought of those things too late. The old man had embarked on what obviously was going to be a long story, and he forced himself to listen. ". . . saw, in the well of the deck, the Moors standing with their scimitars on the throats of his crew, ready to cut them. So de Ruyter said, 'I see. I suppose I had better have a word with your sheik,' and the Moor said, 'We brought a horse for you.'" The old man chuckled, filled his glass again, took a sip, washed his mouth with it, swallowed and belched, staring at the stars. He was enraptured by his story and Peter felt a sudden violent dislike for him. It was wrong that a frail, garrulous old man like that should have so much power. He was something half human, a sprite, a grandfather who had dodged the lasso of time and now roamed the plains of life like a cheerful hyena. Heavens, that stuff must be stronger than he thought. He tried to listen, but he felt quite giddy. No wonder, he had not eaten since that morning. "Then the sheik lifted his veil and said in Dutch, 'Well, Captain, down to business.' It was a Mr. Van der Plas, of a rival company, from Haarlem." The old man laughed, took a long sip of his drink and showed the stars the empty glass. "That, my friend, was Holland. But nowadays . . ."

"Yes, how true," Peter said, melodiously, holding on to the arms of his chair as it started to swing toward the stars.

"It's not the captains that have changed," Captain Van der Pink went on, "but the companies. The companies!" he snorted. "That's why our merchant navy is doomed! When I started out in the business, to be a ship's Master meant to be somebody. The moment you left Holland you were on your own. All decisions were yours. You had to make out as best you could. You were skipper under God. But now? Since the war, with the communications we have now, a captain is tied hand and foot. He can't even buy a dozen pencils in Punta Arenas without first asking permission from Amsterdam. Skipper under God has turned into skipper under a junior clerk of the home office. No, sir. They couldn't keep me, and they won't be able to keep any young man with pride and adventure in his guts. They have turned our navy into another *Pollux*, a flat-bottomed imitation of the original that will turn turtle at the first breath of wind. Cheers." He drank and seemed to emerge sober. "Here I am," he said, "Mr. Van der Plas from Haarlem, sitting in God's copper frying pan, without a company."

"And how do you like it?" Peter asked cordially, as if this were a conversation between two tycoons in the Industrial Club.

"I feel lost, occasionally," Captain Van der Pink confessed, after pursing his lips and frowning, trying to focus his eyes in thought. "Perhaps because no man, whatever his age, can do without a father image. I was an orphan, so I suppose my lifelong battle with the company has been largely symbolical. What was your father? A clergyman?"

"No," Peter said, smiling fondly. "The reverse."

"What the hell is that?" the captain asked, raising his eyebrows.

"He was an atheist and a very ardent one."

"Pah," Van der Pink said, deflated. "Same thing. Atheism is one of the most exacting and puritanical religions. No, I won't be tricked into calling myself an atheist. I know He's around, all right. He's somewhere, the old bugger. I'm not going to make a fool of myself by heaving a deep, happy sigh and saying, 'He does not exist.' No, sir. He exists all right; He's everywhere. He's right there, now, this minute, eavesdropping out there, listening with pointed ears to what we're saying." His old finger pointed at the window, the tennis racquet and the stars. "But don't ever let yourself be tricked into thinking that you can do a deal with Him, for He has no heart, no pity, no compassion, no weakness, nothing human at all, except some traits that have led me to believe that, if I had to pin Him down, I'd say He's a Dutchman."

"My father always said . . ." Peter started, but the old man was not interested.

"God of love!" he cried. "Phooey! All you need do, to find out that all the clergy of all time have been meowing up the wrong tree, is to sail on convoy duty during a modern war. I've seen more men praying, sticking Bibles in their breast pocket to stop bullets, fingering strings of beads, clutching plaster statuettes to be saved from drowning than I care to remember. I've seen people start out in a lifeboat after their ship was torpedoed singing 'The Lord is my Shepherd' and I've seen them die as rabid cannibals that had to be shot as you would shoot famished beasts of prey. No, sir. If I could write, I'd write a book called *God and the Convoys, a Bible for the Young*. And do you know what my conclusion would be? Scum, sir. Mankind is scum, a disease of the planet. The cancer of the earth. Look how we multiply, look how we scar and gut the body of this globe, and now we've got the atom bomb it won't be long before we go the way of all voracious microbes. We'll destroy the body we feed on, and by doing so commit communal suicide. Cheers." He lifted his glass and put it to his lips, then he said, before drinking, "What am I sounding off for? You as a police inspector must have arrived at the same conclusions long ago."

"As a matter of fact, I haven't," Peter said, and he was struck by the boring sound of his own voice. "I think that mankind has more to it than that. I think we may have made such advances in tech—techno—technical things that our—our old spiritual symbols no longer can keep up with—er—with them." He rubbed his eyes and thought, how did this happen? I came here to arrange for her passage to Palestine and here I am, defending mankind. Then he looked at the old man across the table, who sat with his legs crossed now, Arab fashion, glass in hand, his piercing blue eyes taunting God to show His pointed ears in the window frame. "I think that all this talk about God and what He's like is stupid," Peter said. "I think we've been pestering God for two thousand years now, it's time to leave Him in peace. I think that all we can hope for right now in our relationship with God, if He exists. . . ." He almost had it, the answer to all questions, the ultimate solution to all problems; it lay on the tip of his tongue; then Captain Van der Pink leaped to his feet with a shout, ran to the window, grabbed the tennis racquet, took up a stance and waited motionlessly with fierce concentration until a little winged body came flitting toward him. He batted it back at the stars and cried, "Fifteen-love!"

A volley of winged balls came soaring at him in rapid succession, but he nimbly served them all back, crying the score as he leaped. Then one of them got in. The little animal, terrified, fluttered around the room and Peter put his hands over his head, a feminine gesture, thinking sentimentally of a story his mother had once told him about a little mouse seeing bats for the first time in its life and running back into the family hole crying, "Mummy, mummy, I've seen angels!" Then the old demon slammed the little angel back through the window into the night and cried, "Game and set! Aah!" He put down his racquet, rubbed his hands and came back to the table to fill his glass. "I suppose I'm the only man in Africa who has God for a sparring partner," he said; then he peered at his guest, still slumped in his chair with his hands over his head, and he added, malevolently, "Ah! I forgot! You are a humanist. Vegetarian, perhaps?"

"No."

"Then what on earth put the crazy notion into your head of taking a Jewess to Palestine?" He drank. "Well?"

"Common decency," Peter said, fuzzily.

"Poppycock!" Captain Van der Pink retorted. "Mind you, it's no criticism. After all, I need people like you to sail my launches. You're all the same. Crusaders, desperadoes, child rapists, ship sinkers, homosexuals, collaborators, pyromaniacs, Christians; all of you have one thing in common: a secret. A guilty secret. The worm in the apple. Cheers."

"I think I had better begin thinking of making my way home," Peter said, trying to shake off the giddiness. He succeeded for a moment and saw the white old man uncurl his legs and rise, one crumpled trouser leg halfway up a thin, varicose calf. "All right," the voice snapped. "Go and see your Mr. Cohen tomorrow and tell him to contact me if it's okay. The stairs are to the left. Good night."

Peter drifted down the stairs, feeling skittish and playful, humming a new tune. The hall porter rose behind the reception counter and blinked at him sleepily, looking like an attendant in a furniture shop, with all those leather chairs lined up against the wall. In one of them a muscular young man sat behind a newspaper, and the amusing thing was that he had an open book lying face downward on his knees. Peter read its title, and shook his head as he wormed himself out of the confusing revolving door. Three cheers for the spread-eagled blonde and the British Intelligence Service.

He wondered whether he should go back to tell Captain Van der Pink, but he shrugged his shoulders, muttered, "Phooey! Tomorrow. Tomorrow is another day," trying to pick up the tune of his new song as he skated down the narrow street with controlled, graceful movements. The night smelled of urine.

He found the hotel in the end, but by the time he did so he was sick. He could barely make it to his room; there he fell on his bed in the darkness, moaning. He felt so sick, so weak, so miserable that he sobbed on his pillow; then a door squeaked and Anna's face floated toward him through the darkness, smiling. She held a candle, sheltering its flame from the draft with her hand. She looked down at him; he closed his eyes when the candlelight hit him and groaned. He heard the small sound of the candlestick put down on the bedside table, fifty times magnified with a series of diminishing echoes, then he felt somebody fiddling with his feet. He gave a ticklish shout, opened his eyes and saw she was taking off his shoes. He wanted to tell her to stop that, to go back to her room and to bed, for tomorrow was another day, but she smiled at him with implacable serenity and he suddenly realized what she was doing. She was treating him like a child.

His last strength of character rallied inside him in rebellion, and he rose on his elbows crying, "No!" But it came out weak and tearful and he sagged back, overpowered by the irresistible force of her gentleness. He could not hold back the tears; it was humiliating and wonderful to bawl his head off. Then he felt her hand on his forehead and a great, clean peace came over him, like a sunny morning in winter, and he heard her soft voice say, with tinkling clarity among the icicles, "Don't worry. We'll get there."

Overcome with wonder, he fell asleep in the snow.

He dreamed of Amsterdam. It was night, the lights on the other side of the harbor made quivering trails across the water, from the shipyards came the blinding blue pinpoints of welding. The harbor was empty, except for the occasional ferry; he sat watching the water from jetty South 16, where the patrol boat of the harbor police used to moor, close to the underpass to the East Dock. Overhead wheeled the gulls that never slept; at the next dock, on the mail ferry about to cross the Zuyder Zee, old men were turning on lights in galley and engine room. Soon barrels would start to roll and crash on board from the quayside, and the first passengers would turn up: country-women in old-fashioned black clothes with lace caps and string bags full of shopping, dredger boys on their way to build the dikes for the new land, carrying duffel bags on their shoulders and rubber hip boots around their necks, soldiers returning to camp after their leave. Later, the first wave of bicycles would come rushing down the quayside, clattering and jingling, to pile onto the large car ferries that were to take them across the harbor. He knew how the harbor looked at every hour of the day and night, who would be there, what ships and what people; right now he knew that the lonely voice singing behind him across the road was a fireman polishing brass in the fire station; the new shift had just come on. But the song of the fireman detached itself from Amsterdam, became alien, Oriental; he slowly woke up with a feeling of doom in the hot hotel room and heard the muezzin chant through the open window. The voice sounded very close, it must be a loud-speaker.

As he got up his head seemed to remain behind on the pillow; he clutched it, moaning, and remembered how drunk he had been the night before and he cursed

16

Captain Van der Pink. He washed his face, feeling sick, and decided that he could not do anything, not even think straight, until he had had some fresh air. He opened the squeaking door to the corridor cautiously, so as not to awaken Anna, and tiptoed down the stairs. The house still smelled of mothballs; in the dimly lit hall an Arab night porter sat dozing behind the counter. He remembered that he should have sent her some magazines and some chocolates the day before; now it was too early, the Arab did not look as if he would understand, he gazed at him across the counter with glassy eyes and watched him go out through the swinging door without moving his head.

The street outside looked like a furrow in which the night lingered; overhead the sparse, harmless little clouds turned pink with the day. He walked idly past the sleeping houses; after turning a few corners and crossing a square he found himself facing the harbor. Across the basin a few rusty tramps were tied up to wharves piled high with crates and timber; the quay onto which he had emerged obviously skirted the fisherman's port. A row of fishing boats lay on the mud, from which small, surreptitious jets of water squirted that must be shellfish hidden under the surface. A rust-streaked wooden trawler lay anchored a little way out, swinging in the tide; she looked as if she had been picked up as a derelict at sea and now lay there, rotting, while waiting for her fate to be settled in some courtroom, far away. The waterfront consisted of dingy shops and dark archways; in one of them a sleepy Arab was plaiting a fender out of a piece of old hawser.

Peter stood staring at the water and the ships for a while, feeling lonely and despondent. It was not the pastis, it was the dream. He was homesick. He strolled back to the town, dejectedly, found a café open on the main street, ordered a cup of coffee and wrote a postcard to Susie. There was much to tell her, but all he could find to say was, "All going well so far. The weather here is very hot. Please write % Captain Van der Pink, Hotel Tarzan, Tangier. Love P." It was not only inadequate, it was stupid. He should not give Van der Pink away. He tore up the postcard and put the pieces in his coat pocket. The coffee tasted bitter and gritty, the bartender switched on a radio from which came the squeals of two tomcats fighting over a banjo. The bartender, cutting cake, hummed with them and started to wriggle his hips as he worked. In Amsterdam the first fast motor launches would now be setting out to take the dayshift across to the yards, and the first trams would come squealing around the bend from the underpass. He sighed, paid for his coffee without having finished it, and went back into the street that had become livelier now. There were few Europeans about, most of the passers-by were Arabs in white burnooses talking together excitedly, who fell silent as he approached, averting their eyes, to take up their chatter again as soon as he had passed. It was an alien, hostile world; he had never realized how many of the passers-by on the Amsterdam waterfront he knew by sight. He tried to visualize their faces as he walked along, but he found that he could not remember any, only the policemen.

The watch shop Captain Van der Pink had mentioned looked very modest, with its two dingy windows barred with heavy mesh. The door was still locked and he was looking for a bell when a voice behind him asked, "Can I help you?"

He turned around and saw a young man with an earnest, weak face and big, moist eyes gaze at him. He wore a little straw hat and a blue-and-white-striped summer suit and carried a brief case. He seemed to belong anywhere but here, among the Arabs and the overflowing dustbins.

"I am looking for Mr. Cohen," he said.

"That's me," the young man said. "How do you do?"

"I am Inspector Jongman from Amsterdam, Holland. Could I see you for a moment?"

"What about?" the young man asked warily; the word "inspector" had put him on his guard.

"Captain Van der Pink sent me. I have a customer for transportation."

"Oh, I see." He seemed only slightly reassured. "Come in, please." He opened the door with a key; as they entered the dark little shop Peter said, "I'm sorry to be so early, but this was my first night here and I didn't sleep very well."

"I understand," the young man said politely in the darkness. "It does take some getting used to. This way, please." He switched on a lamp over a desk in a small office, and asked Peter to sit down. Staring suspiciously across the desk with his big, moist eyes, he looked earnest and worthy and very tired. The harsh light of the desk lamp glinted in beads of moisture on his forehead and his upper lip; his pink, soft hands lay on top of one another on the blotter as if they were asleep. "Well?" he asked, almost apologetically. "What can I do for you?"

Peter explained, and the young man seemed to grow more tired as he listened. Finally he said, "If she can identify herself and substantiate her claim, I may be able to arrange it. But what is your function in this business? Are you related?"

Peter explained some more, and the young man listened earnestly. His hands on the blotter seemed to lead an independent life; they stretched themselves and looked for something to play with. After some tripping and touching, they found a pencil and started to roll it about. "I see," the young man said, a little confused by Peter's story. "Well, I suppose if all the details are settled to our satisfaction, she will be able to leave in about three or four weeks."

"I'd like her to see a doctor," Peter said. "Do you know of a good man here?"

The hands dropped their pencil to listen. "Certainly," the young man said. "As a matter of fact, it's imperative. You see, one thing I did not mention is that those who are obviously unable to make the trip have to be hospitalized first. Can she walk?"

"Of course," Peter replied hastily. "I'm sure there's nothing seriously the matter with her. It's just that I think she should have a check-up, if only to put my mind at rest."

"All right," the young man said. "I'll write down the address for you and find out when he can see her. One moment, please." One of the hands leaped to the phone, the other greedily jumped on the pencil now all its own, and started to roll it up and down the blotter again. The bell at the other end of the line went on ringing for a while, then he put the receiver back and said, "Too early." The hand that jumped off the telephone ran to wrench the pencil from its playmate but, before either of them had won, the right one shouldered the pencil and started to write on a pad, held down by the other. "Here it is," the young man said. "Doctor Mitropoulos, a few blocks down to your right. You take her there in, say, an hour. In the meantime, I'll tell him to expect you. By the way, how old is she?"

"Twenty-one."

The young man frowned. "H'm," he said. "I hope she really is, we have had great difficulties with minors. Well, I'll see what I can do. Normally, I should want some documentary proof that her parents or her guardians agree, otherwise a documentary proof of their death. Would that be difficult?"

Peter got to his feet and said, "Yes. They were killed in a camp. Shall I see you later?"

"Come and see me after you've seen the doctor," the young man said, and one of the hands leaped into the air. Peter shook it gingerly; it was clammy.

He walked back to the hotel past the mirroring shop-windows, the Arabs, the dustbins; the hall looked even more bleak and dismal than it had at dawn. The chairs and the tables had been herded together by two Arabs who had hitched up their burnooses with large safety pins. The carpets were rolled up and the hall reverberated with the nagging whine of two ancient vacuum cleaners. For some reason the counter was covered with a dust sheet; behind it, as if standing watch over the bier, was the pallid, ageless European clerk he knew. They wished one another a formal good morning, ignoring the chaos that surrounded them; the Arabs were now slyly chasing one another with their vacuum cleaners in an infantile game. The clerk eyed them over Peter's shoulder with disgust.

"I'd like to buy some chocolates," Peter said. "I thought I saw some yesterday on the counter."

"Certainly, sir," the clerk said. "But those boxes are dummies. Chocolate melts, you know, in this climate. I'll have to order some from the kitchen, but I'm afraid it is not open yet. Breakfast is prepared in the pantries."

"I see. Well, in that case, I'll take a magazine."

"Certainly, sir."

The clerk pulled up the dust sheet with a gesture that made the magazines seem scabrous. Peter chose two English ones, far out of date, one called *Country Life* with a picture of a tomb, the other called *Picture Post* showing a pig on a tricycle with the legend, "Moscow Circus." As an afterthought, he also bought a French thing called *Elle*, which depicted a young woman in a bathing suit and a hat, peering condescendingly through a V sign. The clerk said, "The lady ordered her breakfast while you were out. Shall I put these on your bill?"

He said, "Yes, please," and went to the elevator. The clerk took him up. "Our boy is a little late this morning," he said, closing the gates. "Punctuality, you know, is linked with culture."

The corridor of their floor smelled faintly of sleeping people. Outside the clergyman's door stood a pair of high laced boots; amazing to what lengths these English went.

He knocked on her door, she opened at once. Her bed was made and there was no trace left of her breakfast. On the tallboy, inside the door, stood a tray and some crockery that had obviously been washed in the bathroom. She was wearing the soft slippers they had bought in the Belgian village. He wondered whether she had brought her clogs too.

"Good morning," she said cheerily. "I thought you were still fast asleep."

He said, "No," awkwardly and gave her the magazines. "I must apologize for last night and—er—thank you."

"For what?"

"Oh, well, you know, I must have been quite a handful. It's those Dutch sea captains. This Van der Pink certainly ran true to type."

"Oh, how kind of you to bring me these," she said,

as if it were an expensive present. "I've heard of this one. I've wanted to buy a copy for ages."

"The stuff he gave me tasted like aniseed and made me feel like a butterfly as long as I was sitting down, but when I got up it turned me into a caterpillar."

"No need to apologize," she said, smiling. "What was he like?"

"Very Dutch, if that means anything to you. Tough and businesslike on the outside, but he plays tennis every night with God."

She was not listening. "Is he going to take me on?"

"Of course. It's all settled, except for a few routine things. I went to see the contact man of the American organization this morning; he started by wanting documentary proof of all sorts of things, but I got him down to just the medical check-up, and that's all."

"Check-up?" she asked, and her face changed. It was almost like a hallucination. The calm, serene girl he had come to know vanished behind the mask of the one that had sat listening to Susie. He saw, in front of his eyes, the life drain out of her face and retire behind that no man's land, devoid of feeling and awareness.

"Doesn't mean a thing," he said. "It's only a formality. They only want to make sure that you are fit for the trip. Surely you can understand that?"

"Yes," she said, but it was not an agreement. It was meaningless, a word echoing across a void.

"The moment they see you come in, they'll know," he said persuasively. "The mere fact that you walk into his office looking the way you do will be enough to convince the doctor that you can make the voyage. Look how far we've come. It's a formality."

"Yes."

For some reason her passive acceptance that had once moved him now irritated him, he felt like shaking her by the shoulders and saying, "Don't be silly. Nothing is going to happen. They won't hurt you." But then he remembered the medical-research camp and he realized that she must be terrified of doctors beyond imagination. He felt ashamed and gently took her arm and said, "Let's go."

She obeyed; it seemed as if she delivered herself completely into his hands and by doing so escaped from reality. They went down the stairs, across the hall, out into the early sun that already shone hot and dazzling on the pavement, and they started to walk. Instead of going toward the doctor's office, he led her in the opposite direction. They walked for a while in silence, his hand on her arm, guiding her. It felt like guiding a blind person. They went through archways and alleys, through smells of bedding and coffee and sweat, underneath the still rows of laundry hanging like wet flags; then they turned the corner to the wide-open shell of the sea and the sky with, glistening in its heart, the harbor, a mirage from *A Thousand and One Nights*. The Oriental fishing boats lay sleeping over their dreamlike reflections, rippled and slurred by the wind and the tide. The derelict trawler had now swung around at her anchor; the squirting shellfish in the mud had been covered by the sea; across the shimmering water the rusty freighters looked like angular monsters hewn out of red sandstone. In the dark archway of his shop the Arab had finished half of his fender, plaiting the frayed rope with graceful, feminine movements of his hands. The eternal gulls sat dozing on the rampart that felt hot to the touch as he leaned on it. While he stood looking at this vision of a quaint and distant land, he felt that she cautiously, incredulously, hazarded out of the fortress of her soul.

"Is . . . is it here?" she asked, in a small voice.

"Yes," he said. "This is as far as we'll go. I am not going to take you to the doctor if it upsets you. It isn't worth it."

"But wasn't it—wasn't it their condition?"

"Yes, their condition; not mine. I'll take you to Palestine without the Americans."

"But how can you?"

"By selling my services to Van der Pink. He has already stung me for two trips as a mate on one of his launches for going with you. If that's his price for a passage, I'll make four trips. It makes no difference."

She did not answer. He turned his head toward her, shielded by a smile; when he saw her eyes, his smile faded. She stood staring at him with such tenderness that he cleared his throat and averted his eyes.

Then she said, "All right. Let's go." Her voice was different, and he knew that she was no longer sheltering behind her passivity. She was once more the girl who had sat knitting by his side in the wheelhouse in silent contentment and unobtrusive strength.

"Are you sure?" he asked.

She smiled and said, "Of course. I'm sorry. Let's go."

They went back through the arches, the alleys, the dazzling street where the traffic roared. The doctor's office was only a few blocks away from the watch shop; he shared the house with a lawyer, a ship chandler and an exporter of rugs. The waiting room was dingy, almost shabby. On the wall was an ornate map of Israel with pictures of Biblical battles, miracles and migrations. On a low table lay a stack of magazines, most of them issues of *Palestine Today*, the rest copies of *Paris-Match* and *Radar*. A door opened in a wall of frosted glass and a slight young man appeared against the light. "Hello," he said. "Are you the girl from Holland? Steve told me you were coming. Well, welcome to Tangier, my dear. You're over the hump now. I'd say, let's go ahead and get it over with. Will you wait here, sir?"

"Yes, if I may."

"We won't be long. Make yourself comfortable. All right, my dear. What's your name?"

"Held."

"Don't be silly. What does *he* call you?"

"Anna."

"That's better. All right, Anna, let's go inside. We'll take it easy. He's got plenty to read there. Now tell me, how old . . ." He closed the door and his voice became a murmur.

Peter closed his eyes in weariness, and was overcome unexpectedly with the wish to be able to pray. He picked up the first magazine at hand and started to turn its pages. He looked at photographs of young, bronzed farmers with spades and guns, at tough, booted girls in slacks, wearing helmets and pistols while driving a tractor. There were maps of the future, with dams in the River Jordan and fields of corn where now the desert shimmered in the sun. The more images he saw of the Promised Land, the more he realized that she had no business there.

As he reached that conclusion, he shied away from it. It was nonsense. She had come this far, she would be able to do the rest of the voyage with ease. Nothing could be more taxing than to look after two men on board a barge. He closed his eyes and saw the ship. The hatches, the bows, Coba, the horizon. Brandt would have finished unloading by now, perhaps he had found a return cargo for Holland. Who would take their places? Perhaps Brandt would try to sail the ship alone, or tandem up with a neighbor. Suppose she arrived in Palestine in a few weeks' time, what would he do with himself after that? He opened his eyes and picked up another magazine. At this moment, all that counted was to get her into Palestine. To think of the future beyond the goal of their journey was to undermine his strength.

He sat leafing through the stack of magazines for what seemed like hours. The doctor's voice mumbled occasionally in the distance, sometimes there was a tinkle of metal on glass, but most of the time there was nothing but silence; a vague shadow moved to and fro on the frosted glass. Then, suddenly, the outside door opened and Cohen came in from the passage. He blinked myopically in the half-light; his hands, eager piglets, hopped to the back of a chair. "She still in there?" he asked in a whisper.

Peter nodded.

"How long has he been?"

"About an hour."

"Oh. Well, it shouldn't be long now. I came to fetch him for lunch." He sat down, his hands drummed on the arms of the chair as if they were straining at a leash. "Your first time in Tangier?" he asked.

"Yes."

"How do you . . ."

The door in the glass wall opened, and the doctor came out, closing it behind him with a movement of secrecy. "I must talk to you," he said, his voice low and urgent. "It's very important and I don't want her to hear. Go across the hall to where you see a door saying 'Doctor Berlin.' There's nobody in there. Wait inside and I'll join you in a minute. Here's the key."

"Something the matter?" Cohen asked, unnecessarily. Peter's heart had sunk.

"Hush," the doctor said. "Hurry now. I'll be there right away."

They got up and crossed the dark landing. Cohen fumbled with the key, finally let him into a small waiting room that seemed an exact replica of the one they had just left, only it was darker. Cohen tried to switch on the light and said, "He must be out of town. The main switch is off."

"What do you think is wrong?" Peter asked; he could not help himself.

"I have no idea," Cohen said, sincerely. "He's a very good doctor, you know, and you can count on it that, if it's at all possible, he'll send her on. He may run into trouble soon for we've already had protests from Haganah. It's not that they don't want invalids, they admit any Jew, every Jew that wants to come home, but, right now, with the British chasing them all over the beaches, one person unable to stand the strain may change the fate of scores of others. So . . ."

The door opened and the doctor came in. He was still in his white coat. There was something oddly nervous and tense about him for a medical man; he almost stammered when he said, "Impossible. She cannot possibly make that trip. I . . . I haven't seen anything like it in my life. I mean, she should receive medical care at once. I think, Steve, that you should have her shipped to the States as quickly as possible. This is unbelievable; I mean, I wouldn't have believed it if I hadn't seen it with my own eyes. She must be photographed, a clinical report must be made by an international committee of doctors and the material must be sent to Nuremberg at once. Anyone seeing those photographs will hate and despise the Germans as long as he lives."

Cohen said, "What . . ." but the doctor went on.

"It's the most horrifying sight I have ever seen. They have made skin grafts that . . . that are the work of sadistic lunatics. I . . ." He clenched his fists and struck them together in an odd gesture of rage and incoherent despair. "I knew that these things had happened, but I had never seen them. And that is not all. They have . . . well, let's grant her the grace of some discretion. If you were her parent or her husband, it would be different, but . . . you understand, surely. In any case, I cannot possibly let her go. It is out of the question. I am sorry. You know that I am the last man to keep anyone from returning, but this time, I . . . I can't find the words to describe it. It's . . . it's a nightmare."

Peter's hands had gone ice cold as he listened. But the disembodied detachment that had sustained him before enabled him to ask, with quiet composure, "But what about *her?*"

"What do you mean?"

"You say she must be shipped to America as soon as possible. I assume she is very ill. Will that save her?"

The doctor glanced at him; then he answered, "No. Nothing, nobody can save this girl. Apart from what they have done to her, she has tuberculosis of the lungs. I don't know whether they induced it on purpose or whether it is the result of conditions in the camp. Anyhow, she is in the final stage. It's a miracle that she has held out this far, but then these miracles do happen. I mean, I talked to her and she told me about her desire to get to Palestine, it's amazing how this vision of the homeland can sustain a person who scientifically should be in a coma."

"In that case, don't you think she would be sustained by that vision until she gets there?"

"No."

"How can you be so sure? She has come this far. Where do the circumstances change so abruptly? All she has in front of her is a short sea voyage, isn't that so?"

The doctor laughed. It was not a laugh of amusement. "You don't know what you are talking about," he said. "That short sea voyage is more than even a healthy man could stand. These people are transported on vessels and in conditions that defy description. Your countryman Mr. Van der Pink is a true offspring of the old slave traders."

"All right," he said calmly. "So the conditions are bad. I'll be there with her, she won't be alone."

"It's more than that. Those vessels that Van der Pink uses are so small that people get seasick, and it's not the seasickness of a pleasure cruise. They get seasick to a point that they don't care if they die. She will."

"But what makes you so certain that she won't be able to stand it? What symptoms would there be if she undertook the voyage?"

"I can't give you a reliable prognosis, because her reactions so far have not been normal. But I can tell you this much. She will die by suffocation, or drown in her own blood. Before she finally succumbs, she should be given injections of pain-relieving drugs and receive all the medical care she can get. It is a simple question of humanity, of mercy. When I say that she cannot make that trip, it is because I want to save her a Calvary."

"Does she know about this?"

"No, but I think we should tell her. Perhaps not in so many words, we don't want to add the load of anxiety to the burden she already carries. I think she should be given a choice. We, the three of us, will know it's not a real choice, but let's put it to her that she will do more to help her people by going to the States and having herself submitted as evidence at the war-crimes trials, than by arriving in Palestine as a helpless invalid. You see what I mean?"

Cohen said, "Sure, sure," and he turned to Peter. "What do you think?"

He did not answer straight away. He tried to think, but his mind was a blank. He was numbed by the horror of it all. He just could not cope with a nightmare of these proportions. "I think it is the only way," he replied at last. "She will have to be told and make up her own mind."

"As long as we make certain that we put the choice to her in such a fashion that the outcome is certain," the doctor said, "for her own sake. Believe me, I have her interest more at heart than I can put into words. I know that if we want to help her, we must load the dice. All right?"

"All right with me," Cohen said. "Just tell me what you want me to say."

"Just agree with me and follow my reasoning as I go along. All right with you, sir?"

Peter said, "All right," but he wondered. He foresaw that she would not be fooled by these two well-meaning men.

"I'll get her," the doctor said. "Just stay here." When he had his hand on the doorknob, he turned around and said, "This may not be necessary, but try not to show pity or any emotion that might give you away."

Cohen said, "Of course," but sounded unconvincing.

They sat in silence for a while, each with his own thoughts; then Cohen said, wringing his hands in an oddly nervous way, "People just don't understand. They don't know. They can't imagine. Sometimes I think there is only one solution—to kill them, all of them, man, woman and child. They are not human, they are . . ."

There were steps outside, the door opened and she

was ushered in by the doctor. She looked calm and composed. It was a relief at first, then it became unbearable.

"Well, my dear," the doctor said, with admirable control. "We won't beat about the bush because you know as well as we do that you are not exactly a healthy girl. Now, we are faced with a choice, that is to say 'we' is only a figure of speech. *You* are. All we can do is to formulate the choice for you and leave it to you to make up your mind. All right?"

"Of course," she said quietly. "You are Mr. Cohen, I suppose?"

"Oh, yes, of course, I'm sorry," the doctor said, his composure faltering. "I should have introduced you. I didn't realize you hadn't met."

"How do you do?" Cohen said in a small voice, half rising, while one of the piglets leaped at her guilelessly. She touched it and said, "I'm pleased to meet you. I'm sorry for all the trouble I'm giving you."

"Oh, it's no trouble, no trouble at all," Cohen said, clumsily sitting down. "It's—it's a pleasure."

"All right, my dear," the doctor said. "Let's get down to business. You must forgive me if I mention private matters here, but my reason for doing so will become obvious as I go on. What I mean is this: what happened to you in that medical camp is evidence that we may not suppress if we want to see justice done. Let me put it another way. You are on your way to Palestine, not only because you want to return from the Diaspora but because you want to help as a nurse, isn't that so?"

"Yes."

"Well, it now turns out that, in our opinion, you can be of infinitely greater help to our people, your people, by allowing the prosecution at the Nuremberg trials to expose the truth of what happened to you. Because," he added, watching her closely, "we want to prevent something similar occurring again in some distant future, we must establish here and now what anti-Semitism leads to in the end. What you have to show the innocent victims of the first seed of anti-Semitism is the flower that will spring from that seed, whether they want it or not. For the difference between saying 'I wish those Jews would move out of our neighborhood' and your fate is gradual, not basic. Do I make myself clear?"

"Oh, yes," she said, still with the composure that had made Peter avert his eyes.

"If you should agree with me on this, we will arrange for your transport to America at once, tomorrow. You will be admitted to the best hospital, you'll be cared for by the very best doctors, with the newest drugs, but all this is secondary. It's, how shall I say, a lucky circumstance for you. Your crucial choice is: shall I serve my people by revealing my fate at the hands of those—those men, or shall I press on to Palestine and become a burden to the homeland? For you see, my dear, you are not well enough to do any work, and you won't be for a long time to come. Your only hope of ever getting to Palestine as a nurse is by going to America first. It's your only chance to get well. If you set out for Palestine now, in your present condition, you—you will never get well." He laughed nervously. "Now I hear myself say this, it doesn't seem much of a choice, does it? I'm sorry, that was not the idea. I want you to decide, not the circumstances. So, tell me. What do you think of all this?"

Peter looked up and saw her gaze at the doctor's eyes. He had the eerie feeling that she not only knew everything, but that, at that moment, she was thinking of them rather than of herself.

"May I think it over?" she asked matter-of-factly, without any sign of concern.

"Of course," the doctor said, almost relieved, "by all means. I don't want you to feel that you are being steam-rollered into something. Only, I'd like you to decide to-day. If you should decide to go to America, we should waste no time."

"All right," she said. "I'll let you know tonight. Thank you very much." She turned to Peter. "Shall we go?"

Peter rose silently to his feet. Cohen still sat wringing his hands, but his eyes were brimming over. The doctor shook her hand, his jaw set. He looked, at that moment, like an illustration from *Palestine Today*. "Good luck, my dear," he said. "I'm sure you'll make the right choice."

"I think so," she said with a smile. "Don't worry."

Peter opened the door for her and followed her onto the dark landing. He turned around for a last look at the two men watching him, their faces now unguarded. He mumbled, "See you later," and closed the door.

"Gosh, it's dark," her voice said. "Can you see? I'm here, by the banister. You'd better go to the other side, the steps are very narrow here."

"You must have cat's eyes," he said, groping his way along the wall.

She said, "I have."

As they emerged into the blinding sunlight, she took him by the arm. "Let's walk, shall we?"

"But you should have some lunch."

"I'm not hungry. Are you?"

"No, but I think you should eat something."

"I'd like to go back to the harbor," she said.

They walked back the way they had come an hour before; or was it two hours, or three? He had lost all notion of time. The street was hot and noisy. When they turned the corner and entered the narrow alley leading to the harbor, the laundry was still hanging motionlessly in the windless air; when they emerged on the quayside, the trawler had turned with the tide once more, and the Arab in the dark archway had finished his fender. They leaned on the parapet as they had done on the Thames Embankment. He felt a hollow sickness, a wordless despair that made him close his eyes in an effort to escape. Then he heard her ask, "What do you think I should do?"

He opened his eyes and looked at the water and the fishing boats and the small white clouds in the vast blue sky. "I heard the doctor put your choice into words," he said, carefully. "I'd like to hear your own version of it."

"Why?"

"I think that may help you to find the answer." He looked at her and saw her smile and said, "Whatever you decide, I'll help you without reservation."

She said, calmly, "Do you know that you are a wonderful man?"

He put his hand on hers, a quick, shy gesture of tenderness.

"And quite reckless," she added.

He glanced at her; her smile brought a lump to his throat. "Tell me," he asked, "what is it to be?"

"America, of course."

He instantly realized that he should under no circumstances betray his surprise. If this were her choice, she should be allowed the grace of utter certainty. He said, "Of course." His voice was hoarse, he cleared his throat.

Her eyes looked suddenly sad. "Let's go to the hotel," she said. "It's getting rather hot now."

He took her arm and guided her back across the cobbles to the alley and its smells of cooking and poverty. He tried to clear his thoughts of all questions; whatever he did, he must not betray that her answer had taken him unawares. All he must do was what he had done all along: help her to fulfill her destiny, whatever it might be. He tried to chat cheerfully about the shops, the weather and the Arabs as they walked along, but he realized that she was not listening. When they stood at last in the draft of the fan in the hall of the hotel, she said, "Would you mind going and telling the doctor and his friend? I'd like to lie down for a while."

"Of course. Are you sure you're all right? Don't you want to eat anything?"

She smiled a wan smile, moving in its courage, and said, "No, thank you. I'm just a little tired. Don't you stay in the sun too long. We're obviously not used to it."

"I won't," he said. "I'll be right back."

He went back into the sunlight and the heat and the noise; the dustbins that had still not been emptied began to fill the still turgid air with a stench of decay. He went first to the doctor's office; when no one answered the bell he retraced his steps and tried the door of the watch shop. It was closed too and he remembered they were going out to lunch together. They might not be back for hours, to escape the noonday heat. He felt hot and tired, but restless. He should go back to the hotel, but he was not hungry and he could not face the thought of lying on his back on his bed in that stuffy room, staring at the ceiling, a prey to the feeling of despair that threatened to engulf him the moment he let it encroach upon his mind. Yet he had to face it and he did so as he walked aimlessly through the torrid sunlight. Why had he been so sure of her choice? Who was he, to feel that she had made the wrong decision? What was this nonsense, that he should have been so certain the child would choose the nightmare of the trip, the pointless return to the Promised Land where she would only be a burden to her people? Of course to go to America was much more sensible. It was the only reasonable thing to do, and she would certainly, as the doctor had said, be of much more help to future generations if she were to reveal the truth of what the Germans had done to her. And suddenly, as he thought about it, a feeling of hatred swamped him. He stood still on the sidewalk, unseeing, breathless, choked by a hate against the Germans that he had never felt before. His hands hurt as he dug his nails into his palms; he stood there shaking with anger and a blind, raging lust for revenge. Then he slowly relaxed, deflated, as he realized what would happen should he ever get that chance: the same thing that had happened in London. He would turn away at the last moment and let the guilty go.

But what difference would that make? He might turn away, someone else would do it for him. She would; all she need do was to show her scars and she would kill the guilty as surely as if she had pulled the trigger of a gun. Then despair assailed him and urged him on, and made him walk aimlessly under the arches, as that one word repeated itself, senselessly, in his thoughts. It was wrong, wrong, wrong. But why? Why, for God's sake should it be? What was it that gave him this feeling? All that would happen would be that she let herself be photographed and justice would be done and people for generations to come would see with their own eyes where anti-Semitism would lead them in the end.

But would they? Or would the death of the madman who had abused her be the crushing of just another beetle on the senseless road to nothing? When all was said and done, it would only close the vicious circle once more. Revenge would bear the seed of revenge that, given time to grow and mature, would cause another holocaust of murder and horror and despair.

She could have broken that vicious circle. Her choice must be wrong, it must be, for what she had made him feel about the Germans at the thought of what they had done to her she would make others feel, when the truth about her body was projected on the screen in the hushed courtroom at Nuremberg. But why shouldn't she? Who was he to disagree with the highest court of law in the world? He, a policeman?

He turned a corner and found himself in a square that seemed familiar. He looked around and saw Hotel Tarzan. On an impulse, he walked toward it. He might as well tell Van der Pink how matters stood now he was there.

Van der Pink was in. The porter he had seen behind the desk the night before took him up in the elevator and knocked on the door and when a voice called, "Come in," he opened it. The captain was sitting at his desk, which had been partially cleared to make room for a ledger and an old-fashioned inkpot. He looked like an old, benevolent professor. The bed was still unmade, the windows stood open and showed flat roofs, a minaret, the sky. He told the old man in a few words what had happened and as he did so, the burden of despair seemed to lighten until it had almost disappeared. He knew a short moment of relief and certainty, then the old man behind the desk said, "Well, well, that's an unexpected development, isn't it? I'm sorry, because I could have used you. But let me be magnanimous and congratulate you. You are the lucky exception."

"Why?"

"Your chief of police will certainly let bygones be

bygones, now you're not going through with it, and so, I'm sure, will your wife. So you are saved at death's door, one might say. Let it be a lesson to you. Goodbye."

As the old man bent over his ledger once more, Peter suddenly understood everything. He took a deep breath and said, "I'll be back, sir. I'm sorry," and before the other could open his mouth, he left.

He hurried back to the hotel, running more than walking; everything was clear now, he knew why she had done it. He knocked on her door and when there was no answer, he cautiously opened it and found her lying, fully dressed, on her bed. Her leather slippers stood on the rug, the door to her wardrobe was open, revealing her raincoat, her one pair of old shoes with worn heels and her clogs. The sight of those clogs in Tangier made him waver; he turned to sneak out again. Then she opened her eyes and saw him and asked, in a weary voice, "Have you told them?"

"No."

"Why not?"

His certainty had left him, and he answered lamely, "They weren't in."

"Oh," she said and she rubbed her eyes. He saw that beside her, on the bed, lay a little book face downward, open. It was a Hebrew Bible.

"Did you have something to eat?" she asked.

"No."

"But you should."

And then everything he had wanted to say came to nothing as he cried, stupidly, "I can't!"

She closed her eyes and turned her face to the wall and he felt clumsy and stupid, a coward, who by his sheer dithering had done the opposite of what he had come in to do, and he pleaded, "Anna," and as she did not react, "Anna, listen to me."

She turned her head and opened her eyes and asked, "Yes?"

Now he had to say it. Now he had to gather his wits about him, or he would ruin everything for ever. "Are you . . ." he started, and then he plunged. "Are you sure of your motives?"

After a moment of blank amazement, a smile dawned on her face.

"What's so funny?" he asked, bewildered.

"Remember? I asked that same question in the Chinese restaurant, the first night."

"Oh . . . yes," he said, bewildered. He must not let her sidetrack him. He must face her with the fact that he knew the truth now. "What made you ask that question at the time?"

"I thought you were in love with me."

"Well," he said. "There you are."

"What do you mean?"

"Now it's my turn to ask that question."

"Oh."

"Are you?" It had been the right question to ask, but somehow it sounded wrong, the way it came out.

"Of course I am," she said. "You are the only living being in my world. You and Coba."

"I am serious," he said. "You must not think of me when you decide. You must think only of yourself."

"Whatever put that idea in your head?" she asked, lifting her head. Her astonishment looked sincere, and he felt a sickening quiver of doubt.

"Van der Pink did," he said.

"When did you see him?"

He told her how he had walked about and found himself in front of the hotel and gone up to tell the old man. And then he started to lie. "I went to tell him that I would take his offer," he said, "despite the fact that you would not go after all. Because even if I could get my job back, I don't want it any more. That trip on the barge has opened my eyes to what I really want. I want to sail a ship, any ship, I don't care where, I want to live on the water because there I feel at home and at peace with myself, and Van der Pink has offered me a salary that would mean my wife would be better off than she was before. So, you see, your decision makes no difference to my future, only to your own."

"But I would be a burden to everybody," she said. "What good would it do, what purpose would it serve?"

"Don't," he said. "Don't ask for the purpose. Ask for . . . for. . . . You must realize what consequences it would have if you let them use you as evidence in those trials. Do you realize that?"

"Why?" she asked, warily.

"Do you?"

She did not reply. She suddenly seemed to drop a mask, and reveal another face, a person he had never seen before: the true Anna, who had survived everything because of her indestructible core. Now, at last, she showed that core. It was hatred.

He went quite cold, but he urged her on. "Do you?"

She looked at him calmly, implacably, as if he too had changed into another person, and then she answered, "Yes. They would hang him."

He felt as if, suddenly, he emerged into the open. A great, tired peace pervaded him, and he knew that, at last, they were facing the ultimate truth. He went to the door, turned, and said, "You are now facing the same choice I faced. The choice your father faced. I—I cannot tell you why we chose the way we did. All I can tell you. . . ." He tried, but he could not think of any words in which to put it, so he said, "I'll be back," and went to the door.

"But why?" she cried. "Why may I not punish them? Why may I not use the only power I have ever had? What good would it do to anyone, anywhere in the world, if I went on to Palestine and let them get away?"

And then he said, knowing that he was taking on a terrible responsibility, "You would have chosen mercy over revenge. You would carry something to Palestine that would break the curse of violence." He groped about in his thoughts for the word that would convey it all. "Instead of carrying a message of hate to Palestine," he said, "you would be carrying a message of love."

She looked at him with such stupefaction that he suddenly wished he were far away. Somewhere, where he would be alone just with himself, out of harm's way, the the harm he seemed doomed to bring to others. He hurried out, onto the landing, down the stars to the hall where he sat down in one of the deep chairs, his face in his hands.

He was called to the desk by the clerk half an hour later. "The young lady would like a word with you," the clerk said, holding out the telephone.

17

"Hello?" he asked. "Yes?"

"All right," her voice said. "You may go and tell them."

"Ah?" He did not dare to ask what she had chosen; he realized he was supposed to know, but he did not. "Before I do, I—I think we should have a word about it. I mean—shall I come up?"

"No," she said. "Please go, and tell them. I know what they'll say. I know they think I won't be able to stand the voyage. But we'll make out."

"If you think so . . ." he said.

"Yes, I do." Her voice sounded cold. "I'll be seeing you when you get back?"

"Are you sure you . . ."

"Yes," she said. "I know. If you think you can face it, I can."

"All right," he said. "I'm sure we will be all right. I mean—I won't be long."

When he stood on the hot, empty street in front of the hotel, he faced what he had done. He had enticed her into what the doctor had called a Calvary. But he could face it without flinching, for as he walked to the doctor's office he was sure that she had made the right choice. He entered the office building briskly, eager to have it over with.

He found both of them in the dingy waiting room. They sat opposite one another at the little table with the magazines, a Thermos flask between them, and they were drinking coffee from paper cups. They looked up at his entrance in a way that gave him the feeling they had been talking about him.

"Sit down," the doctor said. "Cup of coffee?"

"No, thanks. I have come to tell you her decision. She asks to be excused, she felt a little tired."

"Ah?" The doctor gave him a probing look.

"She does not want to go to America. She wants to go to Palestine, as planned."

For a moment, both men looked at him in astonishment, then Cohen cried, "But why?"

He told them that it had to do with serving as evidence at the trial; the doctor looked at him without sympathy, as if he were aware of his part in her decision. But when finally he spoke he said, "I was afraid of that. She's too far gone to be amenable to reason. You know. . . . But let me ask you something first. Does she talk about love for mankind? And not only mankind, but animals, even objects? If she does, it is a sign that she has entered the schizophrenic stage of the euphoria that precedes the annihilation. I mean, she cannot be taken at her word. It is a symptom of her condition rather than, how shall I say, a spiritual achievement. Am I being too technical?"

"No," he said, "I think I understand what you mean, but this is what she wants."

"But surely something can be done to make her change her mind!" Cohen cried. "We can't let her do this to herself!"

"I doubt whether we can do anything," the doctor replied. "Only a person whom she trusts implicitly could hope to steer her away from self-destruction."

"I am certainly going to try!" Cohen said, with an almost humorous effort to appear masterful. His eyes blazed with virility, but his soft, wet mouth belied it and his unruly hands played leapfrog on his lap, mocking his determination. "You go and tell her!" he said. "She will receive no money, I cannot possibly include her in any of our convoys, nor can I finance her trip with Van der Pink. We will not cooperate in her landing. This means that it will be impossible for her to land."

The doctor sighed irritably. "Don't exaggerate, Steve, she needs our help; obstructing her will only stiffen her determination. People in her condition derive a new stimulus from each obstacle." He turned to Peter and asked, "What gave her this notion of forgiving her enemies? Because that's what it amounts to."

"A religious consideration," he answered, not knowing how else to put it.

"I don't believe it," the doctor said firmly. "It is not Jewish. Our God is not a God of love like yours, he is a God of righteousness."

He looked at the young man, at the nervous face and the alien eyes, and gave himself a few seconds to overcome his anger. Then he said, calmly, "I am no expert on anybody's private God. All I know is that here is a child who, in what you call the euphoria that precedes her annihilation, wants to carry a message of love to the land of her fathers. Any God who would frown upon that dream in righteousness is not a God, but a malevolent monster, the incarnation of all that is evil in those who created Him after their own image." He smiled apologetically and said, "Sorry, that was quite a speech." He was shaking like a leaf.

"You must have misunderstood me," the doctor said quietly. "It was not intended as a criticism of her. I am just trying to understand what drives her to this decision. There must be another motive, for it does not fit in with the conception of God handed down to her by her environment."

"Which environment?" he asked. "The extermination camp?"

The doctor looked at him for a moment; then he said, "There's no need, sir, to be aggressive. I am not censuring her, nor you for that matter. . . ."

"Look, gentlemen," Cohen interrupted, "let's continue this some other time. Right now we should occupy ourselves with the practical question: what can we do to stop her?"

"Not a thing," the doctor said. Then he turned to Peter. "But maybe you can. Have you tried?"

"No," he answered. "I think she should be allowed to do as she thinks right."

"But you don't know what you are letting yourself in for!" the doctor cried. "Believe me, I am not an alarmist; I've seen many patients die in agony and I've never shied away from human suffering; but to care for a dying consumptive, in the conditions you are going to face, would make me throw in the sponge. I am frank with you."

"Why?" he asked. "Why throw terror into me when you know that neither you nor I can change her determination, or rather, could, but may not."

"Why not?" the doctor exclaimed. "Why in the name of humanity may we not spare her being garroted in terror and torture, if we have the scientific means to guide her gently, kindly, painlessly across the border of death?"

"But won't the drugs take care of that?" he asked. "Can't I administer them if it should become necessary?"

"But you—you—you don't understand!" the doctor cried, stammering in a desperate effort to find the words that would convince him. "You have no precedent, no means of knowing what you are talking about with such horrible self-assurance. Those boats they sail on have no sanitation, no proper food, no privacy, let alone the means of regulating the temperature or the degree of moisture in the air or the percentage of oxygen. She needs specialists to determine those delicate quantities, she needs professional nursing day and night, all the amenities only the most advanced hospitals in America can give her. You are talking about her illness as if all she were going to suffer from were a bad cold. How can I get it into your head that she is heading for a purgatory that no sane man can visualize?"

His mind was a blank, he was driven back against the wall of his senseless, dogged determination. "Those—those drugs," he asked. "Won't they help?"

"Certainly," the doctor replied, tired.

"Can I administer them?"

"Certainly."

"How?"

The doctor took a pad out of a pocket underneath his gown and a pen from another. "I'll prescribe two drugs. One of them may only be given in the exact quantities, widely spaced, unless—circumstances should make you decide otherwise. Do I make myself clear?"

"Yes," he said, not understanding.

"I hope I did," the doctor said, and he started to write. Cohen and Peter watched him in silence. He tore off the prescription, held it out, and said, "Take this to the pharmacy a few blocks down to the right. Also get a hypodermic needle with attachments; you can get a small metal traveling kit. Have you ever given an injection?"

"I learned how to do it once. I've never actually had to give one. . . ."

"As long as you know the basic rules, you'll find them on a folder inside the kit. These injections will be sub-cutaneous, so they are given in the rump. As long as you don't hit any nerves or veins, you can't do much harm. The other prescription is for pills. When she gets a coughing fit, she should start taking the pills. When the pills are no longer effective, you must start on the injections. It is there that the quantity and the time lapse prescribed must be adhered to most rigidly, unless—unless you decide otherwise. Good luck."

"Thank you," he said. "Goodbye."

Cohen did not answer, he did not even look up when he opened the door.

He stood a moment motionless in the darkness of the landing, then he went slowly down the stairs. This must be the worst moment of his inner torment; it could not get worse or he would be driven out of his mind. Yet he was unable, even by an act of will, to shake the determination that drove him. To take her to Palestine at whatever the cost was still his irrevocable mission, but only now was he able to visualize what the cost would be. To carry out his mission seemed, at that moment, stripped of all sense and even humanity. The only justification was that, by going, she chose mercy instead of revenge. But what had given him the right to bring about her fateful choice? What was his role in all this? What was it that drove him?

All he could conclude was that, out of millions of well-meaning but ineffectual middle-aged men, fate had appointed him to undo a crime some other middle-aged man had perpetrated on the innocent. The horror of the crying children herded into the fake shower rooms of Auschwitz to be gassed by uniformed henchmen was so unimaginable that perhaps human conception was also incapable of fathoming the purpose of what now seemed an errand of pointless cruelty. Anyhow: whatever he might think, whatever doubts and waves of weakness might assail him, he would take her to Palestine, even if he had to carry her dead body through the surf.

He went to the pharmacy and ordered the drugs and the syringe, which he would have to collect later in the day. When he stood outside, he knew he could not face her yet. A reaction had taken hold of him, he trembled and was damp with sweat. He had to talk to someone, anyone, to clear his mind of this turmoil; talk about anything, anything at all, as long as it was not about her and his responsibility for what lay ahead of her.

Although his funds were getting precariously low, and the price of the drugs and the kit would probably be exorbitant, he took a taxi to the Hotel Tarzan.

When Peter came in, Captain Van der Pink was no longer sitting behind his desk. He now lay on the sofa, feet up, glasses on the end of his nose, his untidy hair sticking up at the crown. The bed was covered with a counterpane that seemed to be made out of cut-up old neckties; the window was still open, showing the minaret, the roofs and the sky; on the desk a space had been cleared for a tray with tea things. He was reading.

18

"Well, what do you know!" he said, looking over his glasses. "I wondered what you meant when you said you'd be back."

"Things have changed," Peter said. "She is not going to America after all."

"Ah?"

"So, I'd like to arrange for her passage with one of your boats, if that's all right with you."

"Of course," the old man said, with wonderfully soothing calmness. "What about some tea?"

"I'd love some."

"Press that bell there, by the door. Sit down, kick off your shoes, take that silly waistcoat off, you look like an anachronism anyhow. Is that the way police inspectors still dress in Amsterdam? They looked exactly the same when I was a boy. Or can't you take it off, because you are wearing a dicky?"

It was a relief to be ragged like this. The old man could not know how he helped him. He rang the bell, took off his coat, his waistcoat, his shoes.

"What about that monstrous tie?" Van der Pink asked. "Why don't you take that off, too?"

"No, thank you," he said. "I'm fine," but he loosened it, and let himself down into one of the chairs with a sigh of relief.

"You can have a cold drink if you like," Van der Pink said, "but I wouldn't advise it. Hot tea, as the Chinese knew five thousand years ago, will keep you cool. What made you change your mind?"

"Plans have been changed. When could we leave?"

"Are the Americans paying her passage?"

"No."

"I put your passage at two trips as a mate of one of my launches. Her passage, of course, is a different thing."

"Why?"

"No need to look at me like that, I'm not a demon. I'm a Dutchman, like you. What would you think of me if I didn't press my advantage?"

"I might think that you had a heart, after all."

"Poof!" the old man cried. "That's a beauty! Listening to you is like walking down the Warmoesstraat in Amsterdam; brothels on one side, mission posts on the other." It had obviously triggered off a memory, for his face changed. "I wonder if the club of 'The Youths of St. Paul' is still there," he mused. "We used to go and beat them up when I was a pupil on the *Pollux*."

"Any particular reason?"

"Just that they were naturals for persecution. They used to stand at the bottom of the gangway on Saturday afternoons and hand out mimeographed invitations to us to come to Jesus at three o'clock, admission one cent. The fact that they charged admission was their saving grace, of course. But it took me fifty years to find that out." There was a knock at the door; he went to open it and let in the surly old porter, who entered carrying a clattering tray. "Damn," he said. "Who told you to bring pastis? It isn't six o'clock yet. When I ring before six, it means tea."

The old porter did not deign to answer. He carried the

tinkling tray to the table and dumped it there. Van der Pink shook his head and sighed; after the door had slammed he said, "As you see, to rule an empire doesn't mean one has authority. I'm afraid it will have to be pastis again."

"Oh, no!" Peter said. "Not this time. I'll have a glass of water, or the rest of your tea."

"All right," Van der Pink said cheerfully. "I'll have to sacrifice myself." He poured a glass, mixed it, dropped in two cubes of ice and said, "Cheers."

Peter watched him drink; his neck was thin and scraggy, the Adam's apple bobbed up and down greedily. As he put back his half-empty glass he smacked his lips and said, "All right, I'll take her to Palestine if you sign a contract for a year as a skipper on one of my launches."

Peter's heart skipped a beat. "Don't talk nonsense," he said.

"You'll have to get used to the idea," Van der Pink replied calmly, "because that's what it's going to be. Look, be sensible. I'm not proposing slavery, or even servitude. I'm proposing to let you sail as a captain without asking for your papers, at a salary with which I could bribe any prime minister in any of the European countries, our own included. Your wife will be able to live it up like a queen, you'll be messing around with boats: if I read you right, you'd do it for nothing, but your salary will be five hundred dollars a month plus, of course, your keep. As you will be selling your dollars in the black market, multiply that amount by five, and you have your guilders. Well?"

"Can I pour myself some tea?"

"Go ahead. You'd like to sail as soon as possible, I suppose?"

"You are jumping to conclusions."

"Of course I am," the old man said peremptorily, "if they are this obvious. If your conscience bothers you, all you need do is rise just a little bit above the backs of the herd, for what is against your conscience is in accordance with somebody else's. Take for instance Captain Ayoob, one of my best. He's an Egyptian; every time he smuggles something for the benefit of the Jews into Palestine, he beats his forehead with his fists; it's against his conscience, for by doing so he betrays his own people; he has sold his soul to the devil and his price was exorbitant. Then there's Captain Nachtgeist, if you want to call him captain; he is a Polish Jew who sails his launch as if he were Lohengrin astride his swan, because he is fulfilling a historical mission. As he sails for nothing, the one balances the other in my books. So you see: in this year of our Lord, on this sea, anything you consider a crime is considered an act of patriotic idealism by someone else, it depends on which side of the fence you find yourself. You won't be on either side, you'll be sitting on it. The only circumstance that justifies your salary is that occasionally you may be shot at, but whether they score a hit is entirely up to you. No one can pull a six-inch gun on you as suddenly as if it were a revolver. You'll see the gunboats train their sights on you in plenty of time to scurry for shelter, for my boats are faster than anything afloat on the Med'."

"What will the cargo be?"

"Why?"

"The other night, you mentioned a bonus."

Van der Pink smiled and said, "Jongman, my boy, you're a true Dutchman. How much do you want for *your* soul?"

"I see no point in bargaining with you," he said. "Tell

me what you had in mind and then let's talk about something else."

"All right. You'll make two trips as mate for nothing; if your work is satisfactory, you'll get your own boat, and your salary will start. If I should get a shipment, I'll let you make a trip with immigrants before I shift you to cargo runs, when your share will be one per cent of the net profits. I'd like to see how you make out on your own before I risk any money on you."

"No financial risk in immigrants, I take it?"

"No. All other cargo is cash and carry, immigrants are paid for in advance." He said it guilelessly, as if it were only a matter of logic.

"Does the human side never bother you?" Peter asked.

"What do you mean?"

"The way you talk about me trying my hand on immigrants before you entrust me with cargo."

"Look, Jongman," the old man said, patiently, "this is a perfect example of muddled thinking. The Jews want to get into Palestine, I take them in at a price that I can justify to any level-headed businessman, considering the risks involved. Now what do you mean by the human side? Do you want me to pay a penalty in money, to prove to God that I value the Jews more than cargo? Is that it?" He looked at him with narrowed eyes, his smile was still there but it had become a little sharper. He began to look as he had the night before: a crafty animal, a fox ogling its game. "Let's get down to brass tacks," he said. "You'll sign the contract?"

"I'd like to think it over."

"Don't be a fool. These are my conditions, and I'm holding the trump card. Be a man and face it. Will you sign the contract?"

He could always change his mind before signing it, so he said. "Yes."

"All right, so we'll take her on. Why won't the Americans pay for her? Because of her physical condition?"

"Yes."

"That means we have to treat her as a special case. Let me think." He got up and wandered with his glass to the open window, where he stood with his back to the room.

"By the way," Peter said, "I forgot to tell you, but I think I am being followed."

"By whom?"

"When we flew down here, an English clergyman boarded the plane in Madrid. We talked; he registered at the same hotel here. I wouldn't have given it a second thought if I hadn't come across him last night when I left you. He was sitting in the hall downstairs reading a newspaper."

"How old is he?"

"Thirty or so."

"Sounds like my friend Dickens," the old man said, amused. "They must have sent him to Madrid to meet you." He laughed. "I should be used to it by now, but it surprises me every time how clumsy those people are. The bureaucracy in the secret service is even worse than in so-called organized crime, which, God knows, is pretty terrible."

"If that is true, it should be easy to shake him."

"I'm not sure that we should. Let me think." He looked at the window again. The minaret had turned pink in the setting sun. Somewhere in the distance a mechanical muezzin began to chant his metallic prayer; a loud-speaker in the minaret opposite took up the chant, a tuneless braying that sounded alien and mechanical, the prayer of an electronic brain.

After the muezzin had finished and Van der Pink could make himself heard again, he said, "We may be able to use that young man. It depends on whether he chose his disguise because he is a frustrated parson at heart, or because he hates the clergy."

"I'm afraid I don't get you."

"Does he know you spotted him?"

"I don't know."

"Has he avoided you since?"

"I haven't seen him, but I haven't been in the hotel much."

"All right. Try and contact him tonight. Have your meal in the dining room of the hotel and see if he turns up. If he doesn't, go to see him."

"Then what?"

"Confide in him. Tell him the situation: that here's a Jewish girl who, after having been used as a guinea pig in an experimental medical camp, wants to return to Palestine with the last strength left to her. If he is a frustrated parson, he'll feel embarrassed that he should be the one to prevent a dying girl from fulfilling her last wish. You might make a deal with him."

"How?"

"Tell him that it would, of course, be the easiest thing in the world to shake him off if we wanted to, but that in this particular case we are appealing to his humanity. That we'll make this a special trip, just for her. No other immigrants. Just you and her and a skipper, probably Ayoob. He's the best."

Peter could not believe his ears. "You mean you are willing to—to transport her alone?"

243

"Indeed."

"But isn't that uneconomical?"

The old man smiled. "Not really," he said. "It will be your trial run, and also, if we want her to be received by the Jewish underground on the beach, we'll have to run in some nominal cargo so they'll be there to pick her up. See what I mean? We won't tell the Jews she'll be landing, we'll announce it as a cargo run."

"What will the cargo be?"

"Oh, anything. Canned fruit, as far as I'm concerned. It's just a device to get the Jews on the beach without giving them a chance to rile about her condition. Does that satisfy you?"

"Yes," he said, uncertainly. "I must say, this comes as a surprise, from you."

"Don't start idealizing me, my boy," Van der Pink said, "All I am doing is making the best out of a bad situation. Now, get along with you. Start plotting."

"I'll see what I can do. I hope your conception of the British secret service is right."

"Don't worry. I know the English. Try for his co-operation first, but be prepared to settle for his negative help."

"How do you mean?"

"That he shall omit to report your departure for Palestine to his superiors. If even that is too much, try and make him accept a phony lead. Say, for instance, that you are leaving tomorrow week, at dawn, with *Le Bien-heureux Monsieur Rostand.*"

"Who is that?"

"That's the name of a trawler I use."

"I see." He put on his shoes, giddy with exhaustion.

"So turn on the sincerity, and keep me posted," the old man said, watching him put on his tie, his waistcoat and his jacket. As he did so, he realized he had not had anything to eat since the plane. "All right, I will," he said. "I . . ."

Outside, the electronic brain began to bawl once more at the top of its metallic lungs. He said goodbye in sign language and left the old man gazing after him with a benevolent, paternal smile.

When he stood outside in the square, it seemed hotter than ever. To the stench of decaying fish and refuse were now

19 added the nauseating smells of Arab cooking. He knew it was extravagant, but he asked the old porter to get him a taxi. He sat waiting for it in the furniture shop, eyes closed, legs stretched out, trying to keep awake. The taxi took a long time; when it finally turned up, darkness was falling outside. It was not a Rolls-Royce this time, but a historic old American limousine with headlamps that must once have been chrome but now were polished brass.

He gave the name of the hotel, leaned back in the cushions that smelled moldy, closed his eyes and it seemed to him as if the present were a dream, from which he was about to awaken. He felt like telling the Arab to drive him to the airport. It was only a moment, then he thought of the girl lying in the hotel, waiting, and he remembered the drugs he was supposed to collect before closing time.

He found the pharmacy still open, and paid off the taxi. His parcel was ready and the price was even more exorbitant than he had expected; next time he saw Van der Pink, he would have to ask for an advance on his salary. On his way to the hotel he realized that the old man had him in his power now; he would have to accept his conditions whether he liked them or not. But he did not care; he was beyond caring. To take her to Palestine was more than his mission now; it was the only positive thing left in his life.

He knocked on the door of her room; when he received no answer he opened it quietly. The room was dark; all he could discern was her vague form on the bed. He tiptoed to the chest of drawers underneath the window and laid the parcel on it. She startled him when she asked, "Where have you been?"

"To see Van der Pink," he answered, casually, "and the doctor."

"Did he give you the medicine?"

"Yes."

"Is that it?"

"Yes."

"Let me have one."

"Have you—have you been coughing?" he asked.

"Just a little. It's nothing."

"But you're not supposed to take these until you really need them . . ."

"Don't worry," she said. "I know what I'm doing. You go downstairs and have something to eat. Please."

He gave her a pill, a glass of water and went to help her as she sat up.

"Do go," she said, "I'm all right, honestly."

He went out, and closed the door quietly. He felt uneasy about the pills as he went down the stairs, although the doctor had warned him only about the injections. He hoped with all his might that they would sail soon.

The dining room did not look inviting. It was a high, dark vault like a chapel, Arab waiters in incongruous tail coats hovered in the gloom like ushers, and one of them came tiptoeing towards him to guide him to his pew. Then he spotted the curate alone at a small table in a corner. He indicated that he would like to join him; the Arab waiter preceded him silently. The curate sat, chewing cheerfully, underneath a big portrait of General Franco, now adorned with the flags of the United Nations since the Spanish had handed back the city to international control. The young man, looking up from an anonymous paper-backed novel, cried, "Hello there! How are you? I say, do sit down."

"Thank you, if I may."

"Rather! I was just thinking of passing up my sweet. It's frightfully gloomy here, isn't it?"

"Yes," he said. "What have you been doing with yourself since last night?"

"Last night?" the religious halfback asked innocently.

"Yes," he said, taking the menu from the waiter's brown hand. "Remember? Hotel Tarzan." Then he concentrated on the menu, while the other cried, "Of course! I say, I had forgotten. So much has happened today, and it's been a regular scorcher, hasn't it?"

The waiter went into a recitation of the day's specialities, but the curate cut him short. "Take the lamb stew," he said. "It's the only possible thing."

"All right," he said. "I'll have that, and some red wine."

"A bottle, sir?"

"No, a carafe will do." Then he looked at the young man opposite and said, "If I hadn't known you, I would have thought last night that you were a special agent."

The young man's face remained blank for a moment, then his eyes turned surprisingly cynical. "I'm sorry about that," he said in a voice that was obviously his normal one. It sounded courteous and yet contemptuous; only the British had the secret of the mixture.

"Don't let it worry you," Peter said. "It's just that I'm an old professional. No one else would have noticed."

"Thank you, sir," the young man said politely. "I'm afraid this may prove a mite embarrassing, but I was instructed to make myself obvious enough for you to spot me."

His smile did not falter. "I see," he said. "Forgive me. Have you any idea why?"

"It was London's idea of subtlety. They obviously assumed that, with your background, just to spot me would be sufficient for you to get the message. A gesture of consideration toward a colleague, one might say."

"The message must be pretty final, to warrant such consideration."

"It is, I'm afraid."

"Let's have it."

"I am detailed to report on all your movements and relay them direct."

"To whom?"

"To Naval Headquarters. I'm sorry."

He smiled. The old detachment, weary and familiar, rallied to sustain him once more, and made it all seem far away and unimportant, happening to someone else, not to him. He tried to remember the boy's name. Charles somebody. "All right, Charles," he said, kindly. "Do you mind if we talk about it?"

"Please do, sir. But I'm afraid the name is Roger."

"Sorry. I thought I remembered . . ."

"Second name's Dickens, sir," the young man said blandly. "It's a common mistake."

The waiter came, bent on his own esoteric business, and took away his knife. When the man had moved out of earshot, he said, "Could you relay a message to London on my behalf?"

"With pleasure," said Dickens, surprised.

"The girl has not been accepted by the American contact because she is dying."

Dickens looked at him stonily and said, "I'm sorry to hear that."

"She has one last wish," he continued. "To go to Palestine. The time to get her there is so short and her case so pathetic that I have been wondering whether we couldn't declare a truce. I am in a position to guarantee that only she will be landed and no one else. It will be what you might call a voyage of mercy. Do you think you could pass this on?"

"Certainly. I doubt, though, that it will do much good."

"Why?"

"Is this an arrangement suggested by Mr. Van der Pink? Don't answer if you don't want to, but I think it might be a good idea to give London as much information as you can."

"All right, it was."

Dickens smiled ruefully. "In that case, you might as well save yourself the trouble," he said. "Mr. Van der Pink has passed the point where any proposals coming from him can be taken into consideration."

"I'm sorry to hear it, but as he is the only one who has offered to help us, I'm afraid I have no choice."

The young man looked musingly into the distance. "Was the word 'mercy' actually used by him? If it was, I would be very careful, if I were you."

"I'm afraid you are being obscure."

"Have you any idea of the conditions in which he transports his occasional immigrants? I mean, not only the accommodation, but the type of vessel, the qualifications of their operators, the prices?"

"I gather the ships are rather small."

"It is the worst case of cynical exploitation I've ever come across. The pirates of the east coast, shipping Negro slaves to Arabia, are organizing Pullman trips in comparison. The word 'mercy' in the mouth of Mr. Van der Pink means, to me, a call to battle stations."

"I think I am in a position to give you some guarantee. You see, he is not doing all this for nothing. I am paying a price, and it's a stiff one."

"All right," Dickens said, after a scrutinizing look. "I'll let them know. But, offhand, I'd say that if they were to consider this at all, it would be on conditions that would exclude any possibility of double-crossing on the side of Mr. Van der Pink. What's more, I think it would be helpful if we could substantiate your diagnosis of her condition. My information is that she is just another illegal immigrant."

"I could take you to see her doctor."

Dickens smiled politely. "I'm afraid London might consider him biased, sir."

"Why? He's a doctor."

"He is also the representative of Haganah in Tangier. I suppose I would do the same in his situation, but should there be any conflict between the Hippocratic Oath and his oath of allegiance to Palestine, there is no doubt as to the outcome."

The waiter arrived with a tray and they watched him in silence as he put the dishes between them. He filled Peter's glass; Dickens put his hand over his.

"Wouldn't you like a glass of wine?"

"Not right now, thank you. Thanks awfully."

The waiter left.

"Has Van der Pink ever met the young lady in question?" Dickens asked.

"No."

"Have you known him in the past? I mean would you consider yourself his friend?"

"No. We have mutual friends, and I am also a Dutch-man."

"I'm afraid that's not enough to warrant any faith in the captain's altruistic motives," the young man replied. "You may have come to expect anything from a human being in the way of cruelty and treason during your years under the Nazi Occupation, but believe me, sir, you have seen nothing yet. The Med' has turned into a jungle, where wild beasts are on the prowl, devouring anything they can lay their claws on, including one an-other. I don't know whether it is the outcome of the war, or what, but I don't think the world has ever seen worse gangsters and more ruthless pirates than you'll find on this sea right now. Human life is worth its weight in flesh. Illegal immigrants are herded, shipped and un-loaded as if they were cattle on the hoof. Any agree-ments, any deals, any promises among the boys them-selves are only their way of weeding out the suckers. So you see why I'm somewhat skeptical, as far as Captain Van der Pink's voyage of mercy is concerned. Why won't you let her go to America?"

"You know about that too, do you?" Peter asked, wearily.

"I'm afraid the communicating doors in this hotel are rather thin."

"Thank you. I'll keep that in mind."

"As our cards are on the table, I don't see why I shouldn't tell you. But you didn't answer my question. Don't, if you don't want to," he added. "Only, it seems to me that you haven't got a chance to get her into Pales-tine. All your moves are watched."

"You don't think London will relent?"

"No. I even think you'd be wise to leave them out of this. You see, the further away people are from this sea, the less they can visualize what's going on. It's only natural, I suppose. They have never seen any immigrants intercepted. They have never heard their wails, or seen old women burst into tears or, well, etcetera. You know the kind of thing. The Navy has, because it's they who do the dirty work."

"Do you suggest we contact the Navy?"

"I suggest you send her to America and go home. I'm sorry if this sounds presumptuous, but believe me, sir, I'm only telling you what I would do, if I were in your shoes and knew all the facts."

"Are you sure you know them?"

"I'm afraid so."

He looked at the young man, who sat there with the courteous self-assurance of a Roman centurion discussing the terms of an armistice with a defeated barbarian chieftain. "Thank you," he said. "You have been most helpful. Now will you have some wine?"

"With pleasure, sir," Dickens said.

Peter filled his glass and his own and, for the rest of the meal, they talked about other things. Any moment, he expected the young man to put the question, "What made you bring her here in the first place?" But he never did. He was not interested in the chieftain's motives, only in his orderly surrender.

When he knocked on her door, later in the evening, he again received no answer. He opened it cautiously and peered inside.

20

The curtains were not drawn, in the reflected light from the street he saw she was lying on the bed exactly as he had left her. He tiptoed to her side, bent over her and saw she was asleep. In the half-light her face looked ageless, a mask. There was no innocence or defenselessness in the mask; it looked like death.

He bent over her with a sudden feeling of horror, and heard her breathing. It came falteringly, almost inaudibly; he wanted to shake her to try and wake her up from this eerie, moonlike sleep in which she seemed to hover on the brink of darkness. There was nothing left around her of the euphoria that preceded annihilation; there was only a chilling sense of dwindling light, a slow sinking back through time, back into the sea from which life had crawled at the dawn of creation.

During the few moments that he stood there in the lucidity of exhaustion, he seemed to discern what lay ahead of them. During the long peaceful hours at the wheel of the barge, he had visualized their arrival in Palestine as a moment of exaltation. It was not going to be like that. He felt as if he stood at the entrance to a dark tunnel of horror, through which he had to carry this dying child to her grave. Already her soul, her consciousness, her love, those gossamer things of which Anna Held was made, seemed blown into space, lost for ever. The body that lay there, the cavernous mask, the faltering breath, had no longer anything to do with the unique, irreplaceable girl who had run through a forest after a tank with a star of David on its side. As he stood looking down on her in the half-light of that room, where death was now an almost tangible presence, he felt as the father must have felt, who went on carrying his son; then she sighed.

It was the hesitant, unconscious sigh of a dreaming child, and it called him back from the brink of darkness, ashamed. He had nearly convinced himself that the sense and the meaning of what he was doing had vanished, that she was almost gone. If he deserted her now, she would indeed lose her identity. He was the last man on earth to know Anna Held; the odd thought struck him that she had handed over her identity to him as she lay there, unconscious, her senses blunted by the brutal blow of the drug. He bent his head and thought, "God of Israel . . ." But he could not go on; even for her sake, he could not go on.

He left the room, closing the door gently behind him. He went into his own room, turned on the lights, sat down at the desk and wrote a letter to Susie on the stationery of the hotel. "Dearest," he wrote, "I have good news. Thanks to a compatriot whose name I was given by a friend, I have found a job that will solve all our financial problems. It will mean, I'm afraid, that I have to stay here a little longer than we anticipated, but on the other hand. . . ." He sat staring at the paper for a while, felt the impulse to tear up the letter and drop onto his bed, but continued, ". . . we have to face the unpleasant fact that we need the money. Please write to me % this hotel and mark the envelope 'To Await Arrival.' Let me know about Betty and Albert and when the wedding will be, so that I may send them a cablegram and a present. There is much to tell but it is late and I want to write you everything at length. You'll be hearing from me again soon. Much love, Peter."

He put the letter in an envelope, addressed it and propped it up against the lamp. Then he undressed, washed, and went to bed.

He was dragged out of the depths of sleep by a persistent knocking on the door. It took some time before he realized where he was, even after he had groped about and pulled the light cord. He called, "Yes?"

The door was opened and there stood Dickens, his boyish hair disheveled, his eyes light with sleep, in a silk dressing gown and Arab slippers. "I'm sorry to call you," he said, "but I think there's something wrong next door."

"Next door?"

"She seems to be in pain, or something. I was woken up by her moaning. I think you'd better go and have a look."

"Yes," he said. "Yes, thank you." He put on his raincoat and his shoes without socks, went out into the passage and opened her door. He was standing with his hand on the knob when he heard her, a faint hopeless cry, like a child calling in the dark.

He went in without turning on the light, leaving the door open. She lay on the bed exactly as he had left her, her body still seemed immobilized by the weight of the drug, but her head moved from side to side on the pillow in agony. She groaned; it was not a call, it was not a human sound at all. He switched on the light beside the bed and put his hand on her forehead, trying to stop the thrashing of her head.

"Anna," he said. "Anna. Wake up. You are all right."

But she was beyond the reach of his voice; she was alone in a world he could not penetrate, a world of fear and pain and darkness. He only realized that Dickens stood beside him when he heard him mutter, "For God's sake. . . ." He looked up and saw him stare at her in horrified pity.

He put his arm under her and lifted her shoulders so that she sat up, leaning against him. It was only a clumsy gesture of protection, for he did not know what else to do, but somehow it seemed to penetrate to her that she was no longer alone. She rested her head against his chest and sighed and mumbled something that he could not catch. But the thrashing of her head stopped and she no longer moaned. She just sat leaning against him, asleep.

They sat like that for a long time. When, finally, he lowered her gently back onto the pillow and took his arm from under her, he saw Dickens sitting in the chair, staring at him with eyes that were no longer those of a young centurion. "I think she'll be all right now," he whispered. "I'll open the communicating door so I can hear her."

They tiptoed out of the room; when they stood in the corridor the young man said, "I never thought I would see one of them alive. It's hallucinating."

"One of whom?" he asked, tiredly.

"I was with the first troops to get to Belsen, and I saw the stacks of emaciated corpses," Dickens said. "She looks as if one of them had got up and walked away."

"It's the drugs," he said. "I've never seen her like this. Once she wakes up, you'll see she's quite different."

Dickens stared at him, still under the spell of what he had seen. His eyes seemed young. "I'm sorry if I sounded skeptical last night at table," he said. "I had no idea. I see now why . . ."

"Yes?" he asked, when the other faltered.

"This is indeed a case for mercy. I'll take it up with Malta direct. See you in the morning." Then he turned away and vanished into his room.

He was about to go back into his own when he realized that, in order to open their communicating door, he should unlock it on her side first. He went back into her room, but instead of unlocking the door he stood once more beside her bed. She seemed at peace now, her breath came softly and regularly. He wondered whether it had only been her sitting up and resting against him that had alleviated her pain; she had seemed conscious of his presence. Or maybe just somebody's presence. It did not matter, as long as she had felt that she was not alone.

The dark tunnel ahead of them had not changed, but he was no longer afraid. He settled in the chair and stretched his legs and closed his eyes; this was where he would sleep from now on, every night, until they left.

As the first light of dawn rose over the domes and the spires of the city he dozed off, a haggard man in a raincoat over rumpled pajamas, shoes with dangling laces on his bare feet. Then the muezzin started to call the faithful with his reverberating bugle call, and he woke up to the miracle of her smile.

She sat watching him, her eyes twinkling, and as she saw his gaze focus on her, she said, "Wow! For a moment I thought you were going to win the contest with that loud-speaker!"

"Huh?" he asked, hoarsely.

"Isn't your throat terribly sore after snoring like that?"

"Oh," he said. "I . . . I'm sorry. How do you feel?"

"Fine. My headache is completely gone. Why are you sitting there?"

"I? Oh—I just wanted to make sure that I was at hand in case you needed me."

"That was very sweet of you," she said. "But you

needn't have done it. That pill I took last night made all the difference."

"Oh?" he said. "That . . . I'm glad to hear it."

"Do you think we could have some breakfast?"

"Yes." He got up. "Yes," and he went to pick up the telephone.

As he stood with his back to her, waiting for the porter to answer, he closed his eyes in a wordless prayer of gratitude to God, whatever and wherever He might be.

"Well?" Van der Pink asked. "How did you make out with our friend Dickens last night?" The old man sat behind his desk; a space had been cleared among the books, the ledgers and the letters for a breakfast tray. He looked spry and full of vitality; to see him sitting there made the morning seem hotter.

21

Peter told him about Dickens.

"H'm." The old man finished his egg, thoughtfully. He looked more like a fox than ever as he drank the rest of his egg from its shell, his head back; then he wiped his lips and his whiskers and said, "Experience has taught me not to rely on midnight humanism. When he comes to take up contact with Malta this morning, I can't see him pleading the case of a dying girl to his opposite number, sporting a set of headphones. No, it won't do."

"I think he was sincere."

"Of course he was." Van der Pink put the empty egg shell upside down in the egg cup, like a child wanting to fool his nanny. "But just because *you* made an unrealistic decision as a victim of your conscience, you mustn't expect him to go through a conversion like that. You are an exception, my friend. Given a good lawyer, your family could easily have you committed. No, no. We must help Mr. Dickens to do the human thing by making it carry a bonus. Let me think." He rolled up a napkin which looked extremely dirty, and put it in a ring. Then he got up, showering crumbs off his lap, and went to the window, one of his trouser legs halfway up his calf again.

"While you are thinking," Peter said to his back, "you must take into account that her condition is getting worse. We should not wait any longer than is strictly necessary."

"You mean she might die on us?"

"Yes," he said, flatly.

"We can't have that." The old man came back into the room, his mind made up. "All right, here is what we'll do. You two will leave tonight with the trawler, under Captain Ayoob. She's slow, but it's all I have available at the moment. You'll have to pick up your cargo somewhere on the way. I think I'll let you have an odd lot of K rations that I have sitting around in a warehouse in Brindisi; I've been trying to fit it in with another shipment for some time. But what can we do to make sure that the British will let you through the Palestine blockade? There must be a way to make them cooperate."

"Is their blockade very effective?"

The old man was not listening. "There's only one solution," he said, after a short, tense silence. "They will let you through if they are convinced that you are not bringing something in, but taking something out. If we could make Mr. Dickens conclude that I am using the girl as a decoy to take a leader of Haganah out of Palestine for a secret conference, our bed would be made. Perhaps it's better not to be too precise. Perhaps all we should let him conclude is that we are going to take something or somebody out. He must be led to believe that he sees through my game."

"How are you going to do that without making him suspect anything?"

Captain Van der Pink smiled, and his eyes became benevolent and paternal once more. "You are," he said. "You are going to put that flea in his ear, because you have the most priceless asset in any business: sincerity."

"I don't think I'll have it in this instance."

"Oh yes, you will, because it's the only way to make sure the girl reaches her destination."

Peter looked at the old man for a moment without

speaking. "All right, sir," he said, getting up. "I suppose all that's left for me to do is to thank you."

"Not quite," the old man said with a smile. "There is the little matter of our contract. Let me see; I put it here somewhere." He started to rummage among the chaos on his desk and finally brought out a paper from underneath a stack of magazines.

"Read this at your ease," he said. "There is no small print, but you might like to change something. Here, by the way, is a month's salary in advance." He handed him an envelope from his coat pocket.

The contract was a simple letter in which the conditions of one year's service as a skipper on one of the company's launches in the Mediterranean at five hundred dollars a month were stipulated in return for one passage to Palestine. The only new item was the name of the company: "Charity A.G." of Zurich, Switzerland. After glancing through it, Peter signed it with the old man's pen. "Just as a matter of curiosity," he said, "suppose you were to break this agreement, what redress would I have?"

The old man grinned and patted his shoulder and said, "What you really mean is: what would happen to you if you walked out on me?"

"What would happen?"

"You'd be shot."

Peter laughed and said, "I see." Only as he walked through the alleys on his way back to the hotel did it occur to him that Van der Pink had meant what he said.

When he arrived at the hotel, the clerk told him that
Miss Held had just come in and gone upstairs. He found
her in her room, lying on her bed, tired but cheerful. "Where have you been?" he asked.

22

"I went to buy a summer dress," she said.

"You did what?"

"I had to. You men can take your coats off, but we
are condemned to swelter or put something else on."

"Nonsense," he said, and when she looked astonished,
he added, "Come on. Tell me the truth."

"Oh, all right," she said, trying to sound offhand, but
she was obviously delighted. "I didn't really need it, I
just felt like doing something silly. When we walked back
from the doctor yesterday, I saw a dress in a shop window that I liked. Would you like to see it?"

"I'd love to."

As she unwrapped the box and opened it he wondered
whether he would ever understand a woman. There she
had been, leaving the doctor's office like a prisoner walking out of the courtroom after being condemned to
death, and while he had gently guided her along the
street, overcome with sorrow and commiseration, she
had, out of the corner of her eye, spotted a summer
dress in a shop window. It was like her laughter when
he told her that Thorens was a white-slave trader who
had intended to ship her to South America.

"Like it?" she asked, holding up a white-and-yellow-
striped dress in front of her. It looked very simple. For
some reason, he had expected something with a lot of
bows.

"Looks all right to me," he said; at the look of disap-
pointment on her face he added hurriedly, "Put it on and
let me see it properly."

"All right," she said. "Turn around."

He turned around and looked at the chest of drawers beside the window and the other parcel, hastily opened: the drugs and the syringe. When she said, "All right, you may look now," he turned, stared, clasped his hands in admiration and said, "Wonderful! I didn't realize it would look like this on you. Let me see the back."

She turned around; the price tag dangled on her back; below the skirt that was too long were the slippers they had bought in Loozen.

"I think you look adorable," he said. "Where did you get the money?"

"That's the thing," she said guiltily. "They are on approval. I thought I would ask you to advance me the price of the one you like best."

"You have another one?" he asked, managing to end the phrase on a tone of pleasant surprise.

"Yes," she said. "Like to see it too?"

"Put it on," he answered. "I can't judge it properly if you just hold it up."

He turned around once more and looked at the window. Her waking up this morning looking so mischievous, her going out to buy these dresses with her last strength might be part of the same thing: her desire to make it as easy as possible for both of them. Perhaps not even a conscious desire; perhaps she really had no memory of what had happened last night. But she too must be conscious of the encroaching darkness; he should help her by realizing her every whim.

"Yes, you can look now," she said.

He turned around. It was a good thing he was not color-blind, for it was exactly the same dress, only the stripes were green and white.

"Show me the back," he said, "slowly."

She turned around like a fashion model and he said, "I'd keep both."

She looked startled. "Both of them?"

"Yes. I think they are so flattering, I mean adorable, that I wouldn't know which one to choose. And I just received quite a lot of money, so . . ."

She threw her arms around his neck and kissed him on both cheeks. He patted her awkwardly on her back, and felt the price tag.

"Which one shall I wear first?" she asked.

"You want to go out?"

"I must. I must pay for them."

"I'd say, the yellow one. But don't you think we should have lunch first?"

"What's the time?"

"Half-past twelve. The shops are probably closed until four o'clock. They all are here, I think."

"Oh."

"I'll tell you what. I'll go downstairs and wait for you in the dining room. I want to have a word with our clergyman friend anyhow. Maybe he is there."

"All right," she said. "I'll change quickly. Is the length all right?"

"Yes, I think so. Ask the shop what the latest fashion is, I may have lost touch."

As he went downstairs he remembered buying a dress for Betty when she was eleven years old. He had gone to fetch her from school; the wet streets had mirrored the light from the shop windows, decorated with strings of colored lamps because it was Christmas time. She had stood still, open-mouthed with admiration, in front of a window full of mannequins in evening dresses, holding sequined purses with long white gloves, standing on cotton wool and with snow in their hair. He had been so moved by the child in the rain, pressing her hands against the window and gaping at those lovely ladies, that he had taken her inside and they had asked to see some party dresses. It had been heartbreaking to watch her try them on, one more florid and satiny than the other; in the end he had bought one that had made him laugh with tears in his eyes; she looked like a fairy princess, wearing galoshes. They had carried their treasure home, feverish with excitement, but Susie had not shared their rapture. The child did not need a party dress, when on earth was she going to wear it? Susie had changed it the next day for a sensible winter coat and made him promise not to buy any clothes for the child without her in the future. Maybe that was why he had expected Anna's dress to be full of bows.

"*Déjeuner?*" the Arab headwaiter asked. He saw Dickens sitting at the same table as the previous evening. "I'd like to join the gentleman over there," he said, "but I am expecting a young lady. Will there be room for the three of us at his table?"

"Sure, sure," the headwaiter said with an incongruous American drawl. "We can always add a unit."

Dickens smiled as he reached the table, but he did not look as if he had good news. "I'm afraid we haven't much time to talk right now," Peter said as he sat down. "Anna is joining us in a moment, if that's all right with you."

"Oh, rather," Dickens said, astonished. "Is she about?"

"She has even been out and bought herself a couple of dresses."

Dickens' mouth fell open, then he said, "Remarkable."

"We are leaving tonight, by trawler."

"Trawler?"

"That's what Van der Pink said. The *Bienheureux Monsieur Something.*"

Dickens frowned.

"You know the vessel?"

"Yes. Have you any idea what else he is taking?"

"You mean cargo?"

"Yes."

"Nothing, as far as I know."

"How big a crew?"

"Just me and an Egyptian captain. Ayoob, I believe."

"I don't get it," Dickens said, as if to himself.

"Why? Anything wrong?"

"The *Rostand* is the slowest ship in his collection. It'll take you a fortnight to get to Palestine."

"He says there is no other boat available right now."

"H'm. In that case he must be doing a lot of business just now; he has a fleet of six M.T.B.'s, twenty-five knots, based in Spain. It would take one of them just a few days."

"Well, I'm only telling you what he told me. Did you get a chance to speak to Malta yet?"

Dickens looked shifty and Peter knew that Van der Pink had been right. "I'm sorry, but I'm afraid, on second thoughts, that it will be impossible to make the Navy agree to let her through. I have some good friends in Malta who are as little hidebound by rules and regulations as I am, but no matter how much we want to co-operate with you, there is no solution."

"Solution to what?"

"When the Navy stops your trawler, as they are certain to do the moment she enters Palestine waters, they will find an illegal immigrant on board. She may be in a critical condition and every man Jack among them will want to help her as much as he can, but the fact remains she is an illegal immigrant; there is no official ruling that allows them to make an exception. She will be interned, like the rest of them, in Cyprus."

"I see."

"Believe me, I have been racking my brains all night,

trying to find a means of inducing the Navy to let her through. But I have been unable to come up with anything. It's impossible, I'm afraid."

He tried to make it sound innocuous when he muttered, "Captain Van der Pink said something that made me think." He looked up and saw Dickens stare at him, his eyes very British indeed. "Did he?" he asked, then he beckoned the waiter.

They ordered a drink; when the man had gone, Dickens said, "Well, let's have it. What did he say?"

"Nothing in particular, but somehow the thought struck me that, as well as taking someone in, we might be taking something out."

"What?"

"I have no idea. But it must be something important. Or someone, perhaps. I don't know, but, like you, I can't quite believe Van der Pink to be as altruistic as all that. This would make sense to me."

Dickens looked at him for a long time without expression, then he said, calmly, "Indeed."

"Of course, it's just an idea of mine . . ."

Dickens silenced him by lifting his hand. "Let me think." He thought, as old Van der Pink had thought that morning, gazing into space. They were like chess players, absorbed in a game in which Anna was but a pawn. He felt the unreasonable urge to get up and leave the young man to indulge in his game alone. He felt like picking her up in his arms and starting to walk along the shore of the Mediterranean, until he found someone with a boat who had the simple charity of a decent man, as everyone had had before the German madness poisoned the soul of Europe.

"Right," Dickens said. "I'll take the chance. I shall advise Malta that the trawler may be going to fetch someone; if they think as I do, they'll let her through and intercept her on her return. Yes," he added, after a moment's reflection, "they will. But there is a possibility that Captain Van der Pink may be planning to take something in as well, besides her. If that cargo is not on board when you sail, you may be going to pick it up somewhere on the way. If Malta decides to let you through, they'll want to make sure they are not being hoodwinked. They will keep you under observation twenty-four hours a day."

Peter shrugged his shoulders. "What of it?"

"If you are observed taking on cargo, you will be stopped at the three-mile limit," Dickens said, "and she'll be arrested as an illegal immigrant."

"Well, that's a gamble I am prepared to take. All we can do is wait and see."

"Indeed," said Dickens.

The waiter arrived with their drinks and they raised their glasses to one another and said, "Cheers."

She came down a few minutes later. She wore the yellow-striped dress and had pinned up her hair. As she came toward them, guided by the effusive headwaiter, she looked charming; but when she sat down at their table, they saw she looked ill. Make-up could not hide the dark rings under her eyes, the waxiness of her complexion; there was something in her movements that made Peter realize she was under a great strain. While she listened, smiling, to Dickens being entertaining, he noticed small beads of perspiration appear on her upper lip and on her forehead; her hand trembled as it crumbled a piece of bread while she listened. She must be running a temperature.

He wondered whether Dickens noticed; but if he did he did not betray it. He told them long, involved stories about his wartime experiences, which seemed to have been exclusively humorous; she seemed to enjoy it at first, but soon her cheeks became flushed and her eyes feverish, she laughed more and more at jokes that became less and less funny, in the end Dickens realized that he should try to calm her down rather than animate her any further. He started on a rambling survey of the history of the Church of England.

It seemed as if the end of the meal would never come. She ate very little; it became obvious that she should not have come down at all. But Peter did not know how to interrupt and take her upstairs, without forcing them all to face the truth about her condition. At last he saw a chance; Dickens mercifully turned down his dessert, so Peter could say, "I am sorry, old man, I don't want to rush you, but I must see to some business before we leave. Could you tell me what time the bank closes?"

Dickens said it closed at two o'clock, so he had better hurry; as they stood up he added, "I'll be around later, to give you a hand with your luggage."

"That's very kind of you," Peter replied, "but don't bother. We haven't got much."

"All right," Dickens said pleasantly. "In that case, *bon voyage;* I hope we'll meet again."

She managed to go on behaving as if nothing were the matter. When they reached her room she said, "Does this mean that we are leaving already?"

"Yes," he said. "But not before tonight, so why don't you lie down for a while?"

"All right, I think I'll do that. Thank you for a lovely meal." She opened her door, then she suddenly turned around and said, "Oh, heavens, I forgot! I have to pay for the dresses."

"I'll do that. Just give me the address."

"It's the little shop on the left, a few houses down the street. But, honestly, don't you think you should take one back?"

Her face looked so strained and anxious now that he felt like picking her up in his arms and carrying her to her bed. "Certainly not," he said. "I want you to keep them both."

"All right," she said, and she managed a smile. "Give me a call when you come back."

She closed the door behind her. He listened at the crack, ready to follow her if she needed help. He heard her start coughing, then the tap ran, the bed creaked, and everything fell silent. He wondered whether he should stay within call, but there seemed to be nothing he could do. The best he could do for her right now was to leave her alone.

At the desk he asked for a local newspaper to look up the tides. The pallid clerk, seeing him scan the pages, said, "Low at ten twenty tonight, at the breakwater."

He said, "Thank you." So the clerk knew the tides by heart! He must be somebody's secret agent too.

As he walked along the shady side of the street toward the bank, he remembered the dress shop only after he had passed it. The bank was about to close, so he continued on his way. He sent four hundred and fifty of his five hundred dollars to Susie, went back to the shop and paid for the dresses; back in the hotel he paid their bill. It left him with four dollars fifteen, barely enough for tips; but he had planned it that way. He wanted no part of that money; it was his only feeble defense against the encroaching notion that he had signed on as a pirate.

23

Le Bienheureux Monsieur Rostand, the little windows of her wheelhouse aflame with the reflected sunset, could only be reached by rowboat. An Arab fisherman took them there, after they had been deposited on the quayside with their luggage by a taxi.

As they were slowly rowed toward the ship across the oily water, Peter felt as if this had happened to him before. For a few moments he seemed to personify all the young mates who had ever been rowed toward their new vessel at the beginning of a long voyage and tried to size her up as they glided toward her.

The trawler was the derelict he had seen from the quayside during the day. Her white hull, streaked with rust from her chain plates, was topped by a poky wheelhouse, the roof of which followed the sheer of her deck in an attempt to lend grace to her lines. She carried one steel mast with two derricks, painted black, from which dangled some shrimping gear: a torn net and a heavy wooden board, sea anchor for her trawl. That morning Peter had watched her as part of the seascape of the harbor; now the sight of her made his heart sink. She would roll like the devil, with that high iron gear aloft; as he saw the peeling paint, the dry rot in her rails, the spots in her planking roughly nailed over with tin and tarred paper, he knew what her quarters would look like.

He climbed on board ahead of Anna and cast a look inside the dark wheelhouse. It smelled of bilges, rotting wood and mildew. Behind it was a cabin with two bunks, one above the other; from one of them dangled a dirty sheet. Behind the cabin was a galley: rusty stove, cracked sink, on the wall a calendar with a lascivious nude, compliments of Francesco Albertini, Commissionario di Bordo, Bari, Italia. The stench was sickening.

He thought of calling the whole thing off and sending

her back to the hotel, while he went to ask Van der Pink what the hell he meant, sending a dying girl on a two-thousand-mile voyage in this foul-smelling wreck, without privacy or sanitation, with only two bunks in one pigsty of a cabin for three people. But he realized that, if it would not mean canceling their trip altogether, it would certainly postpone their departure for days; and after last night he knew that every day counted.

If there were indeed a God of David Who turned darkness into light for His chosen children, here was His chance. Here was the blackest darkness they had faced together so far. He went to the rail and looked down; she sat patiently in the rowboat in her new dress, the box with the other on her lap, her small suitcase beside her with her shabby coat over it and, beside the suitcase, her wooden shoes. The Arab fisherman looked up at him, showing a gap in his teeth as he opened his mouth greedily like a baby bird feeding.

"Anna?"

She looked up.

"Let me help you on board."

She wanted to pick up her belongings but he said, "Leave them. The man will hand them up to me." He stretched out his hand to pull her up, but she gave him the box with the new dress instead; she obviously did not trust the Arab with it. He took it, and put it gingerly inside the rail, then he pulled her up while the Arab leered. When she stood on deck, he called down, "All right, there. Give me the rest."

The Arab woke up from his obscene reverie and scrambled over the seats of his boat to grab her suitcase and her coat. When he picked up her wooden shoes he gaped at them and got lost in dreamland once more; it took a sharp word to wake him up and make him hand them over, reluctantly. There followed an almost Biblical scene of haggling over the price; the Oriental histrionics of the Arab as he expressed his indignation would have been fascinating under other circumstances. Now Peter was conscious of the girl behind him, in her new dress that was too long, holding on to the box she cherished, staring at the black hole where she was supposed to live the last weeks of her life. In the end he threw some more coins into the boat and turned away, leaving the Arab wailing as if he were burying a relative.

She was not behind him. He hurried into the wheelhouse; she was not there. He found her in the cabin, standing in the gloom, exactly as he had known she would be standing, holding the box with her new dress, looking around incredulously. Now he saw her, his compassion turned into rage. He felt like taking Van der Pink by his scraggy neck and slamming his vile old head against the wall.

"Smell them?" she asked, in a whisper.

He stared at her in bewilderment. "What?"

"People. Dozens of them must have slept here."

"How do you know?"

"The boxcars smelled like this. Do you think they were Jews?"

"I—I suppose so," he said; then she cried, "Look!" and pointed at the inside of the door. Her thin marked hand touched the grimy panel, and he saw a small, lopsided star of David drawn on it in pencil. "So they *did* get there," she said, awe-struck. "Now I believe it."

He realized that the stench that had driven him to despair had finally convinced her that she was indeed on her way to the Promised Land. He did not know what to say; he just stood there and looked at her.

"You know," she said, "ever since yesterday, when I said I would not go to America, I have been afraid."

"You aren't, any longer?" he asked.

She looked around the cabin and said, "No." Then the cabin darkened. Peter looked around and saw the silhouette of a huge man standing in the doorway.

"I am Captain Ayoob," a voice said, soft and melancholy. "Are you the passengers for Palestine?"

She answered, "Yes."

The man in the sunset was an Arabian giant with dark, velvet eyes and a huge hooked nose over a mouth that was almost feminine in its gentleness. His shirt and trousers were filthy and he smelled of diesel oil. On his head he wore a grimy cloth cap, on the front of which was printed "Peabody's Paints."

"I am Peter Jongman. How do you do? This is Miss Held."

The Arab bowed and shook Peter's hand gingerly. Then he said, "Honored," and "Welcome," and "Shall I show you the ship while the lady makes herself at home?"

"In here?" he asked.

"Yes. It is the only cabin."

"Where are you and I supposed to sleep?"

"In the wheelhouse, no?" Captain Ayoob looked at him shyly, as if it were a daring suggestion.

"You can't get two beds into that wheelhouse."

"But don't we need only one?" the Arab asked, a huge hand over his right breast. "One of us will be at wheel while the other sleeps. Could we not put paliasse down there?"

"Paliasse? Oh, I see. Yes, I suppose we could."

"I will be very happy to sleep there," the Arab said with conviction, "but if you have another suggestion. . . ."

"No," he said. "Anything, as long as Miss Held is comfortable. You know she is ill?"

The Arab bowed in reply.

"What kind of food have we on board?"

"It is not here yet, but will come."

"Who is going to do the cooking?"

"We will, ourselves. But most of it is cans," he added hastily, seeing the dismay on Peter's face. "Nice cans. Let me show you engine room."

Peter followed him through a narrow hatch, down a Jacob's ladder, into a poky hold where he could not stand upright. The Arab turned a switch; a light went on over an old-fashioned diesel engine with a big flywheel. "I will have to tell you about engine before we leave," the Arab said earnestly. "Afterwards there will be no chance, until we break down."

"Are we likely to?" he asked.

Captain Ayoob gave the matter courteous consideration, then he answered, "I do not think so. I have sailed with this engine many miles. She has often—how do you say—made faces of stopping, but she never did. She will, sometimes, make stopping noises. You understand?"

"I think so," Peter said. "What's through there?" He nodded toward a narrow door in the bulkhead.

"The holds," the Arab said. "Place for cargo." He opened the door and squeezed through. Peter followed him; when he emerged on the other side his stomach turned at the stench. The Arab fumbled in the darkness and turned another switch; a naked electric bulb at the ceiling revealed a small hold, smaller than Peter had expected. They stood for a moment side by side, mutely, both overcome by an odd feeling of shame. Then Peter asked, "Jews?"

"Yes," the Arab said.

"How often?"

"On this ship, under my command, two times."

"How many at a time?"

"Five hundred."

"What?" he cried in horror. "How, for God's sake?"

"Oh, standing up," the Arab replied, shyly, "close together. Also on the decks. But do not pity them. They have their God."

"I see," he said grimly.

"I mean it," the Arab continued in his soft melodious voice, "You will see. She is very sick, no? You will see: Palestine." He stretched out his huge hands in a weird gesture of blessing and praise, while his face took on an expression of rapture. "Palestine!" he repeated. Then he lowered his hands. "To them, it is land of God. When they come to that land, they are like wave of the sea. No one can stop them. You stand there, your hands high, crying, 'Slow! Slow! Easy! Please!' But they flow, unseeing, like water; and when they have washed past, you are left with envy. They possess nothing, nothing at all, no money, no health, no youth, nothing. But they have God. Now I show you steering gear."

He vanished in the darkness and Peter followed him, stooping under the low beams of the deck. "This bearing must be greased every watch," the gentle voice said in the darkness. "It is the gland, if you forget it starts to make noises. Who is that?"

He wondered what the man was talking about, then he listened with him and discerned the sound of oars, followed by a bump and a scraping against the hull.

"Must be the food," the Arab said. "Excuse," and he went ahead, back to the deck.

It was Dickens, with a small bunch of flowers in his hand. "Oh, hello there," he drawled. "I thought I'd drop by to say adieu. Where is our girl?"

"In there," Peter answered, pointing.

"Mind if I pop these in to her?"

"By all means. She'll be delighted."

Dickens tripped toward the doorway of the wheel-house like a suitor; Peter went to the rail and looked overboard. There was no boat; the longshoreman who had brought Dickens was on his way back to the quay. So he intended to stay until they left; he was not taking any chances.

When Dickens came back from the wheelhouse, with-out the flowers, his face was grim. "Would you mind if I had a look at the rest?" he asked with restraint.

"By all means," Peter said, "unless Captain Ayoob objects. Do you two know each other?"

The Arab bowed; Dickens said, "I'm afraid we don't. My name is Dickens." He did not hold out his hand. "May I take a look around?"

Captain Ayoob made a gesture that seemed to include not only the ship but the harbor and the sky. "It is yours," he said in his polite, gentle voice.

"Thank you." Dickens turned away; when he had van-ished through the engine-room hatch, Ayoob asked, "British agent?"

Peter nodded.

"I thought so," the Arab said, musingly. "I was told to expect such a man. He will stay until we leave?"

"I don't know. Any reason why he should not?"

"No, no," Ayoob protested hastily, as if a doubt had been thrown on his hospitality. "He most welcome. I hope food will arrive soon so we may offer him some tea."

Dickens came back a few minutes later, his face frozen into a cold fury.

"Seen the holds?" Peter asked.

"I dare say," Dickens said. "Perhaps now you under-stand why I don't like your Mr. Van der Pink. He incarnates all that is loathsome, diseased and debased in civilized man. For that poisonous toad, Christ has been crucified in vain."

It was the most vehement speech Peter had ever heard made by an Englishman. "Yes," he agreed. "It's quite a sight."

"Unforgettable, one might say," Dickens drawled, and lit a cigarette. "Well—I suppose he has his role in the drama of the Wandering Jew, considering that he brings them home." He flicked his lighter shut; then he added wryly, "I suppose now you are wondering where we fit in?" He did not wait for an answer.

He stayed on board until the last minute. The food was delivered, a boatload of tins and boxes; he scrutinized each item as it was handed up. He seemed reluctant to accept the fact that there was no other cargo; as the hour of their departure drew near, he was obviously nonplussed.

Peter had changed into the overalls he had worn on board the barge and gone down into the engine room with Ayoob. As they leaned on the engine in the semidarkness and the melancholy Arab explained how to grease the bearings while the engine was running, he felt overcome with a bewildering relief. He realized that despite the fateful purpose of their voyage he was happy to be on board a ship again, and he felt a juvenile friendship for the big Arab as he described the warning noises that might be heard, lifting a huge brown finger, pursing his lips and squealing like a dog when someone stepped on its tail. "If you hear that, collar has slipped out of groove. Is not important, cannot do harm, only if not put back it puts bilge pump out of operation. Also if you hear like this . . ." a sound like a clucking hen, "from there . . ." he pointed, "then knock this little lever back at once, it controls oiling of main bearing and the clicking means it slipped off sprocket."

When they came back on deck, Dickens was leaning in the doorway of the wheelhouse, chatting with Anna who was inside, at the same time watching the harbor and the quayside with unflagging alertness.

An hour later Ayoob started the engine. Darkness had fallen, and no one had turned up to substantiate Dickens' suspicions, not even Van der Pink, although Peter had expected him to see them off.

"Well, sir," Ayoob said, "I regret but it is our time to leave. Shall I whistle a boat for you?"

"Yes, I suppose so. Thank you," Dickens said reluctantly.

The Arab produced a whistle and blew it; from the darkness came a wail of acknowledgment and the rumbling of oars as a longshoreman leaped into his boat. When the silhouette of the rowboat detached itself from the night, Dickens turned to Peter and held out his hand. "Well, God bless," he said. "Best of luck. I'll go and tell Gib' you have left." He went to the rail and added, "Say goodbye to her for me, will you, old man? I'm afraid my chatter has been a mite soporific."

"I beg your pardon?"

"She's asleep." At that, he swung his legs over the edge and lowered himself down. The boat, after a few strokes of the oars, vanished in the night.

"All right," Ayoob called from the wheelhouse. "Let's bring anchor up, please. Just pull lever of winch until she's home."

Peter went to the foredeck, and found that Ayoob had already started the engine of the anchor winch for him, all he had to do was to engage the gear. As the anchor chain started to come in, clicking in the sheaf, the ship slowly swung around against the lights on the quayside and the stars. After the anchor had risen out of the water, dripping, draped with weeds, he stopped the gear and signaled to the wheelhouse that they were free. The exhaust behind the roof spewed sparks and black smoke as Ayoob revved up the engine, the old hull trembled and shook, they started to glide toward the breakwater, slowly gathering speed.

Then the sea opened out in front of them, glinting mysteriously in the darkness. As they nosed into the open it was as if they entered a realm of peace and majesty. Their identity seemed to fade away; in the light of those same stars, the Phoenicians, the Romans, the Moors and the Crusaders had left this same harbor. As their lonely hull started to heave and roll with the first swell of the sea, he thought of Susie and was overcome with the sudden yearning to share this with her, to go on a sea voyage together, to look at Italy and Greece and Turkey and the Orient, to do all the things she must have dreamed of when she sailed home from the Far East, a girl dreaming of romance underneath the stars. And then there had appeared the dashing young man on the foredeck of the little patrol boat in the harbor of Amsterdam.

He stood on the foredeck as he had once stood on the little patrol boat, and what had happened between seemed a dream, a restless sleep of hibernation. He forgot that soon he would be an old man and his life would be over; during those few moments of eternity, as *Le Bienheureux Monsieur Rostand* set course for Gibraltar, he was immortal once more, and the future shimmered like a mirage of happiness and fulfillment among the stars. Then, suddenly, he realized he was no longer alone.

He looked around and saw Anna standing behind him, dark against the stars.

"Oh, hello," he said, hoarsely, as if he had not spoken for a long time. "Lovely night, isn't it?"

"Yes," she said, and in that one word she expressed everything, her hope, her faith, her elation. Here she was, the girl lost in the forest, at last facing the night, the stars, the shimmering sea, the road to the Promised Land. She made him conscious of a great presence around them, greater than the sea, the night, a wordless truth, in front of which his father waving his banner of enlightenment looked like a child digging a castle on the beach at low tide. Then there sounded in the darkness a growing roar of engines, like the approach of aircraft.

He looked up at the sky, but there were no lights moving among the stars. The roar grew to thunder, out of the night came a white wave, foaming toward them. Before he realized what was happening, a long, low ship swung around, crashed into them alongside, and tied up to them. The wave he had seen rolling toward them had been its bow wave.

He stood staring at it, open-mouthed with astonishment; the roar of engines grew still louder, became deafening; two more waves converged upon them, then three more; they were surrounded by a fleet of shadows. Their own engine faltered, but a commanding voice barked from the darkness, "Keep your engine going! Keep your course! We'll take care of the loading!"

For a moment he had thought it was the British Navy, coming to check on them, but the word "loading" made him realize what they were: Van der Pink's fleet of fast launches. Men swarmed onto the deck of the trawler in the darkness, threw open the hold, manned the derricks, started to lower crates and objects into it with astounding speed and precision; within minutes all six boats had transferred their deck loads into the hold.

"That's it!" the metallic voice quacked in the night. "Cover up your hatches! Get a move on! They may be here any minute!" Engines thundered, exhausts spewed sparks; they vanished in the direction of Spain like ghosts, their roar raced away into silence.

Peter went to the open hatch and looked down. He had stubbornly clung to the conviction that the cargo which had been transferred into their hold at such hallucinating speed consisted of the K rations Van der Pink had talked about; but as he stared at the oblong crates, the boxes, the parcels wrapped in oilcloth, he knew otherwise. He had seen those packages during the war, loaded into barges.

He closed the hatches, covered them with the tarpaulin, secured them with the wooden pegs; meanwhile, his thoughts were clear and unemotional. Van der Pink had foreseen that Dickens would alert Gibraltar only after their departure; his only chance of transferring the cargo unobserved was immediately after they left Tangier. It was a complicated operation competently organized, executed with speed and skill; a cynical exploitation of the windfall of a dying Jewess. Her pathetic message of forgiveness was now perched on top of a boatload of arms.

She was no longer on the foredeck; he found her lying on the lower bunk in the cabin, her head turned toward the wall, her tattooed hand hanging over the edge. On the floor beside her stood the bottle of pills.

The composure, which had sustained him as the boats came roaring out of the night, cracked under the impact of a blind fury. He felt like shaking his fist at the God of David, cruelty of fate. Then a dazzling light jabbed at him from the darkness, caught him in its blinding brilliance, then disappeared. Ayoob's voice called from the wheelhouse, "The British! Have you covered the hatches?"

He replied, "Yes!"

"Will you come and take over wheel? I must put out log."

"Yes. One moment."

He bent over her. His hand found her forehead in the darkness; he stroked her hair in a gesture of comfort and said, "Don't worry, child. Everything is going to be all right."

Then he went to take over the wheel.

Ayoob took over the wheel at dawn, after a few hours of sleep on a mattress taken from the top bunk in the cabin and put on the floor of the wheelhouse. He needed room to sleep; his arms flailed in his dreams; occasionally he hit the partition at which his snoring stopped for a few moments. When the first pink light of the dawn filtered into the wheelhouse he was lying with his face pressed in the corner, one arm behind him, the other over his head; Peter had to shake him before he woke up. He took over the wheel half conscious, swaying on his feet, gazing at the red and gold of the horizon, yawning.

24

Peter went in to see her; the light of the dawn had not yet penetrated into the cabin but he heard from her breathing that she was asleep. He went aft, gazed into the night behind them and saw a low, gray motor torpedo boat with a large white number on her bow trailing them, radar scanner swinging. She showed no flag, but obviously she was British. As he stood watching her, the radar scanner stopped turning; the gray boat slowed down and dropped behind until she was a pink ghost on the horizon.

On his way back to the wheelhouse he looked in on Anna again and found her still asleep. He told Ayoob to call him if there should be any sound from the cabin, however slight; then he lay down on the mattress, put his head on the pillow that smelled of Ayoob, and before he realized what had happened he was a soldier, slogging wearily through the sand of a desert at night, lugging a pack that seemed to get heavier at every step. A muffled command sounded; others, whose presence he vaguely felt around him, stopped and lay down. He followed their example, knelt in the sand; the weight of the pack made him sag sideways and he rolled over onto his back.

The stars were bright and large, the sky was ablaze with them, he had never seen so many stars before. He knew he would not be able to get up again, but he was beyond caring; then, as he lay gazing up at the night sky, he felt his conscious self leave the body collapsed in the sand. A thousand gossamer tendons seemed to strain as he slowly rose out of the pain, the weariness and the dull despair that weighed him down; he felt them snap softly, one by one, and the stars seemed to increase in brilliance; but then something dark, a cloud, came floating between them and him. The cloud was black and sharp-edged; behind it the day broke, red and gold. He felt tears well into his eyes with exhaustion, he heard the drums roll that called him to his feet. With a tremendous effort of will he started straining at the pack that pinned him down in the sand. He dug his elbows in, strained, opened his eyes, and realized that the cloud was the silhouette of someone kneeling by his side, proffering a cup.

"I made you some tea," a soft voice said. It was Anna.

He said, dazedly, "Thank you."

"The captain asked me to call you, because it is your watch. I would have let you sleep."

He propped himself up against the wall and took the mug from her and sipped the hot tea. Ayoob looked over his shoulder and said, "It is going to be fine today. We are lucky."

"Yes, aren't we?" she said; then she turned to him, her face radiant, and said, "We are lucky altogether."

She obviously did not know what their cargo was; he relaxed with a sigh of relief when he saw her happy face. Yet there was something odd about her, something wrong that he could not put his finger on. "Is there time for some breakfast?" he asked.

_286_

"Yes," Ayoob said. "All food is in the galley. Today I will store it."

"Please," she said. "Let me make you something to eat. You go and freshen up."

"Thank you," he said, wondering what made him think that something was wrong. He washed and shaved absent-mindedly, and joined her in the galley where she had laid out a cracked plate, a knife and a fork on a newspaper.

"I am sorry," she said as he came in. "This is the best I could do." She was wearing her old dress and her apron, as she had done on board the barge; he saw the dark rings under her eyes, her sunken cheeks, and realized how much she had changed in this short time. She said, "Sit down, here is the bread and butter. Do you think this is jam? I'll fry an egg for you if I can find a pan. How about some more tea?"

He smiled at her fussing, but as he did so he realized what was wrong. She was whispering, there was something wrong with her voice.

He no longer listened to what she was saying as she chattered on, looking for a frying pan and lighting the stove with paper and kindling wood; he listened to her voice. He tried to hide his alarm but he must have shown it, for soon she fell silent and, although she went on smiling, a shy, furtive despair grew in her eyes and she avoided looking at him. He tried to make amends by talking, about nothing in particular, just talking, but he could not take his mind off her hoarseness. Was it the beginning of a paralysis? Was it pain? He did not know. But he knew now that the doctor had been right.

When he went to take over the wheel from Ayoob, Anna stayed behind in the galley to clear up. He mentioned it to the Arab. "Don't let her think you notice anything," he said, "just act naturally, but try not to ask her any questions, help her not to talk."

The big man nodded solemnly and his dark, gentle eyes looked at him with the shyness of compassion. "Perhaps she not want to talk," he said. "I know a holy man who never speaks. He listens."

"I am afraid it's not like that," Peter said. "I'm afraid it's the beginning of the end." He said it calmly, the terror and the despair he felt were but a faint quaver at the bottom of his thoughts. He wondered whether he would have the strength to help her without being afraid or stricken with commiseration. He was not a nurse, he could not remain detached; he wanted to take her in his arms and shelter her head on his shoulder from death, but it seemed to be all around them, it rose like the dawn. He wished weakly for a moment that he had let her go to America to be cared for by nurses and doctors in a hospital instead of condemning her to die on this filthy little boat, in the company of two clumsy men who had nothing to offer but their gruff consolation.

"At first I thought he was deaf-mute," Ayoob said, "but then I realized his not speaking was listening. Without him I saw no hope left in life. You know any holy men?"

"No, I'm afraid I don't."

"There are none in your country?"

"I don't know. If there are, I have never come across them."

"I will take you to him when we come back? You like to see the Imam?"

It seemed unreal to talk about what he would do when he came back; the future ended on the beach of Palestine. He said, "I'd love to."

"You see," Ayoob concluded, with a smile, "if he talked, it would not help you. You do not speak Arabic, do you?"

"No."

"You see: now it makes no difference. You talk, the Imam listens."

"Does he understand English?"

"I do not know, but that is not important. He will understand *you*. I try to be silent and listen, like him, but I cannot. I love Ayoob, Mohammed; he pains me, but I cannot forget him. I have learnt nothing from my Imam."

Peter was not sure he understood what he meant, but he wanted to be alone now, to think about her and what he could do to help her.

"What is the course?" he asked.

"East," the Arab said, "still east." With that he turned away and lay down, and yawned, and mumbled, "Perhaps. Perhaps one day."

He fell asleep soon afterwards.

25

That afternoon she cooked a meal, and it exhausted her. She came to tell Ayoob, in a hoarse whisper, that his meal was ready; after Ayoob had relieved him at the wheel, Peter found his meal waiting on the galley table. She had tried to make it look appetizing and attractive by arranging slices of peach like a flower and decorating a plate of beans with beetroot. She was not there; he went to the cabin and saw she had gone to bed. She was asleep, her face turned to the wall; the bottle of pills stood on the floor by the side of her bunk again. He took it to the door and saw it was almost empty. She was taking so many pills that she would soon reach the end of them.

That evening, as the sun sank beyond the cloudless horizon, the gray boat moved in once more, radar scanner swinging. It gave him a feeling of unreality, this silent escort, the oily sea, the first pale stars in the last blue of the day. He felt again as if all this were not something he, Peter Jongman, experienced; it was as if he were taking part in a play, a legend, enacted and re-enacted since the dawn of man, now being enacted once more. If only he knew what the legend was.

Night fell during his watch; he saw the darkness rise and conquer, and it seemed to bring some relief. Despite his fear and apprehension, he began to enjoy steering the ship by the stars. He found that he could keep her on course better if he took a star to steer her by instead of looking at the compass. He tried to steer with a minimum of rudder, and as he began to get the feel of the ship he began to like the rise and fall of her clumsy bow against the stars, the feel of her crude steering wheel, the willingness of her graceless body. She was a good ship; what she needed was a thorough clearing up of her decks, some small repairs, a coat of paint, and she would regain her pride. He identified himself with the ship, plodding ahead underneath the stars; then, suddenly, he heard Anna start coughing. He hastily woke Ayoob, asked him to take over, and hurried to her side.

She was suffering as she had been that night in the hotel, and he saw she had taken more pills, for the bottle was lying beside her pillow. He felt calm and competent as he comforted her with soft gentle words, stroking her hand and her hair and assuring her that all was well. He wondered, as she heaved and choked in his arms, whether he should give her the first injection; but she seemed to calm down under his soothing hands. Finally she relaxed, and seemed to fall into a peaceful sleep; he would have liked to stay with her, but he thought of Ayoob who was taking his watch and went back to the wheelhouse.

"All right," he said. "I'm sorry. I'll take her now. Let's take this hour off your next watch."

"Do not worry," the Arab said in the darkness. "It does not matter." His voice sounded soft and shy. "She is worse?" he asked.

"Yes," he answered. "I'm afraid she is going to die." He said it calmly, no longer afraid. He would meet death whenever it decided to come for her.

"Do not fear," the Arab said. "She will live until she reaches the land of her God. Those who must die, die on the beach."

"Is that so?" he said, feeling a cold horror creep over him once more.

"They kneel and stretch their arms out, and whisper words at the sky, and kiss the sand, and die. Ah," he sighed, "sometimes I am jealous of their God."

"Why?" he asked, to escape from that horror. "Have you no God?"

"Oh yes," Ayoob said. "Of course. Each man has God. But ours so far, so high. You see those stars?" he asked, pointing. "We are in his garden, the stars are his flowers. But the Jews? Their God is not among the stars, he is on the beach, waiting for them. They are consumed with longing, we with loneliness. Well," he concluded, after a silence, "twelve more days and she will be there. She will, like all the others, meet him on the beach, where their journey ends."

Peter felt overcome by sadness. For one unbearable moment he was swamped by the realization of what lay ahead of them. Then a hand shyly touched his shoulder, and it seemed as if a great compassion enveloped him. It did not take away his grief, but it helped him to bear it.

Ayoob had learned something from his Imam after all.

The next day she did not speak at all, not even in a whisper. Otherwise she seemed cheerful and well; she almost made them forget about her voice by fussing over them and enjoying the sun.

26

But a few days later, when she came out on deck to sit in the afternoon sun, she had to support herself on the rail; the slight rolling of the ship was too much for her. She sat down clumsily on the hatch at the foot of the mast and leaned back, exhausted.

Peter was painting the inside of the rail. He had found a scraper, paint and a brush in a cupboard in the galley; he had intended only to touch up the paintwork here and there, but soon he was lying on his back, tongue between his teeth, doing a good job.

When he saw her stagger and sit down heavily at the foot of the mast, he scrambled to his feet and joined her on the hatch, brush in hand.

"It's nice and warm in the sun, isn't it?" he said; then he saw her shiver and asked, "Are you cold?"

She shook her head; then she opened her eyes and smiled at him and put her thin, light hand on his. He smiled back; her hand was burning hot.

They sat for a while like this side by side, then he asked, "Shall I get you something to eat?" and answered himself, "I know! I know the very thing. I won't be long."

He went to the galley, got rid of his paintbrush, washed his hands, and tried to fix something for her that would look attractive. He came back with very thin slices of ship's bread and cheese and some peach halves; she looked delighted but, although she tried, all she could manage was a small piece of peach. When Ayoob called him at the changing of the watch, he helped her back into her bunk before he took the wheel.

The sun was setting; the patrol boat moved in toward them, radar scanner swinging, for her nightly vigil. That night Anna was restless, and coughed so much that when she finally sank into a fitful sleep, toward dawn, the pills were finished.

The next day she stayed in bed but she seemed very alert and cheerful, almost mischievous. She hung on to his hand whenever he wanted to go, she coaxed him into long monologues about his boyhood and his father and the meetings of the atheist society that had been as boring as church services to a fourteen-year-old boy. There had been a string quartet on the podium to relieve the monotony of the speakers, the fat cello player snoozed most of the time, his instrument between his thighs; one day Bobby Streng, who was by far the most courageous of the boys in the back row, had taken careful aim with his slingshot and scored a bull's eye on the cello. The result had been better than they had dared hope; the cellist had leaped to his feet, bellowing like a steer, and the meeting had ended in consternation. She was obviously delighted with the story, and he went on telling her more of his boyhood and his friends, until Ayoob called him for his watch. While he stood at the wheel he tried to recall as many incidents of his youth as he could; he spent his next free watch in the cabin, telling stories. But when night fell he had to admit defeat. Despite his fascinating stories she started to cough, wretchedly, agonizingly; he would have to give her an injection.

It was a moment he had dreaded ever since the doctor had mentioned the injections to him; now it had come he felt calm, almost relaxed as he went through the motions he had rehearsed so often in his mind. He stabbed the needle home in the small patch of skin he had shyly bared, which looked very white and childish and defenseless, and he was sure he hurt her. But if he did, she did not betray it; soon afterwards she fell asleep.

He went to look at her as often as he could that night, but she had not moved. When the sun rose she was still lying as he had left her the night before. He was getting worried, but he did not dare to wake her. When Ayoob joined him at the wheel an hour later after having been to the galley he said, "I do not know, but perhaps you had better look. I think there is something wrong."

He hurried into the cabin, terrified; as he approached her bunk he heard, to his relief, a soft furtive sound. She lay turned toward the wall, her hands covering her face; she was weeping. It was the first time that he had known her to break down.

"Anna?" he asked. "Anna, what is it?" forgetting that she could not answer. He decided to give her another injection; when he bent over her to administer it she clutched the bedcover and kept him from pulling it away with desperate determination. He could not understand; he argued with her, gently, assuring her that if she did not want him to he would not do it, that all he would do was straighten her bed and make her comfortable, that later, after she had rested a while longer, he would come and take her out into the sun. At last she surrendered the blanket, worn out by her feeble resistance. He pulled it back, and then he realized why she had held on to it so desperately. Her body had lost control of its functions. She had wept with shame.

He said, lightly, "Well now, is that what all the fuss was about? Good heavens, the times I've had to look after Betty like this! You just relax, I'll be right back."

He went to the galley to fetch a basin of water, a sponge, soap and a towel. He brought with him the piece of tarpaulin that covered the anchor winch and spread it on the top bunk; then he lifted her in his arms and put her on it. She was alarmingly light; she had lost a lot of weight since he had last carried her. He took the sponge, soaped it, and gently pulled her nightdress away from her; then he stood still, struck with horror.

Her body was terrible to see; he had to use all his self-control to go on washing her as if nothing had happened. Whatever he did, he should never let her realize how the sight of her had shocked him. But as he washed her, gently, cautiously, with infinite care, he heard Dickens' voice say again, that night in the hotel room, "I never thought I would see one of them alive."

He managed to keep all thoughts at bay while he washed her, changed her nightdress and her bed, put her back in her bunk, covered her gently and told her that after his watch they would go out and sit in the sun. But at the wheel, as he stood staring at the compass, the thoughts came crowding in.

He had seen photographs of those horrible mounds of corpses in Belsen; Dickens had been right, she looked like one of them. But not only was her body so emaciated that it looked like a skeleton, it was covered with ghastly scars. What those doctors in the research camp had done to her defied human imagination. He realized, at last, why she had laughed on the Thames Embankment when he told her what Thorens had planned to do with her. Any man uncovering her with lust would have recoiled in horrified revulsion.

It made Thorens look small and stupid, a blundering civil servant of crime. To send this nightmarish body to South America for immoral purposes was the kind of mistake only a petty bureaucrat could make in one of the huge new office buildings that had sprouted all over the earth since the war. The fallen angel, whom he had been too overawed to kill, had been nothing but a bungler.

Later that day he carried her out into the sun; but he saw it was too strong for her, so he brought out her mattress and put it in the shade. He tried in vain to make her eat something. He racked his brains trying to think of something that would tempt her; sitting beside her, covering his eyes with his hand in thought, he fell asleep.

27

He dreamed of a chocolate shop in Amsterdam; displayed on the counter were chocolate animals and dolls. Nurses in white dresses were spraying them with gold dust; he tried to buy one before it was sprayed because he was certain she would not like that. But the nurse would not let him take it and, because he held on to it, his hand was sprayed as well. The gold was burning hot; as he woke up with a start he found her hand resting on his. She was coughing.

He carried her back to her cabin, settled her for the night and gave her another injection. He stayed with her until she was asleep, then he went to the galley to make himself something to eat. In the end all he took was coffee, as strong as he could make it. Then he joined Ayoob in the wheelhouse.

He had lost all notion of time. He did not know where they were and how long they had been on their way; all he knew was the course. His feverish awareness, induced by coffee and lack of sleep, seemed to make all sounds louder, the stars more brilliant, and their ship alone at sea more like a vessel in a legend than before. The weather and the sea seemed full of compassion, the British escort discreet, almost reverent; the whole of nature seemed to be conscious of her dying.

The next morning, as he washed her and changed her bed, he noticed that she seemed to have difficulty in recognizing him. As he watched her, while calmly going about his business as if nothing were the matter, he realized that she recognized him all right but occasionally lost sight of him, as if he were a member of a crowd. Gradually that suggestion took hold of him too; in the eerie unreality of her dying it seemed as if the boat became crowded with ghosts, as if all the corpses of the mounds of Belsen had risen to their feet, followed them, and were now climbing on board.

During the next few days she coughed less and seemed to be no longer in pain, and a strange transformation took place in her. She was turning from a terrified, dying child into someone different, a spirit, yearning for its journey's end.

What could she expect there? If she were to live until they reached the shores of Palestine, what would happen to her then? He saw in his mind's eye the small vessel approaching a coast of dunes, a beach at dawn. "If I take the wings of the morning and dwell in the uttermost parts of the sea . . ." Would the God of David be there to comfort her? Would she kneel and stretch out her arms to the sky and kiss the soil and die, while Jewish soldiers waded to and fro, carrying the machine guns, rifles and mortars that had been smuggled in by virtue of her dying? It was no good, not good enough to make a believer out of grocer Jongman's son. It made him feel like taking up the wrecker's hammer, fallen from his father's hand, to continue smashing the hollow image of a God of love that fooled the innocent. Whatever happened, he would, like his father, devote the rest of his life to protecting the innocent from that last, monstrous deceit.

As the days went by—shimmering, sunlit days of unearthly peace that she seemed to fill with an increasing radiance of hope and joy and youth while her trembling body lay dying—they seemed to move further and further away from reality. Then, one morning, Ayoob warned him to look out for pirates.

"Pirates?" he asked incredulously.

"Yes," the Arab answered. "This is where they may try to board us. See that motor launch in the south on the horizon? They are watching us. They know this boat, they know by water line that we are loaded, they see no people on deck, so they know we carry cargo, not immigrants."

"But who are they?"

"Other gunrunners. Italians, Turks. They have sunk several of us."

"But, surely, they can't do that without being hunted down by warships? Pirates in the Mediterranean, these days?"

"Why not? To the navies of the Allies, we are rats, devouring each other. I do not know where all this will end. Maybe we will end up devouring each other."

Toward nightfall a fast, grimy motor launch came foaming toward them out of the dusk that had begun to settle on the horizon. Ayoob brought out guns from a hatch in the wheelhouse floor; Peter was still undecided whether to use them or whether to let the men board the ship and ask for mercy for her sake when, suddenly, the launch veered away and roared off into the night. They looked around and saw that their escort had moved in close, the M.T.B. was almost alongside, its radar scanner swinging.

"Well," Ayoob said, "this is first time we have been protected by British Navy."

Peter's feeling of being a pawn in a game that he could not understand became stronger than ever. He no longer lived, he was being lived, by something, someone afoot in the night. If only he knew who it was.

She gave the impression, stronger each day, that the fear of death, if it had ever touched her at all, had now left her completely. Despite her agony and the decline of her body she seemed to live in an expectation that had nothing to do with their journey through time, as if they were no longer moving, but waiting.

28

Looking after her took all his attention; he spent every hour he could spare from the wheel nursing her, talking to her, assuring her by the mere fact of his presence that she was not alone. But he had a growing feeling of inadequacy, as if the body he cared for were no longer she, no longer the house of her spirit. As exhaustion began to weigh him down, it made him prone to odd delusions, such as turning around while washing her because he suddenly felt she was standing behind him. One night, steering by a star, he could not believe his eyes when he saw her slight silhouette appear beside him at the wheel. She rested her forehead against the windowpane and stared out into the night.

"What's this?" he asked. "Where do you come from?"

She did not answer. A weary sadness emanated from her, and he remembered the night of the ferry, the promenade deck, her reflection in the glass. He asked, "Are you sure this is all right? Don't you . . ." He did not finish what he was saying, for she disappeared, without moving, like a fleck of sunlight chased by the shadow of a cloud.

The next morning, as he woke up on his paliasse in the wheelhouse, she was sitting by his side, holding a mug of tea, waiting for him to wake up, and smiled as she saw him open his eyes. He stretched out his hand toward her, breathless with surprise, and she was gone.

Those moments were plainly hallucinations, vivid pictures from his memory, for that night, as the sun went down, he saw her standing in the bow of the ship, and as she appeared, the foredeck changed. It lowered and flattened, the anchor winch took on vivid colors, and in the silent spell of the twilight he heard, above the stamping of their engine, Coba's shrill, excited bark.

Surprisingly, those visions did not alarm him, for her last days were different from anything he had foreseen or been led to expect of death. The defeat of her pathetic body was heartbreaking, but brought about its own relief by surrounding her with a peace, a stillness that were unlike anything he had ever known. It seemed as if death were not an occurrence, or a moment, but a slow awakening, an unearthly transition from one consciousness to another. She seemed no longer to be aware of her body, to be no part of it. He gave her an injection every night, it made the desperate coughing cease in total unconsciousness, but it made no difference to the soul that seemed to hover around her, indecisively, as if she were waiting for a call, the arrival of a pilot, a ghost, to guide her to a shore she already seemed to discern on the horizon.

Then there were alarming, chilling moments of a different consciousness, when her unseeing, roving eyes suddenly came to rest on him, and recognized him, and she smiled like the girl he knew, and then her smile would vanish in an inexpressible, paralyzing terror. Somewhere inside her was an evil, malignant kernel of fear; he got the impression that it was his presence that perpetuated it. If he were no longer there for her to recognize in those rare moments of physical consciousness, she might not be terrified any more. But her body, helpless, wasting, depended on his care; if he were to stay away she would die within a day.

Then, one evening, Ayoob told him that they were

about to arrive in the coastal waters of Palestine. Soon they would see the lighthouse on Mount Carmel, and they would beach at dawn. He hurried to the cabin to tell her. He was not sure she heard him when he said, "Anna? We are nearly there! We'll be in Palestine to-morrow morning at dawn!"

Outside, the sun was setting in fiery glory; she stared at him with her large dark eyes in the orange light, as if she were too absorbed in what she saw to notice what he said. He again had the impression that he was one of a crowd, that she was trying not to lose sight of him. Her eyes wandered, she seemed to search for his face among many; then she caught sight of him again, and smiled. It was a wan little smile, all that was left of the Anna he had known. He lifted her gently in his arms and carried her out on deck. Even if she were no longer aware of what was happening, he wanted to show her the lighthouse when it started to flash on the horizon. He settled her down in the lee of the wheelhouse, facing the rising night. The sea was calm, the horizon seemed darkened by a distant shore. They seemed to be sus-pended between sea and sky; although their engine throbbed and they drew behind them a luminescent wake, it was as if they were making no headway, but were churning pointlessly through a world without end, star among the stars.

The first harbingers of the approaching shore were a fleet of small fishing boats, lying motionlessly on their quivering reflections. "Look!" he said, pointing. "Look! There are the first fishing boats! They must be from Palestine!" He turned around to the wheelhouse to ask Ayoob, but saw him standing in the doorway, gazing in the opposite direction. He got to his feet, looked over the rail and saw a slender gray tower bear down upon them with the white wings of a bow wave. So narrow was the silhouette of the thing heading toward them that it took him a moment before he realized what it was; a destroyer, approaching head-on at full speed. Their escort behind them had stopped and seemed to be waiting for her.

She passed close behind them. Although she had slowed down, her wake still made them roll and pitch furiously; crockery crashed off the sink in the galley with the cruel sound of breaking china. He looked around; Anna had fallen over. He hurried to her side, gently lifted her, telling her that it was a destroyer, that there was nothing to be afraid of; she wearily rested her head against his shoulder, her eyes closed.

He carried her back to the cabin, put her gently on her bunk and said, "If we can possibly do without it, I don't think I'll give you an injection tonight, Anna, because we are nearly there. You wouldn't want to be asleep when we arrive, would you?"

She did not answer. She had not heard.

He said, "Of course you wouldn't. Now, take it easy and rest while you still have the chance; I'll be in to see you as often as I can to tell you where we are."

When he came out he saw Ayoob pointing astern. The destroyer had swung around and was now heading back in the direction from where she had come; their escort, instead of drawing closer to them as she had done every night, had fallen in behind the destroyer and was following her at full speed. They were left alone among the fishermen of Palestine.

The little fishing boats, which had seemed asleep like birds on the glassy sea while the escort was still there, suddenly came to life. The whole fleet of them started to move, toward them.

"I do not like that," Ayoob said, frowning, as they fanned out around them.

"You don't think they are pirates, do you?"

"I do not know," the Arab said. "Get the guns."

The fleet of fishermen put itself between them and the two warships, now vanishing in the encroaching night. Small searchlights flashed on, directed toward the disappearing warships, obviously to hide the movements of a fast boat that headed toward them, with the silhouettes of a number of men on its deck, more men than seemed natural for a fishing boat. Peter wondered whether the sticks the men held were guns; Ayoob called, urgently, "Hurry!" The boat swerved around and approached them for a boarding. A voice called across the water, "Friends! Slow down! Haganah! I'm your pilot!"

Ayoob slowed down; the fishing boat bumped against their flank. A number of men climbed on board, all very young, carrying rifles and knives.

"You the captain?" one of them asked, seeing Peter in the doorway of the wheelhouse.

"No," he answered. "The captain is here, at the wheel."

"Where's the cargo?" the boy asked. "Out there? All right, men, uncover the hatches, make ready for unloading." Then he continued, to Ayoob, "I have been detailed to take you in for your landing. The fishermen are screening you from the radar of those warships, so you may change your course to south-south-east now."

"Do you not think they will come back?" Ayoob asked, turning the wheel and watching the compass. "The M.T.B. has followed us all the way from Gibraltar."

"No," the boy said. "Stay on this course until I tell

you. Excuse me," and he brushed past Peter on his way out.

"You see?" Ayoob said, "that is how they are. They look like children, but I do not envy the English over there." He gestured at the horizon, where there was nothing to be seen but the night darkening among the stars.

"How are they going to transport that load?" Peter asked. "There must be more than a truckful."

"Oh, do not worry," Ayoob said with a new bitterness. "They have everything: trucks, armored cars; they raid British camps and take away equipment and hostages."

Outside sounded an incongruous noise: the cheering of boys. Peter looked out of the door of the wheelhouse and saw them dance by the side of the open hatch, slapping one another on the shoulder, shouting with joy. The boy who had given Ayoob the orders stood among the crates; one of them had been prized open, and he held up a tommy gun, as if it were a present he had just unwrapped.

Peter joined them and said quietly, "I am sorry, but would you mind piping down a little? There is someone very ill in there."

The boys looked at him, astonished; then they looked at their leader as he asked, "Who is that?"

"A Jewish girl from Auschwitz, on her way to Palestine. I'd like you to meet her. She will be very happy to see you. She has come a long way."

He did not wait for the boy's answer, but went into the galley to light the lantern that he had used all these nights. As he came out he noticed the silence; the boy in the holds had put the gun back in its crate and now stood beside the hatch, waiting.

"Come along," Peter said. The boy followed him, but

did not enter the cabin; he stayed in the doorway, others looked over his shoulders. Peter lifted the lantern. She lay on her back, her eyes closed; she opened them when the soft light of the lantern shone on her. She did not look at him, she looked at the light on the ceiling; her eyes seemed to try to focus on something that was there.

"Anna?" he said. "Here are some boys from Palestine who want to see you. They are going to take you ashore."

It seemed at first as if she had not heard, then she slowly turned her head and her dark eyes looked at the faces in the doorway. She gazed at them for a long time, without expression; then, for a fleeting moment, she seemed to return to their reality from somewhere far away. Her eyes, large and haunting, looked from one to the other, earnestly; then she looked at Peter holding the lantern, and smiled.

"You see?" he said. "Here they are. It won't be long now."

Then he lowered the lantern because he could no longer bear the way she looked at him. "I'll be back," he said.

He went out into the night; the boys followed him to the aft deck, out of earshot. There one of them asked, "She was in Auschwitz, you say?"

"Yes," he answered. "The medical-research section."

He sat down on the edge of the hatch because, for some reason, his legs had suddenly started to tremble. It must be the reaction. He had slept very little this last week. The boys stood facing him; he again had the sudden feeling that he was one of a crowd, that behind him hundreds of silent faces were staring at those boys, the sentinels of the Promised Land, that he had been chosen to be their spokesman.

He told them quietly and matter-of-factly what had

been done to her by the Nazis, what had happened to her family, how he had picked her up in that station in Holland when she was about to be taken to South America, how they had been voyaging toward Palestine ever since. He did not know whether the boys understood all of what he said, he was not even sure they were listening; but he was certain that the sight of her had made a deep impression on them. When he had finished her story there was a silence, then their leader said, "If he has been able to carry out the raid as planned, he will probably take her into Palestine himself."

"Who is he?" he asked.

"The Commander. He'll come on board when we arrive."

"When will that be?"

"Any moment now."

"I see. In that case, I had better get her ready."

He went back into the cabin, hung the lantern on the wall, and said, "Well, it seems we are about to arrive. How about dressing you in something to fit the occasion? What about that new dress you never wore?"

Her eyes were large and dark. She looked at him as if she were thinking over what he had said, but he knew that she had not heard him. She had been unable to distinguish his voice among the murmuring of the crowd that surrounded him.

"Don't worry," he said, "you'll be all right, you'll see. Let's get started."

He unpacked the dress in the lantern light, lifted it cautiously out of its tissue paper, took off the price tag and laid it out on the lower bunk. Then he turned back her covers and said, "Come, let's make you beautiful."

He washed her, and it obviously tired her out. She lay panting on her back, her eyes closed in weariness;

he decided to pack her bag first, to let her rest for a while. There was not much to pack; he stood looking at her clogs, in doubt, when the engine stopped. Someone knocked on the door, a voice said, "The Commander is coming."

"All right," he answered. "She is ready." He turned toward her and said, "Well, here we go. Let's put that dress on."

It was not easy, and he was not sure whether he put it on the right way. It looked crumpled and shapeless when she finally sat slumped against him, her head on his shoulder.

"My," he said, "you look wonderful. They won't believe their eyes when they see someone like you come out of this boat. Just a moment. I'll see where they are."

He lowered her carefully back on the bunk and went out on deck where the boys were helping a man climb on board. Although he was still night-blind because of the lantern, he could now make out the shore, a low-lying cloud underneath the stars.

"Did you capture it?" a boy's voice asked eagerly.

The man said, "Yes," and they cheered. "Ssh," the man warned. "No noise. Hurry. We have formed a chain to the beach, so start unloading. The trucks are just over the hills."

"Will we be able to keep it?" the boy urged, "Will we?"

"No, we'll have to abandon it, after the operation. It's too easy to trace. But just for tonight it is perfect. Now, hurry!" The boys obeyed; their leader whispered something to the man; the man looked at Peter. "Yes," he said. "I know about her. How do you do, sir." He did not look like a commander at all, but like a genial bookkeeper.

"Won't you come in and say hello to her?" Peter asked.

The man hesitated, then he said, "Of course." He followed him inside; Peter lifted the lantern. She slowly turned her head toward them. Peter watched the man, saw the horror on his face, mastered instantly, and his jaw set in silent rage. He whispered, hurriedly, impulsively, "She brings a message of forgiveness . . ." realizing at the same time how foolish his words were, how inadequate.

For a moment, the other's face seemed to be caught off guard. It looked infinitely tired, an utter weariness, as if in that moment man's eternal longing for a home, children, peace and love overwhelmed him, a wave of unbearable nostalgia. Then he said quietly, "We'll take good care of her," and went outside.

Peter sat down on the edge of her bunk and held her hand, reassuringly, while listening to the sounds of unloading outside. He seemed to sit there for an eternity, waiting patiently, beyond hope or grief; then the commander appeared in the doorway and said, "All right, you can bring her now."

He put his arms under her, carefully, lifted her gently, and carried her out on the deck. There were only a few boys left, vague shapes in the darkness, wearing helmets now, and it was as though they formed a guard. He carried her to the rail; there he saw a small boat waiting for them with the commander in it, holding up his arms to take her over. But when he wanted to hand her over she suddenly, unexpectedly, tightened her arms around his neck and refused to let go of him.

He stood petrified, shocked and bewildered by this sudden resurgence of her consciousness. He had not realized that she knew what was happening to her, and that they were about to part. He felt her fear, her loneliness, her despair, as she clung to him like a child. He whispered, "All right, don't worry, I'll come with you," and he somehow managed, with the help of the boys and the commander, to lower himself into the boat with her in his arms. He sat down clumsily. The last boys followed him, manned the oars, pushed off, and the boat set out toward the shore.

She kept her face tightly pressed against his shoulder, and he was tormented by panicking thoughts. He could not let her go like this, she was terrified without him, he should take her back, or go with her, but he could not possibly desert her now. He tightened his arms in a vain effort to shelter her, to slow down time; he bent his head to kiss her hair; as he did so he looked down, saw the slippers they had bought together that day in Loozen, and suddenly he knew it was all a terrible mistake. She was not a Jewess, returning to the Promised Land from the great dispersion, but a little Dutch girl, far away from home. Then the boat hit the gravel of the beach, the boys jumped out and pulled it higher out of the water. He rose precariously; they helped him step out; when finally he stood up to his knees in the water, about to carry her ashore, he looked at the beach and his heart stopped.

For there, with an ominous rattling and the roar of a huge engine, a monster came lumbering out of the night. Steel crunched and screeched on the pebbles as it bore down on them, lurching; he realized it was a tank. His first thought was that they had been found out, it must be the British; then the tank swung around and he saw, coarsely chalked on its flank, a star of David.

"Look!" he said. "Anna—look!"

She slowly lifted her head, and looked. For a moment,

they seemed to be suspended in a motionless silence, then everything, the night, the sea, the beach, seemed pervaded by her smile.

"Come on! Hurry!" a voice whispered beside him.

He waded ashore toward the tank that stood waiting for her, its engine throbbing. Two of the helmeted boys climbed onto its track, another was waiting in its turret. He carried her to the foot of the tank; then she stretched out her thin arms toward it and the boys took her from him. She did not look back; she was lifted up, gently and swiftly, and lowered inside. Then the lid closed, the engine roared, the tank swung around; with a gnashing of steel and pebbles it ground up the slope of the dunes and rose against the dawn. Its silhouette stood for a moment poised against the sky, angular and grim; then it tipped forward and down, and was gone, and there was nothing left but the dawn over the hills of Judea.

If I take the wings of the morning . . .

He waded out to the little boat that took him back to the ship.

JAN DE HARTOG

was born in Haarlem, Holland, in 1914, son of a Dutch theologian. At the age of ten he ran away to sea and sailed with a fishing smack on the Zuyder Zee. Since then his life has been divided between the sea and writing. His first great success in Holland was the novel HOLLAND'S GLORY, *in 1940. During the war, Mr. de Hartog escaped from occupied Holland and served in England. In the United States, Mr. de Hartog's name has become a familiar one through the success of his five previously published books,* THE LOST SEA, THE DISTANT SHORE, THE LITTLE ARK, A SAILOR'S LIFE, *and* THE SPIRAL ROAD, *and the great popularity of his plays,* THE FOURPOSTER *and* SKIPPER NEXT TO GOD.